GHOSTS, LORE & A HOUSE BY THE SHORE

ALSO BY NELLIE H. STEELE

Secret of the Ankhs

GHOSTS, LORE & A HOUSE BY THE SHORE

A MOTHER/DAUGHTER COZY MYSTERY

NELLIE H. STEELE

A Novel Idea Publishing

For my mom, Stephanie, who inspired the character of Lily!

ACKNOWLEDGMENTS

A HUGE thank you to everyone who helped get this book published! Special shout outs to: Stephanie Sovak, Paul Sovak, Michelle Cheplic, Mark D'Angelo and Lori D'Angelo.

Finally, a HUGE thank you to you, the reader!

CHAPTER 1

*C*assandra Bennett-McGuire stared up at her mid-sized Craftsman. Large, tapered tan pillars held the wide front porch's roof at bay. White wooden banisters framed in the rest. Cedar-shaked dormers rose to create the second story.

The heels of Cassie's black pumps sank into the soil as she stood on the manicured front lawn. She wrapped her arms around her midriff and fought the tears stinging her eyes.

Noise pounded behind her, echoing off the street's homes. A warm arm wrapped around Cassie's shoulders. Fingers squeezed her arms. She caught a whiff of rosewater perfume.

Cassie closed her hand around her mother's. She glanced at her and offered a weak smile as she swiped away the tear that escaped onto her cheek.

"We'll get through this, honey," Lily, Cassie's mother, promised.

The realtor wobbled across the lawn toward them in her smart skirt suit paired with a red blazer.

"We're all set, ladies!" she said in a chipper tone. "It's got great curb appeal. I don't imagine it will be on the market very long."

"Thanks, Gina," Lily answered.

"And, Lily, I'll be by to hang your SOLD sign tomorrow," Gina said, with a wave. "Less than a day on the market. I can't believe it!"

"What a whirlwind that was! But it's a great house," Lily answered.

"I'll call you as soon as I have any news on this one. Hopefully, we'll have the same luck!" Gina waved crossed fingers at them. "Do you need any help with the boxes?"

"No, no, we've got it," Lily answered.

"Okey-doke! I'll get out of your hair. We'll talk soon." Gina patted Lily's arm, before toddling across the lawn to her black BMW SUV.

Lily waited a moment, before she gave Cassie's shoulders another squeeze. "Ready?"

Cassie froze, unable to answer.

"I expected we'd raise our kids here," Cassie answered, after a pause. "And when that didn't happen, I figured at least we'd grow old together here." She glanced at the FOR SALE sign swinging from the post in the yard.

"Why don't you head to the car. I'll grab that last box."

Cassie shook her head and wiped another tear away. "I'll get it."

Lily offered her an encouraging smile. "I'll be in the car."

Cassie sniffled as she trudged to the porch. A lone cardboard box sat near the steps. A frown formed on Cassie's face as she grasped the brown cardboard container and forced herself to turn her back on the house. Without glancing back, she tossed her blonde hair over her shoulder and strode down the walk to her mother's waiting car.

She stowed the box with the others in the trunk and shuffled to the passenger's seat. Cassie slid in as her mother started the car.

Lily glanced at her and grasped her hand. "I know it's not the life you expected. No one expects their husband to die a month after they turn forty. But we'll get through it. We're starting a new chapter. Let's make it a good one." She tucked a lock of Cassie's hair behind her ear, before easing the car out of the driveway and around the corner.

Cassie nodded as the car lurched forward.

"It's not like you expected to be widowed either," she answered, referencing the tragic turn both their lives had taken on the same day. She took one last glance at her former home. She wouldn't spend her life there; wouldn't raise her kids there, or grow old with the man she married there. She had been robbed of that experience by a surprise storm that cropped up over the Rockies.

On a business trip, her husband and father had decided to fly home early to surprise their wives, forgoing a final round of golf at the resort where they stayed. When the left engine of the corporate jet was struck by lightning, there had been nothing the pilots could do. They'd lost an engine and their instruments. They'd struggled to land safely over the mountainous area. The odds were a million to one. They were not destined to be the one.

The plane had not only robbed her of her husband, but also her father. The tragedy had single-handedly devastated both mother and daughter.

Cassie recalled the moment their lives had changed: a few months ago, at 11:23 p.m., the ear-splitting shriek of a surprise phone call had startled her awake. She remembered how she rose from her bed and tiptoed across the hardwood floor to the phone. A man's voice on the other end announced himself as Clayton Bennington.

Cassie's brow furrowed, recognizing the name as CEO of her husband and father's company. She'd enjoyed many dinners with him. Her father, as CFO, had spent a good deal of time with the man. Why was he calling her at this time of night?

"Sorry to call at this hour, Cass," he said, using the nickname he'd called her since she was a child. "I just got off the phone with your mom."

Cassie shook the sleep from her mind as she tried to focus on what he was saying. Her mother? What was he doing calling her mother on a Saturday near midnight? He sighed a shaky breath. The crease in Cassie's forehead deepened.

"I have some bad news."

Clayton informed Cassie her husband, Trevor, and her father had been flying home early when their plane went missing. Emergency responders were searching for the plane and any survivors, but the odds were not good. Cassie's bottom lip quivered as she heard the news. The phone slipped from her hand as she spun and raced to the night table for her cell phone. With shaky hands, she'd texted her mother.

Cassie recalled only one thought bouncing through her mind during the blur of pulling on clothes: they were okay. They had to be. She couldn't lose both her husband and her father in one night.

She drove to her childhood home to wait for news with her mother. They'd cuddled on the couch, squeezed each other's hands, cried together and held each other tightly. As dawn broke, they received the final word. They had found the plane. They had found the bodies. There were no survivors.

In the months that followed, she'd grieved the losses with her mother. Those months had been a mind-numbing whirlwind.

"I don't want to live in this house anymore," Cassie had choked through tears days after the funeral.

"Then don't," Lily encouraged. "We don't need to make any decisions right now, though, honey."

Cassie shook her head in disagreement. "I know you're going to say I'm not thinking straight, but I can't imagine staying here. Everywhere I look, I see Trevor."

Her mother frowned. She nodded, pursing her lips. "It's the same for me. The house felt so empty after you left. Now…" Her voice faltered and a tear slid down her cheek.

Cassie sighed, grasped her mother's hand and squeezed. She nodded her head in a silent affirmation of the unspoken words.

"Let's move," her mother had said. "Let's sell our houses and move."

"Where?" Cassie asked.

"Anywhere." Lily paused. "Let's both move to a new place. Get out of here. A fresh start. Somewhere new."

Cassie chewed her lower lip.

"What?" Lily questioned. "I need a fresh start, too. That house I have is far too big. What would I keep that big house for? Let's both make a fresh start somewhere else. Somewhere new!"

Cassie smiled for the first time since that fateful night. "That sounds nice, Mom."

Lily returned her smile. "There's no reason to rush into anything. Let's both take some time to think about it. If you'd like to sell, when you're sure, I'll call Gina. She's great with home sales. She'll get us a mint for our places!"

"And I'm sure in your neighborhood, you won't have a problem selling," Cassie told her mother.

"No," Lily responded, with a shake of her head. "I've already received a few calls from realtors about the house. Generous offers. Between my house and yours, we could pool our sales and get a nice place. We don't need anything big, but we could go for a new build or something."

"What about my job?" The reality of a big move hit Cassie. She pondered her own question. Her job as an assistant librarian in the neighboring suburb kept her busy and happy, but it wasn't exactly a high-powered career that she couldn't tear herself away from.

Lily shrugged at her. "Find a new job. Hey, maybe we'd have enough left over after the house sales to start a business like we've always talked about. That cute little seaside shop we giggled over so many times."

Cassie offered her mother a half-frown. "I think that's a pipe dream."

Her mother shrugged again. "You never know. Let's see what happens. When you're ready."

She wiped a tear from Cassie's cheek.

"Call Gina," Cassie said, as she grasped her mother's hand. "Let's do it. Let's move."

The memory faded from Cassie's mind as the house slid from her view.

* * *

They'd spent a month readying their respective homes for sale and searching for a new home. The women had expected to wait until their houses sold before diving into the real estate market for a new place, but the wait was unnecessary.

Two weeks after the double funeral, Clayton Bennington called Lily.

"Hey, Lil," he began in a soft, almost apologetic tone. "How's everything going?"

Lily folded a pair of slacks and placed them into a box. "Busy," she admitted.

"Yes, I imagine. With the funeral over, though, hopefully, things will settle now."

Lily smiled to herself as she folded another pair of pants and tossed them into a box. She and Cassie hadn't shared their plans with anyone beyond Gina, their realtor. But they'd all have to hear it soon enough.

"Well," Lily said, as she settled onto the backless beige bench at the foot of her bed, "it won't settle yet. Cassie and I have made a decision."

"A decision?"

Lily fanned herself with her hand, as she formulated the words in her mind before speaking.

"We're moving," she settled on.

"Moving? You moving in with Cassie?" he questioned.

"No, Clay," Lily answered. "We're both moving. Somewhere else. We need a fresh start, and neither of us wants to stay in our respective homes."

Even without seeing him, Lily could tell Clayton was shocked. She could picture the already deep wrinkles on his forehead deepening, and his lips forming the characteristic puckered o-shape indicative of him considering something.

He murmured a few "ahhhs" and "ehhs" before he said, "Did you call Gina? She's the best realtor in the area."

Lily nodded as she responded. "Yes. She's taking care of the sale of both of our houses."

"Has she found either of you a new place? Or are you planning to buy one place and live together?"

Lily sighed. This would be the painful part of this process. "Gina's putting us in contact with a few other realtors in the areas we're looking in. Clay, we're not staying in Oakhurst."

"Not staying in Oakhurst? Your entire lives are here!" Clayton exclaimed.

"Our entire lives WERE here, Clay," Lily corrected.

"That's not true, Lil," he argued. "Your friends, Cassie's

job–this is your home! Listen, I know it's hard right now. This was a shock! I'm still reeling; I can't imagine how you feel. Things are upside down, but don't make a decision this big right on the tail of the funeral. I understand you're both numb, but it will get better."

Lily took a moment before responding. "We don't need these large homes. Heck, Blake and I didn't need a house this large after Cassie moved out."

"Sure, understandable," Clayton answered. "But moving towns? Starting over? Don't leave your friends, Lil. We're all here for you. We want to support you."

"We appreciate that, Clay, we do," Lily answered, "but the memories here are…" She paused with her voice trailing off for a moment. "We need a fresh start."

Clay remained silent for a moment. "I don't know what to say," he murmured.

"How about 'good luck?'" Lily suggested.

Clay offered a quiet chuckle. "I guess I can't change your mind?"

"No," Lily answered. "Sorry to say, you can't. Cassie and I need this. We need each other's support somewhere without the memories here."

"Well, on that note, I may be able to help you with finding that new house."

"Oh?" Lily inquired, uncertain of his meaning.

"That's actually the reason I called."

Lily chuckled. "To offer to buy Cassie and me a new house in a new town?"

"That wasn't exactly what I had in mind, but we wanted to bring you both in to discuss a settlement."

"Settlement?" Lily questioned.

"We carried life insurance policies on both Blake and Trevor. Blake was at retirement age. We need to discuss his pension with you. And, well…" he paused, searching for the words. "According to the investigation completed on the plane crash, the second engine shouldn't have failed when it did. That's what really doomed them. They're offering a settlement. We want to make sure you and Cassie are well-represented in any discussions with them."

Tears formed in Lily's eyes as she listened to those last few statements. Would there have been a chance if the second engine hadn't failed? She shook her head. It didn't matter. Life happened, and it cost her her husband and her son-in-law.

"Al…all right," she responded, as she glanced to the ceiling and blinked away her tears.

"Would this Friday morning work? Check with Cassie and let me know."

"I will. Thanks, Clay."

Lily clicked off her phone and set it next to her. She stared ahead blankly. The conversation replayed again. Had faulty equipment doomed the flight's passengers and crew more than the storm? They' had believed the fateful decision to fly home early cost them their lives. But had it? If not, it may not have mattered when they flew home. Perhaps engine failure would have occurred in any instance.

Lily decided it didn't matter as she picked up the phone to call Cassie. She'd have to tell her the news. She hoped Cassie didn't dwell on the new development. They needed to look forward and keep moving.

She swiped at her phone and scrolled through her contact list, finding Cassie's name. She pressed the phone icon to call her and waited. Perhaps with the settlement, they could open that small shop in the seaside town they'd always talked about moving to. Crazier things have happened, Lily pondered, as the line trilled on the other end.

* * *

Cassie smoothed her dress as she glanced in the mirror. She checked her makeup again. She'd had a weak moment as she slipped on her black pumps, recalling the last time she'd worn them, when she'd buried her husband and her father.

Today, she and her mother would be meeting with representatives from the plane's manufacturer and lawyers from Trevor's company. Her parents' friend, Clayton, had invited them to discuss the terms of a potential settlement in the company's boardroom. He planned to attend for moral support.

Cassie appreciated it. She hoped she could calmly digest and discuss the information presented and make a level-headed decision. Tears threatened again as she considered the prospect of the meeting.

Cassie bit her lower lip and shook her head. She fanned her face with her hands as she blinked back her tears. She blew out a long breath and blew her nose before grabbing her purse and stuffing extra tissues inside.

A horn sounded outside. At least she did not have to drive. Neither did her mother, Cassie reflected, as she hurried down the stairs and out her front door. She stared at the black town car Clayton sent for them. She spotted her mother sitting in the backseat. Her porcelain fingers waved from inside.

Cassie returned the wave and hastened down her walkway to the car as the driver pulled the door open. She slid inside, wrapping her mother in a hug. Tears streamed again.

"Are you ready for this?" Lily asked.

"No, but it has to be done," she admitted, wiping away the tears.

Lily swiped at a wayward tear with her thumb. She offered a reassuring smile, even as her own tears threatened. "Let's get it over with," she said with a quivering lip.

She grasped Cassie's hand as the car pulled away from the curb.

Cassie took a deep breath as the elevator whisked them upward to the twenty-fourth floor of the skyscraper housing HGT, Inc. She watched number after number light up as they rose. Her mother had relayed earlier that Clayton had mentioned life insurances for both men, and retirement benefits for her father. With any luck, the retirement package would allow her mother to live a comfortable life wherever they settled. She'd already begun her job search in several of the towns they'd researched as a distraction from the grief.

The elevator doors whisked open. Glass panels cordoning off the HGT offices stared back at her. The company's associates bustled back and forth inside as she stepped out of the elevator. Clayton met them at the polished, clear glass doors leading into the space. He kissed Lily's cheek and offered another consoling hug to Cassie, before showing them into the well-appointed conference room.

Cassie glanced around the large wooden table as she eased into the thickly padded leather swivel chair. Three men in black business suits sat across from them. Paperwork was neatly stacked in front of each man.

Clayton took a seat at the head of the table, a spot he was familiar with as CEO. To her mother's left, two of HGT's corporate attorneys sat at the ready.

Clayton's administrative assistant laid a packet in front of Cassie and her mother. She poured each of them a glass of water and asked if they preferred any other refreshments. She hurried out the door after they requested nothing else, easing it shut behind her with a soft thud.

Clayton leaned forward and clasped his hands. "Lily, Cassie, these gentlemen represent the plane's manufacturer. They've requested to meet with you regarding a settlement, after an issue was found during the investigation with the plane's engines." He turned to the three men on his right. "Gentlemen, if you'd like to proceed."

The man nearest the head of the table cleared his throat and leaned forward. After offering his condolences, he said, "Mrs. Bennett, Mrs. McGuire, while we realize no amount of money can replace your loss, we have put together what we hope you'll both find is an acceptable offer for each of you."

He offered a brief smile as he slid a proposal across the table. The lead HGT attorney intercepted it. He positioned it between himself and his associates. They shared a glance after reviewing it. He turned toward Clayton and nodded.

"Could you give us a moment?" Clayton requested of the three attorneys.

They nodded and silently left the room. Clayton offered a tight-lipped smile at Lily and Cassie. He slid the paper toward them. Cassie glanced at the black font printed against the white paper. A yellow mark highlighted the amount proposed as restitution for the malfunctioning engine.

Cassie swallowed hard and glanced with wide eyes at her mother. With her eyebrows raised high and her jaw agape, she realized they would never want for anything again.

CHAPTER 2

Cassie pulled another box from the back of her SUV. The cool September wind swept off the nearby bay, rustling the tendrils of hair that were framing her face after escaping from her loose top knot. She glanced out over the water as the choppiness increased. A storm was blowing in. She'd have to hurry to get the last few boxes, she thought.

Cassie set the cardboard container on the wide wooden porch. She took a few steps backward, staring up at the rambling, centuries-old Victorian structure. Tonight they would spend their first night in the house. Her mind wandered to the day they'd toured it.

She recalled the warm August day. The gravel crunched under their tires as she'd pulled her vehicle closer to the beach and the house nearby. Her mother scanned it from within the car as they waited for the realtor.

"It's big," Cassie noted, as she ducked her head to see the top through her windshield.

"Too big?" Lily questioned.

Cassie shrugged. "Maybe not. Let's keep an open mind. Here's the realtor now."

The familiar sound of crushing gravel announced the arrival of the local realtor. Her small blue crossover SUV lurched to a halt behind Cassie's pink Wrangler. The door popped open as the car continued to rock. Black medium-height pumps peeked under the car's door. The middle-aged woman stood and adjusted her skirt suit. She swept a hand through her brunette hair as she reached in for her bag.

As she swung the car door shut, she offered a tentative wave and a faltering smile toward the other SUV in the driveway.

"Ready?" Lily asked.

"Yep," Cassie answered, as they opened their doors and emerged into the warm late summer air.

"Hi, ladies!" the realtor called in a cheery ,though uncertain, voice.

Cassie and Lily joined her at the rear of Cassie's car. "Have you been waiting long?" the realtor asked.

"No, only a few minutes," Lily answered.

The women nodded and smiled.

"I'm Lily Bennett," Lily said, extending her hand to the woman. "And this is my daughter, Cassie."

"Oh, where are my manners? I am so sorry. Lucy Clifford," the woman answered, as she shook Lily's hand, then Cassie's. "Hideaway Bay's newest realtor."

"Newest?" Lily questioned.

"Yes," the woman said, with a bobbling nod, "I just passed my exam six months ago!"

"Ah," Lily answered. "Well, congratulations."

"Thank you," the woman said, with another nervous smile. "Well, shall we?"

Cassie and Lily nodded and followed Lucy to the wide wooden stairs leading to the ample front porch. Ornate pillars rose to hold the roof above. Decorative scrollwork graced each corner. The steps groaned under their weight as

Lucy offered another nervous chuckle, shoving a lock of hair behind her ear.

She approached the front door and fiddled with the lockbox. "Shoot," she cursed under her breath. With an apologetic smile, she tugged at the box until it finally popped open.

As she retrieved the key, she struck up a conversation. "I understand you're moving in together?" she probed.

"Yes, that's right," Lily answered. "My husband and Cassie's recently passed away."

"Both of them?" Lucy inquired, her eyes wide at the admission.

"Yes," Cassie answered. "They were on the same plane."

"Oh, how tragic," Lucy said, as she swung the double front doors open. They creaked on their hinges, offering the first glimpses of the interior.

"Welcome to Whispering Manor," she said as she motioned inside.

Cassie and Lily stepped into the generous foyer. Cassie's eyes rose as she took in the grand space. A wide wooden staircase rose from dark hardwood floors to a gallery-style hallway circling above. Two statues of angels stood on each side of the staircase, holding candles high in the air. A burgundy runner adorned the stairs.

"Whispering Manor?" Cassie inquired.

"Mmm-hmm," Lucy answered with a nod. "Yes."

"Is there a reason for that name in particular?" Cassie asked.

"Well," Lucy answered, as she studied the hardwood floor. She paused and swallowed, pursing her lips before continuing. "Yes. The house is named because of the way the wind tends to sound in this particular spot. Like someone whispering."

"I see—interesting," Cassie answered.

Lucy pushed the other side of her hair behind her ears

and clasped her hands in front of her. "So, this is obviously the entryway. You can see the exquisite and unique details with the carved banister, door casings, statues and the paneled walls."

Cassie rubbed her hand along the carved wood casing leading from the entryway into another room. The details were exquisite.

Lucy stepped through the doorway and into the next room. "And this is your living room," she said. "Well, what they called the 'sitting room' in the day this place was built." She chuckled.

Cassie followed her into the room and stared at the sheet-covered items. "The fireplace is simply striking," Lucy said, as she motioned toward the massive fireplace centered against one of the interior walls. A large chandelier hung in the room's middle. Massive windows looked out onto the front porch.

"Does the furniture come with it?"

"Yes," Lucy answered, as Lily joined them to peruse the room.

They spent another hour touring the sizable home. They ended their walk-through in the house's substantial eat-in kitchen.

"Well, initial thoughts, ladies?"

"It's certainly a beautiful property," Lily said.

"They don't build 'em like they used to," Lucy said, as she smoothed her hair behind her ear for the umpteenth time. She offered another nervous chuckle. "And with the beach-front property, it's really ideal. The beach outside is private. The nearest public area isn't for another five miles." She motioned south. "The property extends on either side, so you have a generous wooded lot which means you'll have your privacy with very little maintenance. And the…"

The woman babbled on about the house's virtues, before Lily interrupted her.

"Well, we certainly have a lot to consider," she broke in.

Lucy offered a wide-eyed, closed-mouth smile and a brief nod. "Hideaway Bay is a lovely little community," she offered.

"Yes," Cassie chimed in, "it seems picturesque. We are still considering several communities. We haven't really settled on anything yet."

"Oh! What are the criteria? Perhaps I can offer some selling points for Hideaway Bay to take the win!" She pumped her fist in the air.

"We'd like to open a small business, so we're looking for an area where we'd have business from both locals and tourists. And one with shop space available, obviously," Cassie answered.

Lucy's eyes lit up and she raised her eyebrows. "Oh, well I can help with that!" she exclaimed. "In fact, I've got the perfect spot for you. It's downtown, right on Main Street. Do you have a few minutes to take a look now?"

"Oh, well…" Lily began. She glanced at Cassie who shrugged.

"Sure," Cassie answered.

"Wonderful!" Lucy exclaimed. "Just follow me!"

They left Whispering Manor behind and followed Lucy's car toward town.

"Now look what you've got us roped into," Lily said.

"Well, we do need a shop! Isn't it best to know if we can get everything we want? There's no sense falling in love with a house and finding out we can't set up shop in town!"

"Falling in love with a house?" Lily questioned.

Cassie glanced at her before returning her eyes to the road ahead. She shrugged. "I liked it."

Lily raised her eyebrows.

"You didn't?" Cassie questioned.

"I didn't say that."

"But?" Cassie prodded.

"I have a few questions for the realtor."

"Such as?"

"Why has that house been on the market so long for starters?" Lily offered.

Cassie considered the question. "Maybe people don't go for that kind of stuff anymore? We are a little quirky."

Lily raised her eyebrows again. "At that price? Come on."

"I guess we could ask her. It's well within our budget."

"That's what worries me. A house like that so cheap? Plus, she seems nervous."

"She's new. Maybe it's her first sale or her first big sale," Cassie suggested.

"Or she's holding something back."

Cassie swung the car behind a row of buildings into an alley just before the town's central Main Street. "Let's see what she's got to show us in town in terms of commercial real estate and go from there."

"All right," Lily agreed, as the car slowed to a stop. She unbuckled her seat belt. "And by the way, I loved the house, too."

Cassie offered a half-smile as they climbed from the car.

Lucy spent the next ninety minutes showing them the available retail space. Five stores up from the town's center, the open spot was sandwiched between a bakery and a book store. Painted in navy blue with large display windows and a striped awning, the storefront had charming curb appeal.

The realtor treated them to pastries from the shop next door and lemonades from the coffee shop across the street as they toured the downtown shopping district.

After inquiring about the store's rent, they'd found it fit nicely into their budget. Though they discussed it at length, both women's gut reaction for both the manor house and the shop was positive.

They'd ended up making an offer on both spaces, and had closed the cash deal within thirty days.

The sound of a honking horn pulled Cassie from her memories. She twisted to face the driveway as a small blue SUV trundled toward her. The horn sounded again in a short burst, before the car rolled to a stop.

Lucy hopped out and waved.

"Hi there! Just thought I'd check to see how the move was going!" she called. She pulled a small flat box from her back seat.

Cassie met her at the open hatch of her own vehicle. "Pretty well," she answered. "We decided to keep most of the furniture in the place, so we only had to move our personal belongings."

Cassie grabbed another box. Lucy pulled the final box from the car's cargo space, setting the flat box on top, and followed Cassie to the porch.

"I saw some movement at the shop," she said, as they ambled up the porch's steps.

"Yes," Cassie answered, "we had the contractor you recommended come in to put a fresh coat of paint on the interior and set up the display cases and shelving."

"They were hanging the sign when I went past," Lucy replied. "And they had completed the window art."

"Oh, great! I can't wait to see it!" Cassie gushed.

Lucy smiled broadly. "'*Buy the Sea*' is such a cute name for a seaside souvenir shop."

"Thank you!" Cassie answered. "And thank you for your help in finding the local artisans to fill the shop with their wares. We're so excited to showcase the town's talent."

"You're fitting in well here," Lucy said with a nod, as they carried the boxes over the threshold.

"You can set that down anywhere," Cassie told her as she dropped her box to the floor near the staircase. Lily shuffled down from the upper floor. "Look who came to visit!"

Lily wiped her hands on the dust rag slung over her shoulder before sticking her hand out to Lucy.

"Did the cleaning company I recommended do a poor job?" she inquired, motioning to the purple dust rag.

"Not at all," Lily answered. "Everything was spic and span when we arrived this morning! Though the newspaper I used to wrap a few items in is another story."

Lucy nodded with a smile as understanding set in. "Can we offer you something to drink? Tea? Coffee?" Lily asked.

"Oh, no, thanks. I just stopped by to see how things were coming along. And to give you this housewarming gift!"

Lucy thrust the flat box forward toward the two women with a broad grin. "Oh, thank you," Lily answered. "How thoughtful."

Cassie accepted the box as she added, "Yes, thanks!"

She slipped off the gold ribbon that stretched around the box and shimmied the bottom loose from the lid. She pulled back the tissue paper to reveal the contents.

"Aww," she murmured, as she shifted the box toward her mother. "How cute!"

Lucy beamed. "The realty company wanted to welcome you to the community."

Cassie lifted the painted weathered driftwood from the box. *Whispering Manor* was painted across it in a sea blue color. A painted recreation of the house stood after it. A chain attached on either side of the sign, making it ready for hanging.

"There's a lamppost at the driveway's entrance with a spot for it," Lucy explained. "The old sign bit the dust a while ago."

"What a lovely thought. Thank you," Lily answered.

"We'll hang it today!" Cassie added.

"Well, I'll get out of your hair and let you settle in. Are you staying here tonight?" Lucy questioned.

"Yes," Cassie answered. "We've got the sheets on the beds and we're prepared for our first night at Whispering Manor!"

Lucy smiled broadly. "Well, on that note, good luck."

Lily's brow creased. "Good luck?" she asked with a chuckle.

Lucy's eyes widened. "Oh, uh," she stumbled. "Uh, I meant, hope you sleep well and, er, welcome."

"Thanks," Cassie answered, as Lucy inched toward the front door.

"Take care!" she called, as she stumbled over the threshold and spun to flee down the porch's three wooden stairs.

"What was that about?" Cassie asked as she heard Lucy's car door slam.

"I'm not sure," Lily answered.

"What an odd sentiment for someone's first night in their new house. Good luck?"

Lily shrugged. "Perhaps she meant with the move and the work."

"Maybe," Cassie reflected aloud. "Well, should we take a break for lunch and hang this sign?"

"Sure. I could use a few minutes to think through where I'd like to place things."

Cassie pulled the sign from the box and they strode out of the house down to the lamp post with the pole. Cassie reached for the old chain, but found it just outside her grasp. After fishing out a ladder from the storage shed near the house, she dragged it to the lamp post and set it up.

"Careful, Cassie," her mother warned, as she climbed higher on the ladder.

As she leaned over, the wooden ladder groaned and shifted on the sandy soil.

"Whoa!" Cassie exclaimed, as she clutched at the sides.

Lily grasped the wooden structure to stabilize it. "Watch it, Cassie!" she exclaimed. "The last thing we need is a trip to the hospital on our first day in town."

"Keep hold of the ladder while I hang this," Cassie requested.

Lily kept her weight on the ladder so it didn't tip as Cassie once again leaned over and removed the old chains from the post. They clanged as she dropped them to the ground. Next, she hooked one side of the sign, then the other. It swung free as Cassie descended the ladder to the safety of the ground below.

She smiled up at the sign. "There!" she exclaimed. "And I didn't have to break a leg to do it!"

As she uttered the last word, the chain on the sign snapped. The sign swung wildly from the one remaining chain, banging into the lamppost and twirling around.

Both Lily and Cassie jumped as the chain broke free. Cassie reached to stop the sign from flailing around in the breeze.

"I hope that's not an omen," she said with a grimace.

Lily raised her eyebrows. "Perhaps we should hang it later."

Cassie nodded her head in response. "Let's head in for lunch. I'll just grab the sign…"

"Maybe leave it," Lily suggested. "I'd rather you didn't climb that ladder again."

Cassie nodded, and they made their way back to the house. As they walked up the drive, Cassie glanced back at the sign dangling from the post. She swallowed hard. Was it a bad omen?

CHAPTER 3

*assie's concern over the broken sign melted as she enjoyed the cucumber sandwiches and hot tea they'd planned for their first lunch in Whispering Manor. The ample kitchen included a large butcher block prep island, surrounded by cabinets and counter space. Offset from the main kitchen was a bay window with a round wooden kitchen table.

Cassie sipped her tea as she stared out the massive bay window to the ocean's rolling waves.

"It really is a perfect spot," she murmured.

Lily joined her, after warming her mug with a touch more hot water and another dunk of her teabag.

"I never realized how much I'd enjoy living near the ocean, but I don't think I'll ever tire of it," Cassie said.

"It's the English in you," Lily answered. "Although, it's been less than a day, so I'm not sure you can comment on tiring from it yet."

Cassie popped open one of the window panes. The sounds of the waves crashing against the rocks and sand floated into the kitchen.

"I feel like that's something Grandma mentioned," Cassie said, as she settled back into her chair.

"That an Englishwoman is always drawn to the sea?" Lily inquired. "Yes, I'm sure she did."

Cassie offered half a smile as she grabbed her mother's hand. "I think we made the right choice moving here."

"I do, too," Lily answered as she squeezed her daughter's hand.

Chimes rang through the house, temporarily drowning out the ocean sounds. Both women's heads swung in the direction of the front door.

Lily raised an eyebrow at Cassie. "Our first visitors!"

"Technically, Lucy was our first visitor."

"She doesn't count. She was our realtor."

Lily offered a coy smile before rising from her chair. They navigated through the house to the front door. A bright pink splotch shined through the door's oval privacy window.

Lily pulled the door open. A tall, lithe woman with a chic blonde bob, dressed in a bright pink skirt suit with matching heels, smiled widely. Next to her stood a shorter, round woman. Her brunette bob mimicked the blonde's though it fell shorter in style. She wore a navy pantsuit and a sensible pair of flats. She clutched her purse in both hands as she eyed Cassie and Lily.

"Hello," Lily said. "Can I help you?"

"Hi!" the blonde said in a cheery voice. "You must be Lily and Cassie." She stuck her hand out. "I'm Tinsley Thompson, Hideaway Bay's mayor and president of the welcoming committee! I'm also your neighbor! Two houses down that way."

She pointed south, then motioned toward her companion.

"And this is Penny Whitlock. She's part of the town's

commerce committee. She reviewed *Buy the Sea's* business proposal."

"Oh," Lily said, as she shook their hands, followed by Cassie, "nice to meet you both. Is there a problem with the business proposal?"

"No!" Tinsley answered, with a laugh that bordered on a cackle. "No, nothing like that. We're here to say a friendly Hideaway Bay hello to the two new gals!"

"How nice," Lily answered. "Won't you come in?"

"Oh, just for a few moments," Tinsley said, wrinkling her nose. "I'm sure you're busy getting settled."

The two women stepped into the foyer. "Oh, it's been so long since I've seen the inside of this old place," Tinsley babbled.

"Can I get anyone something to drink? Hot tea or lemonade?" Cassie offered.

"Oh, a hot tea would be lovely!" Tinsley answered. "Wouldn't it, Penny?" The short woman nodded, seemingly pulled along with whatever Tinsley decided.

Cassie disappeared toward the kitchen to fill the orders of tea, as Lily settled into the sitting room with the two women.

Tinsley perched on the edge of her chair and offered a wide smile to Lily. "It's so nice to see Whispering Manor with life in it again."

"It had been on the market quite a while from what I understand," Lily answered.

Tinsley nodded her head. "Oh, yes, yes. Two years. Though no one has lived here for at least five."

"More than that," Penny interjected.

"Well, I said *at least*," Tinsley retorted.

"Either way," Lily interjected, "we're so glad Lucy showed it to us. We fell in love with the house and the town."

"That's wonderful to hear," Tinsley said with a demure smile, as Cassie returned with a tray of mugs.

"We've only unpacked the mugs. Sorry, no fancy china."

"Oh, it's just fine," Penny answered with a genuine smile, as she accepted a steaming mug from the tray.

"We'll just have to book another tea party with the china once you're settled in," Tinsley said, as she offered a half-smile, half-frown at the bulldog mascot emblazoned on the mug.

"Your business proposal was one of the best I've ever read," Penny said as Cassie settled onto the sofa next to Lily.

"Oh, thank you," Cassie said with a large smile. "Owning a shop like this has always been something we've talked about."

Tinsley raised her eyebrows. "Oh? How interesting. I thought you were a librarian."

"Yes, I was," Cassie answered. "Though after my husband and father passed away, we decided we needed a change. We had always talked about owning a shop and decided maybe now was the time."

"Oh, yes," Tinsley said with an understanding nod and a pout on her face. "What a terrible tragedy. Such a shame." She shook her head and clicked her tongue.

"How is the work at the shop coming?" Penny inquired. "I saw the sign already hanging out front earlier today."

Cassie opened her mouth to answer, but Tinsley beat her to it.

"Oh, Penny, let's not badger them about it on their first day in town! I'm sure they have plenty of settling in to do here before they worry about the shop!"

"Well, we hope to be there…" Lily began, as Tinsley shushed her and waved for her to stop.

"There's no need to explain at all. We understand." She took a sip of her tea as awkward silence fell over the room. "Speaking of signs, I noticed your Whispering Manor sign dangling sideways from the lamppost sideways. I'm not sure if you saw it."

"Yes," Lily answered. "We hung it just before lunch and the chain snapped. We'll need to fix it later. I insisted we have some lunch before Cassie climbed that ladder again."

"Ah, yes. A faulty chain." Tinsley offered a knowing glance. "I'm glad to see you are both so level-headed and didn't give in to the lore."

"Lore?" Cassie inquired.

"Oh, yes," Tinsley said, with a slow nod of her head. "I'm surprised Lucy didn't tell you. Though, then again, she wanted to make the deal, no doubt. And I suppose she's not really required to disclose it. It IS only a rumor. And technically the death wasn't *in* the house."

"Death? Disclose what?" Cassie asked.

"Oh," Tinsley said, flicking her hand at Cassie and shaking her head. She puckered her lips and narrowed her eyes. "Nothing, nothing. Just…" She paused and added a dramatic shrug. "Some people would have read the snapping sign as a harbinger of bad things to come because…"

Cassie raised her eyebrows and cocked her head.

Tinsley glanced side-to-side, before leaning forward and pressing her hand to the side of her mouth. "The house is haunted," she whispered.

CHAPTER 4

Tinsley leaned back in her chair, a half-grin on her face, looking like the cat who caught the canary after her revelation.

"Haunted?" Cassie exclaimed. "You're kidding."

Tinsley gave her head a slight shake, rustling the hair of her bob ever so slightly. "No. No, residents of Hideaway Bay insist Whispering Manor is haunted." She offered that cackle-like chuckle. "Didn't you wonder why it was called Whispering Manor?"

"Lucy explained that," Cassie answered. "It's the way the wind sweeps over the bay. It sounds like a whisper."

"Well, so they say. Others would say it's whispers of past souls, long since forgotten, but not yet gone."

"Any souls in particular?" Lily inquired.

"Oh, yes," Tinsley answered, with a knowing nod. "A few, actually."

Lily raised her eyebrows, and Tinsley continued. "This house has been around for a long time. Somewhere back in the late 1700s, early 1800s, a sea captain owned this house. He went to sea one day, never to return!"

"But his soul returned to haunt the house?" Cassie suggested.

Tinsley shook her head. "No. But his widow awaited his return. She'd go to the widow's walk every evening and stare out across the sea, waiting for her love to return."

"How tragic," Cassie answered, biting her lower lip. A piece of the story resonated with her. She understood the widow's grief.

"Indeed—though the real tragedy comes later."

"Oh?" Cassie prodded.

"The poor girl went mad from her grief. After years of waiting for her lost husband, she threw herself from the widow's walk. It's she who haunts this house! Well, it's she who is *one* of your ghosts anyway. The most famous one."

A hushed silence fell over the room for a moment, before Penny spoke.

"It's a bunch of hooey," she said, with a shake of her head.

"Oh, of course, of course. I'm just ribbing you," Tinsley said, with a cackle that ended in a snort.

"Though there is the bit about the treasure; that's the thing that's always fascinated me!" Penny added.

"Treasure?"

Tinsley offered another coy smile and a nod of her head. "Yes, according to the local rumor mill, the woman's brother was a pirate. He brought treasure and hid it somewhere here." Tinsley rolled her eyes. "Untold riches going unfound for centuries? Now *that's* hooey!"

Cassie offered her a faltering smile before taking another sip of tea. The ladies turned their conversation to the shop opening. Mayor Thompson dropped a few hints about upcoming town events she hoped they would participate in, before they disbanded in the name of allowing the women to continue their unpacking.

Cassie and Lily saw them off from the porch. Tinsley twisted to face them as she strode toward her car.

"You should get that sign fixed," she called. "Before people start believing the rumors." She offered a wink before she mouthed the word "haunted" and gave a fake shiver, her mouth turning in an "O" shape. She waved at them as she began to chuckle, suggesting it was all just a joke.

"Interesting woman," Lily noted, as dust trailed behind the departing car.

"I'll say," Cassie agreed. "Haunted? What have we gotten ourselves into?"

"Less unpacking than we'd have liked, that's what," Lily said. "Come on, I'd like to finish a few more boxes before we call it quits for the day."

"All right," Cassie agreed with a nod. "If you can stand being in there." She fake shivered and mouthed "haunted" to her mother in a mimic of the Mayor's antics.

The two women shared a laugh as they climbed the elegant staircase.

* * *

Cassie wandered into the living room at quarter past one in the morning. Her pink robe swirled around her, and she drew it closer as she shuffled in her fluffy slippers.

"Couldn't sleep?" she asked, as she collapsed next to Lily.

Lily shook her head. "Nope, you?"

"No luck," Cassie answered. "Hot chocolate?"

"Only if you bring cookies with it."

Cassie returned with a tray full of shortbreads and two mugs of hot chocolate. Mini marshmallows floated in the frothy concoction. The two women toasted before taking a sip.

"What's keeping you up?" Cassie inquired. "Ghosts?" She chuckled.

"Something like that," Lily answered.

"You aren't being serious."

Lily smiled at her, taking another sip of the warm chocolatey drink. "The whispering winds are howling tonight," she admitted.

Cassie nodded. "I heard it in my room, too. It really does sound like whispering voices, doesn't it?"

"Yes, and I can understand the name for the house now."

"And its haunted reputation," Cassie said, raising her eyebrows.

Lily chuckled as she bit into a shortbread cookie. "Yes. Though I'm not surprised by the tale."

"Me either," Cassie said with a chuckle. "In fact, I think it's the same tale I've heard dozens of times about haunted houses."

"I think it's almost a word-for-word description of the story they recounted on *Dark Shadows* over fifty years ago."

"Oh, right," Cassie said, with a laugh. "Widow's Hill and the call of the widows." She blew air from her mouth in a "woo" sound. "What about that treasure thing though?"

A loud clang sounded outside, preventing any answer to her question. Both women jumped.

Cassie shook her head. "That sign. I never fixed it. It's clanging around out there under the lamp."

"I guess we're both a little on edge in a new house," Lily admitted, as she spotted the wooden sign twirling on its single chain.

"I guess I should go take it down from there."

"It's not hurting anyone. We shouldn't hear it from our rooms."

"I'm glad you said that. I don't feel like moving anywhere but back to bed."

"Feeling tired?" Lily inquired, as she pushed a lock of hair behind Cassie's ear.

Cassie yawned. "A little. Maybe I'll be able to sleep with a belly full of milk and cookies."

"Let's try it," Lily agreed.

They set their mugs on the tray. Cassie snagged the final cookie from the plate and bit into it.

"Leave those for the morning," Lily said, as she waved at the mugs and now-empty plate.

"You sure?"

"Yeah," she said, as she looped her arm around Cassie's shoulders. "Let's get some sleep."

"Okay," Cassie agreed with a smile, as she swallowed the last bite of cookie.

They took one step toward the foyer when a loud crash sounded from the floor above.

Both women froze. Their eyes floated to the ceiling above them. Cassie bit her lower lip. "*That* wasn't the sign clanging outside," she said.

"No," Lily answered.

Cassie swallowed hard. "Maybe it was nothing? The groaning of an old house." Her eyes slid sideways to her mother.

Lily offered a sideways glance at Cassie. She opened her mouth to speak when another thud sounded, followed by two more in rapid succession. *Thump. Thump, thump, thump.*

A scraping noise emanated from above. The two women shrank away from the ceiling, before glancing at each other.

"What was that?" Cassie asked, her eyes wide with fear.

Lily shrugged and mouthed, "I don't know."

"Do you think it's an intruder? Should we call someone?" Cassie asked. "The police?"

"I hate to do that, particularly if it's a false alarm. The front door looked secure when I came down."

"The back door was still locked, too," Cassie answered.

They waited a moment, weighing their options. "Sounds like it stopped."

As if on cue, another thump sounded.

"Something's up there," Cassie whispered.

"Or someone."

Cassie's eyebrows raised. "Do you think someone broke in?"

Lily shrugged and raised her hands, palms facing up. "Let's do a little investigating."

"Are you kidding?"

"We have to check," Lily breathed.

"Is this safe?"

"We'll get something to use as a weapon."

"Knife?" Cassie suggested.

Lily nodded. The two women crept into the foyer and made a quick dash through, clinging to the walls to remain unseen by anyone lurking on the upper floor.

After retrieving the largest, most menacing knives they could find, Cassie and Lily crept back to the foyer and began to ascend the main staircase.

"Stay behind me," Lily breathed, as she shoved Cassie to the side and stepped past her on the stairs.

"Mom! No!" Cassie hissed. "I've got faster reflexes!"

"Yes, so if something happens to me, you can run away and get help faster than I could!"

"Mom!" Cassie protested again.

"Shh," her mother replied.

They swung around the ornate wooden banister and inched their way toward the room above the living room.

Light shone from under the door. It moved from one side of the room to the other. Tinkling music sounded from within.

Cassie waved her finger toward the moving light beam. Lily nodded.

"I see it," she whispered.

They continued creeping toward the door. As they reached it, Lily drew in a deep breath. She swallowed hard and nodded to Cassie. Raising her fist, she banged against the door.

"Who's in there?" she hollered. "We've called the police. They'll be here any minute. Come out now and we won't press charges!"

Cassie knit her brow and offered Lily an "are you kidding?" stare. Lily shrugged and waved her away, indicating that she didn't mean it.

Thump, thump.

"There's nothing of value in there!" Lily called.

The sound of glass rolling across the floor reached their ears. The light beam shifted again.

"What are they doing?" Cassie breathed.

"Get back, I'm opening the door."

"Mom, wait!" Cassie protested, but her mother had already swung the door open.

Cassie stared inside with her mouth agape. Lily took a tentative step into the room, knife held high.

Boxes were piled in the far corner. One box lay on its side near a closed window, its contents spilled out onto the dark hardwood floor. A small wooden jewelry box lay open. Its musical mechanism slowly played a tune, providing eerie background music for the scene.

A lit lamp lay on the floor. It rolled on its shade back and forth, its light bouncing from one wall to another. A small wooden side table lay on its side, and a glass cat figurine rolled across the floor.

Lily stepped further into the room. Cassie followed, whipping the door half-closed to check behind it. They found no one. Lily tapped her finger toward the partially ajar closet door.

Cassie nodded. She readied for an attacker to spring from it, spreading her legs into a wide stance and raising her knife. Lily whipped the door open.

Cassie blinked her eyes as she rose from her lunge. Her jaw fell open and she shook her head. Though frightened, she had been prepared for a human to emerge from the closet. She'd conjured images of an individual clad in dark clothing, their face obscured by a ski mask, wielding a crowbar or the like. But what emerged wasn't human. Not even close.

CHAPTER 5

*C*assie dropped her knife to her side as she continued to stare at what sauntered from the closet. Lily backed a few steps away, joining Cassie across the room.

"Is that a…" Cassie cocked her head and knit her brows as her voice trailed off.

"Yep," Lily answered her unfinished question with a nod of her head. "A cat."

A black-and-white tuxedo cat sashayed from the confines of the closet. It hunched its back and wiggled its tail, as it slid against the stack of boxes near the window. One yellow-green eye peered at them from within a black spot.

Cassie set the knife on a nearby table and crouched down. "He only has one eye!"

"Poor thing," Lily answered. "I wonder what happened to him."

"At least we know the source of the commotion now," Cassie replied, her eyes still on the furry creature across the room. She held her hand out, palm facing up.

"And at least it wasn't an intruder."

"Well, it was. Just not of the human variety."

The cat stood eyeing the two women. As Cassie inched toward it, it flinched and hid behind the box stack. It peered around the corner at her.

"Poor thing is probably hungry. It must have gotten in with the cleaning crew," Lily surmised.

"How about some milk, kitty?" Cassie asked. Its ears perked as she spoke, but it shied away when she made a move toward it.

"It's skittish," Lily said. "Perhaps we should clean up in here and put out a saucer of milk. We may have some canned tuna, too, and leave it for the night."

Cassie raised her eyebrows at the suggestion, as she picked up the small lamp and returned it to its table. The cat watched her curiously from its safe spot behind the boxes.

"You grab the cat food and I'll clean up," Cassie offered.

Within fifteen minutes, they had restored the room to its previous state. This time, Cassie did her best to cat-proof the items. Lily set a saucer of tuna and another with milk near the furry critter's hiding spot. Before they left the room, the fluff-ball had meandered out and devoured the tuna. Now, it worked on lapping up the milk.

"Aww, he was hungry," Cassie said.

"He? Did you check?"

Cassie nodded. "He's a he!" She slid her eyes sideways to glance at her mother and offered her a coy grin. "Can we keep him?"

"Oh, Cassie," Lily said with a chuckle. "I never thought I'd have to answer that question again after your wedding day."

"I'll run to the pet store tomorrow morning for some supplies," Cassie said, an eyebrow raised.

"Why did it have to be a cat?" Lily lamented. "I'm more of a dog person."

"I'm sure he'll grow on you," Cassie said, as she flicked the light switch off and pulled the door shut to contain the animal for now.

"At least it wasn't an intruder," Lily repeated, as they each headed for their beds.

* * *

Cassie waved a feather plucked from her feather duster at the furry kitty. It playfully batted at the makeshift toy. The small four-legged creature had been less shy after a second round of food this morning.

Lily knocked on the door as she peered into the room. "You heading into town for cat supplies?"

"Yes," Cassie said, as she stroked the unnamed cat's fur, "Do you think he's someone's cat?"

"We can ask around. Though he looks a little scruffy, so I'm not sure."

"All right," Cassie said, as she rose to her feet. "Let's head in and ask around! We can check the progress at the shop, too."

They slid into Cassie's Wrangler and made the short trip to town, parking behind their own shop.

Before they began their shopping excursion, Cassie unlocked the back door to their retail space. They pushed into the storeroom. The smell of fresh paint greeted them as they shut out the bright sunshine of an early fall day. Cassie flicked on the overhead lights and stalked into the storefront. A smile spread across her face as she saw the transformed space.

"Paint looks good!" she called to her mother, as Lily joined her.

"Oh, yeah, the accent wall is great with the nautical stripes!"

The large front windows let in the morning light,

reflecting on the empty wooden shelves and showcases. Shadows outlined the store's name across the oak hardwood floor. The words *Buy the Sea* floated on navy, light blue and white-capped waves painted on the large window and glass front door. A large boat and its billowing sails formed the "B" in the first word.

"I love the name's design," Cassie said, as she unlocked and pulled the front door open. "I want to see it from out here."

"Thanks," Lily said, proud of her design work to create their store's logo. She followed Cassie through the door onto the sidewalk and stared up at the hanging sign jutting toward the street. The women remarked on how great the exterior came together.

"I'm so excited to fill the shelves," Cassie added as they re-entered the store, locking the door behind them.

"If we ever get unpacked," Lily answered.

"Well…" Cassie began, when a frantic knock sounded against the glass.

Both women spun to face the door. A strawberry-blonde woman in a colorful apron waved a drink carrier of cardboard cups. She swayed it in the air, her perfectly shaped eyebrows raised over her flawlessly made-up eyes, as she pointed a finger toward the cups. Her bright red lips formed a broad grin.

Cassie twisted the lock and popped open the shop's front door.

"Hi there!" the woman exclaimed. "You must be Cassie."

"Uh, yeah," Cassie answered.

The woman peeked around Cassie at Lily and waved. "And you must be Lily."

"Hello," Lily called.

"Hi, I'm Meghan McKee! I own *High Grounds*." She noted the blank stare on Cassie's face. "The coffee shop across the street." She pointed to a bright yellow building. Cassie noted the sign. A steaming mug sat atop a mountain of beans.

"I just wanted to stop by and offer the new girls a sampling of my wares! I hope you both like chocolate!"

"I love it," Cassie said with a smile.

"Good!" Meghan freed a cup and handed it to Cassie. "I'm never certain if people like coffee, tea or what. But hot chocolate is usually a safe bet!" She handed a cup to Lily, who expressed her gratitude.

"We're tea drinkers," Lily answered. "Though I always appreciate a good hot chocolate."

"Spending your first day at the shop?" Meghan inquired.

"Oh, not quite," Cassie answered. "We're not completely unpacked yet. We just needed to run into town for a few things and decided to check the progress on the shop."

"Well, it looks great from across the street," Meghan assured her. "I love the name and the boat!"

"Thank you," Lily said.

"My mom designed it," Cassie added.

"Oh, really?" Meghan questioned, arching those perfectly shaped brows again. "Wow, that's fantastic! Do you free-lance? I'd love to discuss a few logo updates for seasonal promotions."

"Well…" Lily began, when Meghan interrupted her.

"After you're settled in, of course," she said, waving her own question away. "So, you're still unpacking?"

Her question was interrupted by another knock on the door. A middle-aged brunette waved from the sidewalk, hoisting an unmarked white box wrapped with string. Her short curly hair was pushed back by a thick headband, and her tortoise-rimmed glasses framed her dark brown eyes.

"Hi!" she called through the closed door.

Cassie stepped over and pushed the door open for their

second visitor. She strolled through the door and waved to the room's other occupants.

"Hi, Genny," Meghan said.

"Hi! Oh," she turned to face Cassie, as Cassie strolled across the room to join Lily. She pushed her glasses further up her nose. "Hi, I'm Genevieve Chastain. I own the bakeshop next door."

"Oh, *Cake My Day?*" Cassie inquired. "I saw your sign when we looked at this property. What a cute name!"

"Thanks," Genevieve answered, color rising in her cheeks. "You can just call me Genny, all my friends do." She waved the white box toward them. "I brought a sampling of some cookies. I saw Meghan heading over and figured she had her signature hot chocolate. What better to go with a warm, sweet drink than cookies! Just a little welcome to the block and the community."

Cassie handed her cup to Lily and accepted the box. She strolled across the space and set it on what would soon become their cash register counter. She grabbed a pair of scissors from behind the counter and cut open the string.

A variety of delicious sights and smells greeted her as she pulled the box lid open. "Oh, these look wonderful!"

She pulled a chocolate frosted sugar cookie from within and took a bite before she offered the box to the other women. Lily grabbed a thumbprint.

"Don't mind if I do. I can't resist Genny's cookies," Meghan said, as she snagged a pirouette from the box.

"So, how long have you ladies been in town?" Lily asked.

"Oh, I grew up here," Meghan said. "I opened *High Grounds* a few years back, after I got my business degree at Pembrook University."

"I moved here fifteen years ago," Genny chimed in. "I worked at a bakery in Chicago before moving here. Couldn't take any more big city life."

"Are you happy with the change?" Cassie inquired.

"Very," Genny said. "I worked long hours in Chicago and it was a real drain. I work long hours here, too, but it doesn't bother me one bit. But enough about me! How are you two settling in?"

"Oh, we're…" Cassie began, her voice faltering as she struggled to come up with a brief answer.

"We had an eventful first night," Lily explained.

"Right," Cassie agreed.

"Oh?" Meghan inquired, with her eyebrows raised high. "Really?" Her lips curled into a smile and her eyes widened. "Did you run into any ghosts?"

"Ghosts?" Lily said with a chuckle. "Heavens no."

"No, neither of us could sleep in the new house. And just as we were about to give it a second try, we heard a commotion upstairs."

"From the ghosts?" Genny questioned.

"No," Cassie said. "A cat."

"A cat?" Both women asked at the same time.

"Yes," Lily answered. "After a good deal of excitement on our part, we found a cat lurking in an upstairs closet."

"A one-eyed tuxedo cat, to be specific," Cassie added. "Have either of you heard of someone missing him?"

"No," Meghan answered, as Genny shook her head.

"You may want to check with Frida over at *Barkaway Bay Pet Shoppe*, though. She's got the pulse on animals, missing or otherwise," Genny suggested. "Just a quick word of warning, though. Frida's a little… ornery."

"Thanks for the heads up. We were headed there next," Cassie answered. "For a few supplies, in case we have a new roomie."

"I think you've already decided we do," Lily said, eyeing her daughter.

"I'm a sucker for a furry face," Cassie said with a shrug.

"So, the house has quite a reputation around here, huh? You both immediately asked about ghosts!"

"It does. It's been empty for several years," Meghan explained. "And even when it's occupied, it's not for long. I've never known occupants to live there longer than two years."

"If they make it that long," Genny added.

"Any reason why?" Cassie asked, as she took another sip of her decadently rich hot chocolate. She had to admit, this was the best hot chocolate she'd ever tasted.

"Because it's haunted?" Genny suggested with a chuckle and a shrug.

"That can't be the reason. We heard the legend of the sea captain's widow and about the treasure from Mayor Thompson. But there are no such things as ghosts," Lily replied.

"Sometimes I wonder if that treasure stuff is all just a bunch of nonsense so everyone can slap pirate-themed items in their shop and make a mint off of the tourists," Meghan said.

"So you don't think there's a treasure?" Cassie asked.

"Nah," Meghan answered, "but there are ghosts."

"Really?" Cassie questioned, incredulous.

Genny nodded and shrugged again. "Strange things happen there."

"Such as?"

"Lights going on and off at all hours of the night. Phantom noises. The sound of crying in the dead of the night. Unexplained smells. Objects moving from room to room."

"So, the usual haunting stuff?" Cassie inquired.

"Have either of you experienced any of these things?" Lily followed up.

"I've never been inside the house," Genny answered.

"I have," Meghan said. "Once. And only once. That house has *always* been a source of gossip. And, like I said, it's been abandoned for years. When I was in high school, people would dare each other to go inside. Spend a night, an hour, whatever.

"One chilly October Friday night, we were hanging out at a friend's house playing truth or dare. I made the mistake of picking dare." Meghan rolled her eyes. "You can guess what I got for the dare."

"A night in Whispering Manor?" Cassie questioned.

Meghan held up a finger. "One hour. They knew I'd never last the night," she said with a chuckle.

"So, we pulled on our coats and walked to the seaside house. No one lived there at the time. I stood for a few minutes staring up at the house's dark form. My knees were like jelly and my stomach was turning over.

"But my friends kept badgering at me. And calling me a chicken and on and on. The whole typical high school thing. So, I walked up the driveway. I took one glance back at my friends—who, by the way, wouldn't even set foot on the property, let alone in the house—and went through the door."

"Did anything happen to you?" Cassie asked.

"Oh, yeah," Meghan answered.

"Really?" Cassie asked, coughing as she choked on a sip of hot chocolate.

"I went into the foyer. Those angel statues were outlined in the dim moonlight seeping through the privacy glass, and they looked very creepy. I figured I'd just stand there for the entire hour and never move. But after a while, my curiosity got the better of me.

"So, I wandered into the room on the right, through the dining room and into the kitchen. I continued back through the dining room and then into the library before I ended up in the foyer again.

"Nothing had happened to me so I got bold. I put a foot on the step leading up. Then I climbed another and another.

Before I knew it, I was standing upstairs. That's when it hit me."

"Someone hit you?" Cassie asked, eyes wide.

"No, not someone. Something. A smell. Like roses. Unmistakeable. I followed the scent down the hall toward the circular stairs leading to the widow's walk."

"Did you climb up?" Lily asked.

Meghan shook her head. "No. I put one foot on the wooden stair when the door at the top opened. A gust of chilly wind blew in and the door banged shut. But just before it did, lightning tore through the sky, and that's when I saw her."

"Who?" Cassie questioned.

"The sea captain's widow. The woman who roams Whispering Manor: Henrietta Blanchard herself."

CHAPTER 6

*C*assie's eyes widened and Lily furrowed her brow. Meghan continued, "She was gruesome. Her dress was bloody and torn. Her dark hair hung in clumps around her gray skin. A big cut oozed blood from her forehead, and her eyes were bulging out of her head. She had long black curling nails, and she was reaching for me!

"I spun around and raced as fast as I could out of that house."

"So, you didn't make the hour?" Genny inquired.

"Nope, not even close," Meghan answered.

"That was a lot of detail to see in one brief lightning flash," Lily noted.

Meghan nodded. "It was fleeting, but that moment has been burned into my memory for fifteen years."

"Did you tell your friends?"

"I could barely string words together when I got out of there. I was shaking all over. We started to walk home but just before we left, I glanced back at the house."

"And?" Cassie asked.

"There was Henrietta, standing at an upstairs window. She had the curtain pulled back and she was sneering at me."

"Wow, that's intense," Cassie answered.

Meghan nodded in a silent response, then added, "I have never set foot in that house since that night."

An awkward silence filled the room, until Genny spoke again. "Well, I guess on that note, we should let you get back to unpacking so you can start your lives here." She offered an awkward chuckle, as though the statement made no sense after the last story.

"Or maybe you'd prefer not to unpack," Meghan offered. "Just in case."

Cassie chuckled. "I think we'll chance it. We're really in love with the house, so I hope Madame Blanchard stays on the widow's walk and doesn't take to roaming inside."

Meghan offered a shrug. "Don't say we didn't warn you," she said with a wink.

Genny looped her arm through Meghan's. "Come on, enough with the veiled threats. Let's let them get on with their business."

"It's not a threat," Meghan argued, as she let herself be led to the door. "More of a warning. No one lasts more than eighteen months in that house!"

"Welcome to the neighborhood!" Genny called back, as she ushered Meghan from the store.

Cassie twisted to face Lily. "Well, that was…"

"Interesting," Lily filled in.

"At least we got a nice cup of hot chocolate and some cookies," Cassie replied.

"Yes, the drink was pretty good."

"Looks like we'll be visiting *High Grounds* again soon!"

"And the bakery," Lily added. "But for now, let's get to the pet store, so we can get home and finish our work there. I'm itching to get in here and get started. Penny said we could do a good business during the October tourist rush and leading up to the holiday season."

Cassie smiled and nodded. After seeing the work in progress, she, too, was yearning to begin her career as a retail shop owner. With the remains of their hot chocolate in hand, they slipped out the shop's front door and walked the block to *Barkaway Bay*.

They pushed through the paw-covered front door and into the pet shop. The large space housed a wide variety of pet-related items. With low shelves and a "Pet's Welcome!" sign, the shop appeared to be set up to appeal to its four-legged customers as much as to its two-legged ones.

Cassie smiled and waved as the woman behind the register greeted them. Her bobbed gray-white hair was pushed behind her ears, framing her tanned skin and makeup-less face. In her late sixties, she wore a simple blue-jean shirt and jeans, her sleeves rolled up to her elbows.

"Morning," she said.

"Good morning," Cassie said, as she browsed a collection of colorful mice in a display bin.

The woman side-eyed them as they meandered around the store.

"Help you find anything?" she questioned after a few moments.

"No, thanks," Cassie said. "Though I did have a question."

"Shoot," she said, wrapping bags of dog biscuits.

Cassie stepped toward the counter. "I'm Cassie McGuire. This is my mom, Lily Bennett. We just moved into Whispering Manor."

The woman lifted her eyes to Cassie and narrowed them. After a moment, she returned to her work with a grunt.

Cassie swallowed, unsure what to make of the woman's response. She noted the name tag pinned to her shirt as she closed the gap between her and the woman. *Frida.* She recalled Genny's warning about Frida's gruff personality. That explained it.

"Anyway, last night, we found a cat inside. We were wondering if he belonged to someone. Genny from the bakery said you would be the best person to ask."

"Probably am," Frida admitted. "Got a picture?"

"Ah, no," Cassie answered, feeling silly for not having taken one. "But he's a tuxedo cat with one-eye."

"He's nobody's," Frida said.

A stunned expression crossed Cassie's face. "Are-are you sure?"

"Yep," Frida answered. She grabbed a card from a drawer behind the counter and slid it across toward Cassie. "Here's the number for animal control."

"Oh, no!" Cassie exclaimed. "If he doesn't belong to anyone, we'd like to keep him. We just wanted to be sure he wasn't someone's pet."

"He's a pathetic little thing. Been here for at least a year. Always begging for scraps at people's doors or nosing in their trash. He's likely got fleas. Maybe worms."

"Well, I suppose we'd better pick up flea meds and a dewormer, along with all the other necessities," Cassie said.

Frida gave Cassie a long, hard stare. She slid the card for animal control back and pushed another card forward. "Local vet. He'll come right to your house."

"Thanks," Cassie said, as she slipped the card into her purse.

Frida offered a single nod. "If you need help, let me know." She gathered up the bags of dog bones and wandered to the shop's front.

Cassie retrieved a shopping basket and filled it with all the necessities for a cat. Lily had already selected a red plaid bed with a matching blanket, red bowls, and a litter box. Cassie added a feather wand toy, a package of colorful mice and a ball. They grabbed food, treats, medicines and litter to round out the purchase.

They approached the cash register with two shopping baskets filled. Frida's eyebrows raised high as she began to ring up the items.

"Lucky kitty," she muttered. "So, you're living at the Manor, huh?"

"That's right. We just moved in yesterday," Cassie answered.

Frida's eyes shot toward them. "You know it's haunted, right?"

Cassie chuckled, but sobered quickly when Frida offered her an unappreciative stare.

"We've been told by a few people at this point," Lily said.

Frida shook her head. "Realtor should have told you."

"She didn't mention it, though a few of the other shop owners have, as well as Mayor Thompson."

Friday snorted a laugh. "I'm not surprised Lucy never mentioned it. She got saddled with that place and was desperate to sell it."

"Lucky we don't believe in ghosts!" Cassie said.

"You will," Frida said. "Give it a few months." She shoved the toys into a brown *Barkaway Bay* reusable bag.

Cassie shot Lily a glance as she plastered on an uncomfortable smile.

"Well, perhaps we'll find a way to coexist with Henrietta," Lily said, filling in the gap in the conversation.

"Henrietta will be the least of your troubles." Cassie handed her credit card over as the final total displayed on the register. "She's not the only ghost in there."

"Oh, she's the only one we've heard about."

"Got at least three of them roaming around that place." Frida finished bagging the items and shoved the receipt in the last bag. She pushed them across the counter toward the women. "Good luck. Maybe the cat'll scare 'em off."

Cassie shoved her wallet into her purse, before retrieving two of the bags. She remained silent for a moment, expecting more information. None came. Frida gave them a definitive nod and busied herself with a box behind the counter. With a glance at Lily, Cassie pulled the bags off the counter, offered her thanks and the two women left the store.

As they carried their purchases around to their car, Lily said, "I guess all he needs now is a name."

"I've been giving that some thought," Cassie answered.

"And?"

"Willy," Cassie answered with a nod.

Lily knit her brow and she shot a sideways glance at Cassie. "Willy?" she questioned.

"Yep."

"One-eyed Willy," Lily responded.

"That's exactly it," Cassie said with a laugh. "With all the pirate lore around here, I thought it was fitting."

"One-eyed Willy it is," Lily answered.

After a brief lunch in town at the local cafe, where they continued to be popular as the new arrivals in town, they arrived back at Whispering Manor in the mid-afternoon. They settled Willy with his new items, and then spent a few more hours unpacking. The chore seemed endless. Box after box emptied, and they seemed to make little progress.

Willy, on the other hand, nosed around at his new things, and, after batting his new ball around for a few moments, settled into his little plaid bed to monitor the women's work. After a few moments of spying the unboxing of sweaters, his one eye slowly closed, and he drifted off to sleep.

The unpacking took the greater part of the week. By the weekend, the ladies took a well-deserved quiet Saturday. Sipping hot tea for most of the morning, the only work they completed was building Willy's new cat tree, which arrived the day before.

Willy's inspection of the new item indicated he approved. He darted up to the top level before taking a flying leap onto the couch, and then bounding to the floor in his version of feline parkour.

"He certainly seems happy," Lily commented as he climbed to the top of the tree again and settled into the round bed for a nap.

Cassie chuckled and smiled at the furry ball in the nest. "Wait until the vet comes at the end of the week."

"Yeah, I imagine he may not be happy about that."

The two women shared a laugh as they curled on the couch and discussed an opening plan for *Buy the Sea*.

"So, you'll handle the interviews, while I do a clean up around the shop?" Cassie asked.

Lily nodded. "Yes, then we'll work on filling the shelves and display cases together."

"Sounds like a plan."

As they wound down with their business discussion, Willy, still asleep on his new perch, popped his head up. Cassie expected to see a lazy stretch before he settled back into his bed. Instead, he swung his head around to stare toward the foyer.

His one eye widened as he leapt to his feet. He arched his back high in the air. His tail bristled along with the fur on his back. He stared, his eye unwavering, his body unmoving other than his swishing tail. His ears folded back against his head and he offered a low growl.

"What is it, Willy?" Cassie inquired.

In response, the cat opened its mouth and let out a hiss, before leaping from his perch. He gave another angry glance in the direction of the foyer as he stalked toward the sofa. With a swish of his tail, he leapt between Lily and Cassie. He rubbed his head against Lily's palm, then Cassie's, before he spun in a circle and settled between the two women.

He curled in a ball, tucking his head near his back legs. His eye squeezed shut. Cassie stroked the fur down his back. He responded by nuzzling further into the couch. A soft purr emanated from the furry animal.

"Must have gotten a whiff of something he didn't like," Lily suggested.

Cassie glanced up at her mother and raised an eyebrow. "Kind of makes you wonder if the joint really is haunted." She offered a chuckle.

"Oh, Cassie," her mother said, with a shake of her head. She rolled her eyes. "There are no ghosts in this house."

"Maybe not, but there is one sleepy kitty."

"No sense disturbing him. Looks like we should settle in for an afternoon movie."

"And a few more cookies," Cassie suggested.

CHAPTER 7

*C*assie swiped at the beige lace curtain covering the large window overlooking the sea in her bedroom. A storm formed in the distance. Gray-black clouds swirled on the horizon, approaching the shoreline at a fast clip. A bolt of lightning lit from sky to sea. The waves swelled, pounding against the rocks and sand along the shore.

Within a few more minutes, rain fell from the darkened skies. A few large drops plopped onto the side porch's roof under Cassie's window. Then the flood gates opened and a deluge poured from the sky, pelting the roof and windows.

Mesmerized by the scene, Cassie watched the stormy sea roll for a few more moments before her attention was diverted. A warm object rubbed against her leg. She glanced down to find Willie's one eye aimed up at her.

She scooped him up into her arms. He snuggled against her, nestling his head under her chin. His loud purring filled the room and vibrated against her chest as she stroked his head.

"Aren't you glad you aren't out in that?" she asked him.

She took his satisfied purr as a yes. They gazed out over

the rough ocean for a few more moments, before Cassie suggested they spend their Sunday curled up with a good book.

"Perhaps we'll find something in that beautiful library," she offered, as she carried the contented cat downstairs.

As she passed between the two torch-bearing angels, Cassie swung right into the ample library. Dark walnut built-in bookcases lined the room on all sides except overlooking the front porch. There, a large window seat, lined with thick blue velvety curtains, overlooked the porch. A thick cushion in matching fabric sat atop the wooden base. Cassie and her mother had added throw pillows in various hues of blue and a warm, furry blanket to complete the space.

Cassie set Willy on the window seat and perused the shelves. As a former librarian, she had been delighted with the space and its collection of books when they'd toured the home. She planned to donate anything she did not want to keep then add to the assortment.

A rainy day like today seemed like an appropriate time to start her survey. Cassie began with the shelf nearest the window seat. A smile formed on her lips as she ran her hand across the spines of the books on the middle shelf. She leaned closer and breathed in the scent. The sweet, musky smell of vintage books wafted into her nostrils.

She pulled one from the shelf. On the cover, a frightened-looking woman, her long hair trailing behind her and her Victorian-era dress flowing in the wind, ran from a dark, gothic castle. Cassie offered the book a half-smile. Apparently, a former occupant was a gothic mystery fan.

She flipped through the pages. A plume of dust billowed in the air from the old book. Cassie stifled a cough as she flipped to the back cover to examine it, before grabbing the next book off the shelf.

As she glanced through the fiction books, Willy plunked

to the floor and stretched before crossing the room. He sat on his haunches as he stared up at one of the bookcases.

Cassie's gaze flitted to him before returning to the bookshelf she'd been systematically working through. "Find anything you'd like to read, buddy?" she questioned.

Willy answered with a trilling noise followed by a meow. His tail swished across the floor, indicating his curiosity. Cassie smiled at him and returned to her book blurb reading. After a moment, he meowed again and leapt to his feet. He stared at the casing around the bookshelf and rubbed his face against it.

He placed his front paws on a shelf and stared upward. Cassie's brow furrowed at his strange behavior. With her curiosity piqued, she shuffled to join Willy at the shelf.

"What is it, Willy?"

She glanced at the shelves, finding nothing out of the ordinary. "Gosh, I hope it's not a mouse," she murmured with a wince.

She spent another few minutes scrutinizing the shelves. Before she finished, Willy's interest waned. He stalked back to the window seat, leaping up and spinning in a circle before settling on top of the blanket.

After a thorough search, Cassie found nothing of interest. At least, not to the cat. Instead, her perusal led her to a small worn brown leather-bound book. She wriggled it free from the other books and flipped to its cover. A blank brown rectangle stared back at her.

She ran her fingers over the soft, cool leather, before thumbing through the small book. A small piece of paper fluttered to the floor, along with a few particles that appeared to be the remnants of a dried flower. Hand-written pages filled the tiny tome.

She retrieved the note before letting the book fall closed.

She flicked open the front cover and stared at the text scrawled inside.

Property of Henrietta Blanchard

Cassie gasped at the name. Henrietta Blanchard–the specter supposed to haunt Whispering Manor. A chill ran up her spine as thunder boomed overhead and she stared at the name inscribed on the yellow-white page. Was this the journal of the woman who threw herself to her death, only to supposedly roam these halls in spirit?

* * *

Lily sat on her haunches as she stretched to reach inside the dark cabinet. The mahogany cabinet, recessed into the wall, with its intricately carved door panels and trim, extended further back than she expected.

With a sigh, Lily glanced at the rain-streaked windows, twirling the dust rag in her hand before trying again. She leaned forward onto her knees and swung the rag into the dark corner of the cabinet.

"I'm going to pay for this tomorrow," she muttered to herself, as her knees creaked.

Her rag swept a wide arc across the dark wood before stopping. A rustling sound reached her eyes and the rag caught on an unidentified object. Lily's brow furrowed and she returned to her seated position. She swept the rag again, snagging it against something.

With her gaze fixed on the dark cabinet, she blindly reached for her cell phone next to her. Her fumbling fingers grazed the cold, hard object and she palmed it, toggling on her flashlight.

Lily aimed it inside the cabinet and leaned forward for a better look. The rag hung on a splintered piece of wood forming the back.

"Shoot," Lily cursed, as she strained toward the sliver of wood on which the rag hung. She tugged at the rag but it didn't budge.

Lily inched closer to the cabinet and reached inside again. She jiggled the rag, but it held. With an annoyed shake of her head, she propped the cell phone against the cabinet divider, with its beam aimed at the stymied dust cloth.

She stuck her head inside the cabinet, blocking some of her own light, and grabbed hold of the cloth. As she jerked at it, she noticed a black bar at the corner of the cabinet. Her eyes narrowed and she puckered her lips as she studied it. She shifted her head, trying to illuminate the dark space. It appeared to be an opening. Did the back piece not fully extend to the corner?

Lily closed her fingers in a tentative grip around the edge of the backboard. With a grunt, she shoved the board sideways. Surprised it had moved, she relinquished her grasp and wiggled backward out of the cabinet.

She grasped her phone and peered inside, finding the gap between the splintered board where her rag still clung and the dark corner larger than before.

"A secret panel?" she questioned aloud.

She leaned inside again and gave the panel another nudge. It slid further to the side, revealing a black space behind it. Lily shined her light inside.

An odd collection of objects met her gaze. A small teddy bear with a dirty red bowtie lay atop a thick book. Next to them sat an antique toy carousel.

Lily reached into the space. She grimaced as her hand

caught on a cobweb and she snapped it back, brushing away the sticky substance. Lily freed the rag and swiped at the opening to clear it of any other unwanted webs.

With the opening cleared of any obstructions, she reached into the hole again and extracted the items. She set aside the dusty and well-used teddy bear. Its squished body lay in a crushed heap next to her.

She studied the carousel. It was large enough to need two hands to hold it. The miniature replica included gold spiral poles, holding horses of every color. Each stood frozen in a different position. A chestnut horse, hooves poised as though in a gallop, held his head high, mane streaming behind him and tail flying in the wind. A white horse stood on three legs, its fourth cocked as though ready to high-step. His mane was braided neatly to the side and his thick tail was interlaced with ribbons. A black horse, his mane wild around him, kicked his front legs as he stood frozen on his two hind ones.

Lily examined the intricate details on the carousel. As she turned it in her hands, she noted a key stuck in the rear. She twisted it, and set the object on the floor next to her. Tinkling music emanated as the carousel spun in a slow circle. Some of the horses bobbed up and down as the replica revolved on its base.

As the carousel crept to a stop, its music slowing to a haunting pace, Lily picked up the thick tome. She ran her dust rag over the top of the red leather. It creaked as she pulled the front cover open.

Lily discovered the thick, dusty book was a photo album. Pictures were scattered on stiff, thick, plastic-covered pages and attached to the spine with a three-ring binder.

Lily paged through them. They began with a picture of a couple holding a new baby. By the looks of the picture, and the clothing, hairstyles and makeup, the year appeared to be in the 70s. Broad smiles gleamed from two faces staring out of the picture. The dark-haired man had his arm wrapped around his blonde wife. They grinned at the camera, proudly displaying a small bundle of joy wrapped in a pink blanket. Lily smiled down at the picture, recalling her first photos with a tiny Cassandra in her arms.

Various pictures of the baby's first few months filled the rest of the page and its backside. Lily chuckled at the picture of the infant in a puffy, lopsided pumpkin costume. The child, now with dark hair and dark eyes, and chocolate smeared from cheek to cheek, grinned at the camera.

As Lily flipped to about halfway through the album, she discovered a large picture which filled the entire page. She cocked her head as she stared at the eight-by-ten. It showed Whispering Manor in the background. A smiling family waved at the camera, a SOLD sign held by both Mom and Dad. Daughter, now about twelve, smiled broadly with her hands clasped behind her back.

Several pages followed showing more birthdays, holidays and other events, now occurring at Whispering Manor. Lily recognized various rooms and locations on the property. Most of the house appeared unchanged by the years.

As she paged through, she came to the child's sixteenth birthday party. The girl stood in a frilly pink dress under a string of letters reading "Happy Birthday, Susan." In another photograph, she sat in front of a large box with a giant pink bow. In the next picture, the box's lid sat next to the bottom. Susan stared at the gift inside, her eyes wide with delight, and a thrilled expression on her features. The third photograph showed Susan holding the carousel and smiling.

Lily glanced at the carousel next to her and smiled. So, this was someone's sixteenth birthday gift, she mused. She caressed the object and returned her attention to the photo album.

She flipped through a few more pages before the pictures

ceased. With about a quarter of the book remaining, Lily assumed they'd not filled the rest of the album–though she could not discern the reason.

On a whim, she turned another page. No pictures were placed on the next page, but she found a yellowed newspaper clipping. Folded in half, the edges had curled, and were now creased from being trapped between the confines of two pages in the thick album.

Lily teased them back as she pried the article open. As she flattened it, the headline of the nearly thirty-year-old article stunned her. Her eyes widened and her jaw gaped open as she stared at a faded picture of Whispering Manor. The headline above read HUSBAND AND WIFE DEAD AFTER TRAGIC MURDER-SUICIDE

CHAPTER 8

*L*ily squinted at the newspaper clipping, cursing
having left her glasses across the room. She made
out the gist of the blurred text. The article indicated
that William Davies fatally shot his wife, Linda, before
turning the gun on himself. Linda's hands and feet were
bound. The gun had been found clutched in William's hand.
The assumption made by the sheriff was that William
murdered his wife before turning the pistol on himself. The
suspected motive was grief and guilt over the disappearance
of his daughter, Susan, nine months prior. Despite her
remains never being found, Susan was presumed dead two
months before the murder-suicide, when a female body was
found washed ashore in Smuggler's Cove, the town south of
Hideaway Bay. The remains could not be positively identified, but all signs pointed to it being Susan.

Pictures of each family member appeared below the
write-up. The tragic event occurred on October 3, 1991, on
what would have been Susan's seventeenth birthday. Lily's
eyebrows raised as she realized the thirtieth anniversary of
the tragedy was approaching in less than a month.

"Poor people," she lamented, flipping the album closed. No wonder this house had rumors swirling around it.

Lily slid the panel back into place, closing the secret hiding spot before she finished her dusting and closed the cabinet, deciding to fill it another day.

With the help of a nearby cedar chest, Lily pulled herself up to standing and dusted herself off. She set the teddy bear aside to be tossed later. A pang of regret at tossing someone's valued item coursed through her, but she had little use for a dirty, well-worn stuffed toy. She gathered the carousel and photo album off the floor, and headed downstairs.

The wooden stairs creaked in their usual spots as she plodded down them. Funny how one became used to the noises so quickly, she reflected, as she anticipated the next groan. She assumed the boisterous staircase would announce her arrival to Cassie, as she stepped onto the thick area rug at the foot of the stairs.

She glanced in both directions, seeking out her daughter. She was about to call out to her, when she spotted Willy curled in a ball on the window seat in the library. Cassie must be in there, she assumed.

She stepped into the open doorway. Cassie stood across the room, peering at a small book clutched in her hands.

"Anything interesting?" Lily inquired.

Cassie jumped, startled by the sudden appearance of her mother. She spun to face her, pressing her hand to her chest. "Stop sneaking up on me," she admonished.

"I didn't sneak. The creaking of the stairs should have given me away."

"It's an old house. There are creaks and groans all the time." Cassie paused for a moment, her brow wrinkling. "Unless that's the ghosts walking around."

"Probably. You're really into this ghost stuff, huh?"

"I'm ruling nothing out."

"I can't believe you believe in ghosts. What kind of daughter did I raise?"

"One smart enough to know we don't know everything that's out there. Anyway," Cassie said, waving the book in the air. "I may have found some information on one of our ghosts! And it looks like you hit a goldmine, too!" Cassie eyed the objects in Lily's hands.

"Oh?" Lily questioned, as she crossed to the window seat. She lay the carousel and album on the cushion, before plopping down next to them. Willy raised his head and sniffed at them, before deciding he didn't care about either item. With a sigh, he settled his head against a pillow and his single eye closed lazily.

Cassie held up the journal, front cover facing her mother. "This is the journal of Henrietta Blanchard!"

Lily raised her eyebrows. "Really? Our widow's walk ghost?"

"Yep," Cassie answered.

"Anything good in there?"

Cassie shook her head. "I'm not sure. I had just identified it as hers when you snuck up on me."

"I didn't sneak up," Lily insisted. She held out her hand in a silent request for the journal.

Cassie held it back. "I propose a trade." She eyed the two items next to her mother. "Yours looks more fun!"

"I beg to differ," Lily answered. "That journal was written centuries ago. Even if she lived a mundane life, how fascinating to read someone's account from hundreds of years ago!"

Cassie narrowed her eyes at her. Lily added, "Yes, you can have the carousel. I brought it down for you. I knew you'd like it."

Cassie handed the brown leather journal to her mother, and snatched the carousel. "Is it musical?"

"It is. Turn the key in the back."

Cassie wound the device using the key and set it on a nearby table. The carousel spun around as tinkling music filled the room. The tiny horses rose and fell as they traveled in their circle.

"It's beautiful," Cassie said, as it rotated in front of her. She squatted down to study each horse as it passed by.

"They don't make them like that anymore."

"How old do you think it is?"

"Early nineties," Lily answered, as she paged through the journal. "Unless it was vintage when they bought it for her."

"Bought it for who?" Cassie asked, her eyes never leaving the spinning object.

"A girl who lived here years ago. Susan Davies."

"And she left this behind?"

"It's quite a story, actually."

Cassie pried her eyes away from the object, and glanced at her mother with her eyebrows raised.

Lily recounted the story of finding the secret panel containing the carousel and the album. She patted the large book. "This contains photographs of the family as well as an article detailing the murder-suicide of Susan's parents after her disappearance."

"Wow, she disappeared?" Cassie inquired, settling on the bench near Willy, stroking the cat's fur as Lily explained more.

"Yes. She had disappeared months earlier. They found a body they presumed was Susan two months before the murder-suicide."

"Wow," Cassie said, returning her attention to the dying carousel. "So much tragedy surrounding this house."

Lily nodded in agreement.

"And then we show up," Cassie continued. "Two widows. We really fit right in."

Lily grasped Cassie's hand and squeezed. "Anyway," she said after a moment, "I'm happy to trade my find for yours." She wiggled the notebook in her hand.

"Good. I'm interested to look through the album. And, of course, I love the carousel!"

"And I will be reading this little prize this evening. A nice way to relax before we start working tomorrow at the shop!"

* * *

Cassie pulled back the fluffy mauve comforter and climbed into bed. She snuggled down under the covers, shivering as the cool sheets momentarily made the September evening colder.

Drizzle continued to fall from the night sky, and a thick fog had rolled in. A glance out of the wide window overlooking the sea showed nothing more than the white mist. Cassie smiled across the room at the tinkling and pirouetting merry-go-round. She patted the covers next to her as, Willy leapt onto the bed and stalked closer.

He accepted her invitation and nestled next to her on his plaid blanket. Cassie pulled the photo album onto her lap. It creaked as she flipped open the front cover and studied the pictures of the happy family.

Cassie paused as she examined the photos of Susan receiving the carousel. Her eyes flitted to the object, which had wound down and ceased its playing some time ago. A chill ran down her spine as she considered it had been the last birthday gift the girl had received.

Tears formed as the familiar ache of grief crept into her heart. With the death of her father and husband still fresh, Cassie could only imagine the depths of grief and despair Susan's parents had felt when she disappeared.

She paged through to the article about the murder-suicide. She gave it a thorough read, gleaning a few more details outside of what her mother already imparted.

Cassie considered the information as she slouched further down under the covers. What a tragic story, she reflected. She glanced down at the smiling faces of the Davies family. With a shake of her head, she flipped the album closed, face down.

Her brow furrowed as she noted a yellowed paper peeking from within the back cover. Her fingers flicked the edge, confirming it did not belong to the album itself but was stuck inside the cover.

Cassie swung the back cover open. Several newspaper clippings spilled out onto her bed. One poked its darkened edge into Willy's side. He snapped his head up and gave it a disparaging glance. Cassie collected the papers into a pile on her lap.

"Sorry, buddy," she said to the cat, as he licked at the spot where the newspaper assaulted him. Satisfied it had done no damage, he settled his head down.

Cassie picked up the clipping on the top of the pile. An advertisement for a wardrobe cabinet was printed on the page. She flipped it over. The headline read LOCAL TEEN MISSING.

Columns of text surrounded a picture of a smiling young woman. Cassie recognized the picture. It captured Susan Davies on the day of her sixteenth birthday.

Cassie scanned the article. Few details were known at this time. The article outlined the last time the family had seen Susan. The teen had been researching local lore about pirates. On a sunny but cold Saturday in January, her father had dropped her in front of the Hideaway Bay public library to continue her probe of the legends. He'd left her with her bike, expecting her to ride the short distance home on her own. After promising not to miss dinner, she'd given him a smile and a wave, propped her bike against the library's beige, stone side, and disappeared through its revolving door.

Susan would not only miss dinner, but she would not return home that night or any other. Her bike was found where her father had watched her place it. The librarians reported assisting her to find materials. She sat at a carrell in the rear of the library. The library assistant had seen her there as late as 3:30 p.m. No one had noticed her leaving the library. Most of the materials she had accessed were still sprawled on the desk. The chair was pushed back as though she'd stood to leave, perhaps to search for more books. But the state of the items on the desk suggested she'd planned to return. Or had left in a hurry. Or had been forced to leave.

Cassie shuffled through the remaining articles. They detailed updates on the case as it progressed. Or rather, as it didn't. No clues could be gleaned. No explanations could be found. No one knew why Susan Davies disappeared. She was not a troubled teen. There had been no trouble at home. She did not have a boyfriend who could have harmed her, nor one she could have run off with. Her friends had no knowledge of any secret meetings with anyone. Her grades were good, and her disposition did not lend itself to a sudden disappearance of her own volition.

The articles continued for several months. Susan's disappearance rocked the small town of Hideaway Bay. The once carefree town became wary of strangers. People began to lock their doors at night.

As the months wore on, Susan's parents appeared on TV asking for help in locating their daughter. The local newspaper reported on the story which had run nationally on a major news program. Tips poured in from as far as California and as close as the neighboring towns. None of them panned out. No trace of Susan existed.

Seven months after her disappearance, a body washed ashore in Smuggler's Cove. Bloated and difficult to identify, the supposition was made that it could be Susan. In a time before standard DNA testing, only identifying marks could be used. While difficult to determine given the body's condition, the coroner found a birthmark on her left thigh which may have matched one Susan had. The proof was not definitive, but the coroner believed the body belonged to Susan.

Cassie returned the articles to the album and closed it again. She shoved it onto her night table and stroked Willy's fur. Halfway through her perusal of the articles, he'd stirred and decided to groom himself.

"What a sad story," she said to the cat. He trilled at her as though he agreed. "Should we get some sleep? I've got a big day tomorrow!"

Willy yawned and rolled back to recline on the bed.

"I'll take that as a yes," Cassie said with a chuckle. She flicked off her bedside lamp and relaxed into the pillows. Visions of a teenage girl floating in a watery grave haunted her night.

* * *

Lily rubbed the lens of her reading glasses with the corner of her robe before she shoved them onto the bridge of her nose as she reclined into the pillows. She hated wearing reading glasses, but she knew trying to read a handwritten journal from centuries ago would be an impossible task without them.

After a few minutes of fluffing and fidgeting, she eased back again, this time pulling the brown leather journal onto her lap. She flipped open the front cover and read the inscription on the first page.

The black script stood out against the ivory paper. Lily flipped to the next page, finding the first journal entry there. Her eyes glided over the stylized text.

November 12, 1797

My name is Henrietta Blanchard.

Lily paused after reading only the first line. She imagined the woman, in her eighteenth-century fashions, perched on a wooden chair at the library's desk with a quill in her hand. In the soft glow of candlelight, she had penned her name without realizing that centuries later someone would read her thoughts.

Lily closed the journal for a moment. Perhaps she shouldn't read them. Perhaps they were the woman's innermost thoughts. Thoughts she never imagined would be exposed. Was this an invasion of privacy?

Lily's lips formed a half-frown as she considered it. Yes, perhaps it was. Though the woman was long since dead. Any secrets she held were surely inconsequential by now.

She pulled the book open again and continued reading.

I have begun this journal to provide an outlet for my thoughts and entertainment to amuse myself on the cold winter nights to come.

This season will provide my first winter in Hideaway Bay. As cold winds already whip from the nearby sea, I wonder what madness may have overcome my mind some fourteen months ago when I accepted the proposal of Captain William Blanchard.

William, or The Captain, as he is oft referred, proved capable of providing me with a life to be envied. Or so I thought. Fourteen months ago, I lived further south in Georgia. What I believed to be cold then would practically be considered balmy here. I am already regretting the chill in the air and my fellow townsfolk have imparted that the weather will further deteriorate.

I cannot imagine it. When William spoke of his home as we courted, I imagined a magical seaside mirage. Instead, I have been brought to a frigid burg where winds howl daily and nightly like a screaming banshee. Gray skies reign from mid-October until late March according to those who have lived here in previous winters.

The cold weather traps me inside for most daylight and night-time hours and, from what I have gathered, will continue to do so until the spring thaw. What a horrible, ghastly concept! Why had William not informed me of this dreadful, dreary weather before we wed?

Others in the town continue on, paying no mind to the frosty weather. Some of them even enjoy it, it seems!

"You will grow accustomed to it," they tell me. I cannot imagine so.

To worsen matters, William has sailed on his ship The Atlantic Queen for trading in southern waters. He shall not return until Christmas at best. If delayed, I shall spend my first holiday as a married woman alone.

While disillusioned, I do not intend to dwell on my complaints. I have written to Mother and invited her, Father and my sister, Carolina, to spend the holidays at Whispering Manor. In my letter, I accentuated the beauty of the home the Captain provided for me. Though disingenuous, I did not mention the terrible cold surrounding my beautiful home.

I hope they shall accept my invitation. Then, I shall busy myself planning for the holiday.

Lily set the journal down and reflected on the entry. How different life had been centuries ago; yet, how much the same. Though the newly married woman had been disenchanted with her new home, she'd eagerly anticipated displaying it to her family.

Lily recalled the first Christmas after Cassie's June wedding. Cassie had insisted on hosting the holiday, eager for her mother and father to see the Craftsman house she and Trevor called home in its holiday splendor.

A smile formed on Lily's lips as she recalled the debate over the phone, in which she'd tried to talk Cassie out of the idea. In the end, she'd backed down and allowed Cassie to play hostess, figuring it was important to her.

A chuckle escaped her as she recalled their Christmas dinner: pepperoni pizza. Cassie's turkey had burned to a crisp, charred beyond any edible phase. Her green bean casserole was an oily overcooked mess, and her mashed potatoes could have been used as a glue substitute. Even her pie hadn't escaped the carnage. With a blackened bottom, it had been dumped into the garbage disposal along with the rest of the meal.

They'd ordered pizza from the only place open on Christmas. Trevor and Blake had traversed through the falling snow to retrieve it. Lily had spent the time alone with Cassie, assuring her that it wasn't a big deal. Cassie had shed a few tears over the spoiled dinner, but she laughed about it now.

"I'm not domestic," she often said. "I have other skills."

The statement was true. Cassie excelled at many things. Cooking was not one of them.

Lily glanced down at the little brown journal laying against her beige duvet. She wondered if Henrietta's meal had gone any better than Cassie's first Christmas as a married woman. She glanced at the clock, then at the journal again.

She'd love to find out, but it was already later than she expected. Despite being sure she wouldn't sleep, Lily decided to turn in for the night. She slid the journal onto her night table, and doused the lights.

CHAPTER 9

*L*ily sipped her tea as the saffron sun peeked over the sea. She'd climbed from bed before her alarm sounded, unable to sleep. She'd spent most of the night tossing and turning, going over the work ahead of her today.

She had six interviews scheduled throughout the day for shop assistants. She hoped to hire at least two to cover shifts after they opened, in order to alleviate her and Cassie's schedules, allowing them to travel and search for unique treasures to fill the shop.

In between those, she planned to help Cassie stock the shelves. They already had acquired a number of unique items, ranging from local home goods to jewelry to display and sell. She couldn't wait to unwrap them all and set out a plan for displaying them.

Her excitement had driven her from her bed far earlier than she would have preferred. With her robe wrapped around her and her plush slippers on her feet, she sat at the kitchen table with her tea and Henrietta's journal.

She leafed through to the next entry, pushed her glasses onto her nose, and settled in.

November 20, 1797

I write today in frustration. I have received a response to my invitation for the Christmas holiday. Mother feels it may be overwhelming to travel north, particularly to a seaside town, fearing it may trigger her bronchitis. Mother's bronchitis is a convenient excuse, in my opinion. And Mother's bronchitis has prevented Father from accepting, and even Carolina, who feels she may become a source of gossip should she travel alone and unwed to Hideaway Bay.

Even now, I can feel angry blood course through my veins as I pen these words. In a fit of fury, I quickly scrawled an ire-filled response and sent it away in the morning post. Nonsense, I wrote! Utter nonsense! The Captain's house is well-built and can provide enough warmth to keep Mother's bronchitis at bay. I scolded her for abandoning her first-born child to a lonely Christmas. I reminded her of William's departure and possible post-Christmas return. And I commented on Carolina's ridiculous reasoning to stay at home. Traveling to her married sister's home a source of gossip? Doubtful, I wrote. And how can she ever hope to achieve a match if she cannot bring herself to leave her home?

In retrospect, perhaps I was too harsh. William often reminds me I should not act with hasty action, but rather with thoughtful intent. Unfortunately, he was not here to temper my more volatile nature. It is too late to recall the letter. I hope it has the intended effect rather than the opposite.

Lily sipped her tea and continued reading, interested to learn of Henrietta's mother's reaction to the angry letter. She just finished the third entry when Cassie shuffled into the kitchen.

"Good morning," she said, with a yawn. Her hair was in a messy top knot and her light pink robe was tied tightly around her. Willy trailed behind her, his tail raised high in the air as he anticipated his morning meal.

"Good morning, Cass," Lily answered, as she closed the journal.

"Did you get any sleep?" she asked, as she popped the lid on a can of cat food. Willy rubbed against her legs, a satisfied purr already escaping him.

"Some," Lily admitted. "Not a lot."

"Too excited, huh?" Cassie chuckled, as she emptied the can into Willy's bowl and set it in front of him. He devoured it as though he was starving.

Lily rose from the table and crossed to the refrigerator. "Something like that. Breakfast? I thought I'd make eggs."

"Ohhh!" Cassie exclaimed. "A hearty breakfast. I won't say no! I'll butter the toast. I'm pretty sure I won't mess that up."

"Only pretty sure?"

Cassie shrugged and giggled. "I could burn it. There's always a chance."

The women set about the kitchen with their breakfast tasks. Cassie eyed the journal on the kitchen table. "Interesting reading?" she questioned, pouring two glasses of orange juice.

"Yes, it is."

Cassie raised her eyebrows as her mother dished the scrambled eggs onto two plates and they settled at the table. Willy stalked over and sprawled near them, deciding this was an opportune moment to groom himself.

Lily shrugged as she finished chewing her first bite. "She's a bit of a brat, but I suppose that's to be expected."

"A brat?" Cassie questioned with a chuckle.

"Mmm, yes. I haven't made it very far, but she's spent the first few entries complaining about living in Hideaway Bay, and her mother's temporary refusal of her invitation to spend the Christmas holiday here."

"She wasn't from here?"

"No, she was from Georgia. A southern belle, through and through. She married a sea captain who brought her to Hideaway Bay. She was not prepared for the first winter here."

"And did her mother end up coming for Christmas?"

Lily nodded. "I just read that before you came in. She pitched a fit and sent them a nasty letter, and her mother gave in and decided they would make the trip."

"Hope she doesn't burn the turkey like I did," Cassie said with a laugh.

"I doubt a woman of Henrietta's status cooked for herself."

Cassie raised her eyebrows again. "Really? Were sea captains wealthy?"

"Some of them, yes. I'd say the row of houses along this road were all sea captain's mansions back in the day."

Cassie puckered her lips as she considered it.

"What about your light reading last night?" Lily inquired of Cassie.

"Well, it gave me nightmares all night, but what a story!" Cassie answered.

"Yes, I felt terrible reading it. That poor family. First, their daughter went missing, and then the grief drove the father to kill both himself and his wife. What a terrible shame."

"There were more articles beyond that one you found."

"Oh?"

Cassie nodded. "Stuffed in the back. A number of articles

about the girl's disappearance and when they found her body. Or what they presume to be her body, I guess."

"It's really a terrible story."

"And strange. She disappeared from the local library!"

"Really?" Lily questioned, setting her knife down after smearing strawberry jelly on her toast. "The library?"

Cassie confirmed it, relating the story of Susan's disappearance after being dropped off at the library.

"That's frightening," Lily answered. "Did they ever figure out what happened? Why she left?"

"No," Cassie said, with a shake of her head. "They went through dozens of conjectures, from Susan being a runaway to being kidnapped–but they couldn't prove anything."

"It's most likely she ran away then. But I wonder why? She seemed happy in her pictures. Unless it was all fake. Just smiles for the camera."

"I'm not sure. According to the reports, there was no trouble at home; she was happy, good grades, no boyfriend. She was a well-adjusted teen."

"What did she go to the library for?"

"She was researching local pirate lore."

"Perhaps she left to check out a local site, and slipped and fell into the ocean."

"That's the only conclusion that makes sense. Though you'd think she would have put her materials away or told someone. She had been seen only about an hour before she needed to return home for dinner. And all her materials were still there like she'd been expecting to return. Even her purse and backpack!"

"Oh," Lily answered. "She left her purse? Well, that sounds more ominous."

"I agree. My mind is churning with questions about what happened to her."

"That's something we may never know, Cassie."

Cassie shrugged as she stacked dishes and dumped them into the sink.

"You don't believe that, huh?" Lily inquired as she joined her daughter at the sink.

Cassie scrubbed one plate with a sponge. "I'd like to see if there's any additional information on the case."

"Cassie, it's thirty years old! I doubt there's anything to find!"

"You never know!" Cassie answered as she dumped the last dish in the dish drainer.

Lily wiped her hands on the dishtowel and pushed a lock of hair behind Cassie's ear. "Don't get your hopes up, sweetie."

"I won't. And besides, I think we'll have our hands full for at least a week or two getting this shop in order. Ready?"

"Yep. Well, as soon as I get out of this robe, that is."

"I suppose it is our store, so if you'd like to go in in your pajamas you could."

"No one wants to see me in my pajamas. See you in an hour?"

"See you then!"

The women dressed and met in the foyer. Cassie gave Willy an extra rub and a kiss goodbye, promising him she wouldn't be late for his dinner. With that, they set off into town in Cassie's Wrangler.

With the early morning sun beating through their front windows, the women entered the shop and glanced around. Fresh paint and new shelving made the space look inviting, though it did nothing to make it less empty.

"Time to roll up our sleeves and get to work, I guess," Cassie said, with an overwhelmed sigh.

"Not me," Lily answered. "I've got an early morning interview first thing."

"Oh, that sounds promising. Early morning. Maybe he or she is a go-getter!"

"She is a she. Amber. And I sure hope so!"

As Lily finished her statement, a knock sounded on the glass door. A girl with ruby red hair hidden under a knitted fashion beanie lifted a hand from her crossed arms and waved.

Lily crossed the shop's floor and pushed the door open. "Amber?" she asked.

"Yep, that's me," the girl said, with a nervous chuckle.

Lily invited her in, introducing her to Cassie before taking her to the storeroom where she'd set up a private space for the interviews. Cassie watched them disappear as the door swung shut. She lifted her eyebrows and glanced around the space. Boxes littered the corners.

"Where to start?" she asked herself.

She busied herself moving and sorting boxes, setting up the cash register, and attempting to connect their credit card reader to the internet. After two unsuccessful attempts, Cassie cursed at the machine.

Lily's next interview arrived within forty-five minutes. Cassie let the young brunette woman, named Chloe, through the door, introduced herself, and allowed her mother to take over as soon as she'd escorted Amber to the entrance, adding a "we'll contact you in the next few days to let you know."

Lily disappeared with her next interviewee, leaving Cassie alone to continue conquering the credit card machine. After another thirty minutes of troubleshooting and consulting the manual, a success message flashed across the screen. Cassie smiled down at the small machine.

Lily emerged from the back room with her latest applicant, offering her the same message before showing her out.

"Well?" Cassie inquired as the door swung shut, the little bell installed above it jingling.

"I think we'll have at least two good assistants," Lily answered.

"Went that well, huh?"

"Very well. Both girls had great interview skills and seemed eager."

"That's great. And you have two more interviews today?"

"Three," Lily corrected. "All this afternoon. Which leaves me some time to help out here before lunch."

"I've got the register set up, and the credit card machine!"

"Whew—you did all the hard work then," Lily joked.

They spent the remaining morning hours stocking the shelves and filling the cases with the unique wares they'd already purchased. They had made good progress by noon, when Cassie stepped out to grab takeout from the local cafe.

They pulled up their stools behind the register counter, using it as a make-shift lunch table. Halfway through the meal, a knock sounded against the glass again. Lily, with her back to the door, froze mid-bite. Her brow furrowed.

"Wonder if that's my one-o-clock interview," she said, glancing at her watch.

"Not unless your one-o-clock is with the sheriff," Cassie answered, motioning toward the individual on the sidewalk outside their shop.

She rose to open the door for the uniformed man. He stepped inside, removing his hat. His thick salt-and-pepper hair was parted down the side and combed neatly into a closely cropped hairstyle. His blue eyes sparkled despite the wrinkles surrounding them. He offered both women a broad smile as his six-foot-two frame stepped inside.

"Afternoon, ladies," he said, in a congenial tone.

"Afternoon, Sheriff," Cassie answered. "Is anything wrong?"

His brow furrowed and his smile faded. "Wrong?"

"Yes," Cassie answered.

"I think she means, is there a specific reason we've garnered an audience with the local sheriff on our first day at the shop?" Lily chimed in.

"Ohhhh," the sheriff answered, understanding dawning on his face. He broke into a smile and chuckled. "No, sorry. I didn't mean to startle you. Just figured I'd stop in and say hello. I haven't gotten out to Whispering Manor yet to introduce myself. Saw the lights on and people inside, so I figured now might be an opportune time."

He glanced at the unfinished lunch on the counter. "Though it seems I've interrupted your meal. My apologies."

"No problem at all," Cassie said. She stuck her hand out toward the man. "I'm Cassie McGuire, and this is my mom, Lily Bennett."

Lily wandered over toward the pair of them and offered her hand. The sheriff shook both of them with a smile.

"Nice to meet you both. I'm Wyatt Cooper."

"Pleasure to meet you, Sheriff Cooper," Lily said.

"Oh, please," he said, with a wave of his hand. "Call me Wyatt. Everyone does. We're a small town; everyone knows everyone."

"Okay, Wyatt," Lily said with a smile.

An awkward silence filled the room as the sheriff stood with a closed-mouth smile, his eyes flitting between the two women.

"So," he said, after a moment, "you ladies bought the old Whispering Manor, huh?"

"Guilty as charged," Cassie said with a chuckle.

"Lot of rumors about that old place," Wyatt said.

"We've already heard a few," Lily chimed in.

Cassie raised her eyebrows. "Yes, we have. The haunting rumors."

"They seem to be a popular yarn among the residents of the town," Lily said.

Wyatt nodded. "Well, when a house has the reputation that one does, it tends to be."

"You don't actually believe the rumors, do you?" Cassie asked.

Wyatt shrugged, his thumbs stuck through his belt. "Maybe not about ghosts roaming the halls but…"

"But?" Lily prodded.

"That house has seen its share of tragedy. It's almost like it's cursed."

"Cursed?"

He nodded again. "Yeah, cursed."

CHAPTER 10

*L*ily and Cassie shared a glance between them, and Lily raised her eyebrows. The sheriff continued as they remained silent.

"Over the centuries the house has stood there, bad things always happened to the people living in it. You know, first the lady's husband dies, then she throws herself to her death. Then the mysterious goings-on there. Always families moving in and out. No one ever stays long. And of course, the tragedy with that poor girl and her parents." The sheriff shook his head ruefully. "Terrible shame. Other than a few renters, that house has sat vacant for nearly thirty years."

Cassie's eyebrows shot skyward and her mouth gaped open. "What? We're the first owners to live there in nearly thirty years?"

The sheriff nodded and gave a half-smile. "Yep. Never thought that place would sell. Been on and off the market for years. The family who owned it before–well, who inherited it from the Davies–couldn't bear to part with it for a long while. When they finally did try to sell it, no one wanted it. Well, 'til you two came along."

Cassie gulped and offered a weak smile. "Lucky us, huh?" she said, with a dry chuckle. "Speaking of the last family who owned it, they never found out what happened to the girl, Susan, did they? We found a photo album and several newspaper articles about her tucked away in the house."

The sheriff rubbed the back of neck. "That was a little before my time as sheriff, but no, they didn't. I remember the case; I was a rookie cop at the time. Her disappearance baffled all of us. And certainly, it's been talked about enough in this town."

"And no one ever learned what happened to her, or why she left the library?"

"Nope. Lots of conjecture, of course, but no one seems to know exactly what happened."

"Well, someone does," Lily said.

The sheriff gave her a hard stare, his face a mask of confusion.

"Susan, for one. Maybe someone else if she was taken from the library," she explained.

"Oh, yeah," he said, as he gave a slow nod. "Yeah, I guess I see your point." He shrugged. "Hideaway Bay's a safe town, though, so I can't imagine a kidnapping happening here. And certainly not when I was younger."

Cassie nodded in understanding. "I guess we'll never know."

An uncomfortable silence passed again until Lily said, "Well, I think we were lucky to get Whispering Manor. It's a beautiful house. Hopefully, we'll be the ones to break that unlucky streak."

The sheriff flashed them his crossed fingers. "Fingers crossed," he said with a grin. "But if you have any trouble, don't hesitate to call. You hear?"

"Thanks," Cassie said. "We almost called you the other night."

"Oh?" he questioned. "Run in with the ghosts?"

"Actually, we thought it was going to be a run-in with a live human being," Lily explained.

"Turned out to be a cat who let himself into the house and decided to have a field day with a few of our things."

"Oh!" he exclaimed with a chuckle. "Well, I hope you had no trouble getting rid of him."

"Well," Cassie said, hesitating a moment, "yes and no."

"Is he still causing you trouble? I can get the dog catcher out." He grabbed his radio from his shoulder.

"Oh, no!" Cassie exclaimed. She waved her hands in the air to signal him to stop. "No, we kept him."

The sheriff replaced his radio and raised his eyebrows. "Oh, huh. Nice, I guess."

"We like him. And the poor fella has only one eye. So, he needs the help," Cassie explained.

"You took in that one-eyed cat?" He gave a mouth shrug. "Huh. Well, good luck with him. He sure is lucky to have two charming ladies like you to take care of him."

They stood for another moment, before the sheriff said, "Well, I better head out. Just wanted to say hello. I'll leave you to your lunch."

"Thanks for stopping by, Wyatt," Cassie answered. Lily passed along her thanks as he ambled to the door.

He paused, hovering in the open doorway before he stepped outside. "Oh, ah," he said, stumbling around to find his words, "I'm really sorry to hear about your recent misfortune. I hope Whispering Manor doesn't bring you any more bad luck."

Both women offered him a tight-lipped smile and a nod as he stepped into the crisp fall air, allowing the door to ease shut behind him.

Cassie took a deep breath, composing herself before speaking. The mention of her father and husband's deaths still sometimes hit her like a brick. She plastered a smile on her face and twisted to face Lily. "Well, that was nice of him to stop by."

"Yes, it was," Lily answered. "It seems like we picked a nice little town to settle in."

"Maybe not a nice little house," Cassie said with a laugh, "but at least a nice little town."

"The house isn't cursed, Cassie."

Cassie nodded with a knowing smile. "Yeah, I found that far-fetched, too, but you have to admit, it is weird how trouble seems to have followed anyone who owned that house."

Lily let the conversation drop as they returned to their lunch. The afternoon passed as they continued to stock shelves, move boxes, and interview candidates for the shop assistant positions. They arrived home sore and exhausted, but pleased with their first day's work.

Willy greeted them at the door. His tail swished as he pranced around the entryway while they shed their shoes.

"Hey, buddy," Cassie greeted him, running a hand down his back and up his tail. "How was your first day alone?"

He responded with a purr and leg rub. "Bet you're hungry," she added, as they all plodded to the kitchen.

Lily collapsed in a kitchen chair with a deep sigh. "I'm hungry, too," she said to the small cat.

"What do you want for dinner?"

"Not a can of Fisherman's Choice," Lily answered, as Cassie popped the lid on the cat food.

Cassie shot her a coy glance. "I was thinking pizza."

"Ohhh," Cassie murmured. "I'm good with that!"

Cassie dumped the cat food into his bowl and set it in front of the eager kitty. She used her cell phone to search for a nearby pizza place that delivered.

"Better check that they deliver here," Lily cautioned, as

Cassie keyed in the digits for *Seaside Slice*. Cassie nodded as the line trilled.

"*Seaside Slice*, pick up or delivery," a middle-aged woman's voice said.

"Uh, delivery if it's available. I'm not sure you deliver to my house."

"Where you at?" the woman asked.

"Whispering Manor."

"Oh… *that* place," the woman groaned.

Cassie swallowed hard. "Yep."

"Yeah, we deliver there. What can I get you?"

"Medium pepperoni and a two-liter of root beer."

The woman repeated the order and gave Cassie the total.

"I'll have it right out to you. Assuming I can convince my driver to venture to *that* place."

Cassie held in a sigh at the mention of *that* place again by the woman, and uttered a "thanks!" Before she stabbed at her phone to end the call.

"I guess they deliver," Lily said as she strode into the room, already changed into her pajamas, robe and slippers.

"They do deliver to *that* place," Cassie said, imitating the woman to the best of her ability.

Lily raised her eyebrows. "We sure can pick 'em," she joked.

"That we can," Cassie answered. "Well, I'm going to go change before the pizza gets here."

"You're going to answer the door in your pajamas?" Lily questioned.

"Heck yeah!" Cassie called as she darted from the room. "I have no shame!"

Forty minutes later, the two women lounged on the couch with their feet up and a tuxedo cat curled between them. A slice of pepperoni pizza sat on each of their plates and a full glass of ice-cold root beer on each side table.

They discussed their day, figuring they could have the shop ready by week's end. They planned a weekend opening. Lily had one additional interview to conduct the next day, but was pleased with the first two interviews from earlier this morning, At least they'd have two shop assistants. Only the third position needed to be filled.

After finishing the pizza, Cassie cleaned up and returned from the kitchen with a bowl of popcorn. Topping off their root beers, she settled back on the couch next to Willy.

Outside, the winds shrieked as another storm blew in off the coast. The familiar whispering accompanied it after each gust. Thunder rumbled in the sky overhead.

"Glad we're in here," Lily said, as her eyes rolled upward.

"Me too. Sounds like it's going to be another severe one."

Lily nodded in response.

"What did you find to watch?" Cassie asked.

Lily raised an eyebrow and scrolled to the movie she'd selected.

Cassie pulled her lower lip down. "Ugh, really?"

"Perfect night for it," Lily said.

Cassie studied the words on the screen. "A Haunting at Hill House," she murmured. With a roll of her eyes, she agreed. "Put it on. I don't want to spend another hour trying to find something else."

The movie began and Cassie focused on eating her popcorn. Willy stretched and hopped to the back of the couch to continue his snooze. Cassie set the popcorn bowl between them, afraid that at the first sign of the supposed on-screen haunting, she'd spill it when she leapt with fear. She hated scary movies.

As the picture-perfect family moved from the big city to the charming, quaint country house, Cassie became all too aware of the similarities with their own move. A house long-since abandoned, offered at a wonderful price, a seemingly charming community, all of which held a deadly secret.

Lily flicked off the light as she downed the last of her soda and only a handful of kernels lay at the bottom of the bowl. The room plunged into darkness, lit only by the on-screen images flashing in front of them.

Tiredness washed over Cassie despite the eerie ambiance enhanced by the chilling music filtering from the surround sound system. She propped her elbow on the cushion and leaned her head against her hand. Before long, her chin dropped toward her chest. Her eyelids drooped shut and she felt herself slipping to sleep.

A loud bang startled her awake. She jumped, staring at the screen. It must have been one of those jarring haunted house moments where the speakers blasted. With a yawn, she shifted in her seat. Lily squeezed her eyes shut before opening them again.

"Oops, I think I nodded off there for a minute."

"Me too," Cassie admitted.

"Looks like the scary movie didn't harm your sleep. Want to head to bed? We can finish the movie tomorrow."

Cassie nodded. She picked up the popcorn bowl as Lily turned off the TV.

"Oh, leave it for tomorrow," Lily suggested.

Cassie agreed with a yawn and set the bowl on the coffee table. She stretched and prepared to stand, when another thump sounded from above. Both women froze.

This time, it wasn't the movie.

CHAPTER 11

*L*ily groaned at the noise. "What's that cat of yours gotten into now?"

Cassie wrinkled her eyebrows as she slowly shifted her gaze to Lily. "Willy's right here." She motioned to the cat sleeping on the back of the couch.

Lily blanched, her jaw gaping open as she realized the source of the sound above them was not caused by their feline housemate.

"Should we call the police?" Cassie whispered.

"Let's check it out first. Take your phone with you, just in case."

"Are you sure?"

"I don't want to call the police if Willy's invited a friend over."

"Good point."

With her phone in her hand, and a baseball bat in Lily's, the two women crept up the stairs. Lily craned her neck to glance around as she inched up the steps. They approached the landing and stood silent for another moment.

A thud sounded to their right. Both of their heads whipped in the direction.

"Down the hall," Lily whispered and pointed.

Cassie nodded in response and they crept toward the source of the noise. The hallway closed around them. Lily tiptoed further, bat at the ready. Cassie pressed her hand against her mother's shoulder in solidarity.

They stopped halfway down the hall near the window. Lightning burst, illuminating the space for a brief second. It showed no one. A bedroom lay at the end of the hall. Was someone lurking inside?

Another gust of wind howled from the sea. After the wind burst, a large branch waved wildly, then snapped against the window. Its branches scratched the glass, and the thick end thudded against the house's siding.

Cassie swallowed hard as Lily lowered the bat.

"We really need to stop panicking," Lily said, as she ran her fingers through her champagne hair and blew out a sigh of relief.

"I guess every house has its noises. Although, this branch wasn't banging against the siding yesterday!"

"The storm came from a different direction yesterday."

Cassie studied the raindrops pelting the window. "You're right."

"Should we head to bed?" Lily questioned.

"Yeah," Cassie said. "I hope I can sleep after all that excitement."

"Me too. We'll need the rest before tomorrow."

"Well, I guess I'll see you in the morning." Cassie pulled her mom into a hug before they parted ways, each heading to their own rooms.

* * *

Bright fall sunshine greeted them the next morning as they slogged into the shop. Lily had already popped a few over-the-counter pain relievers over breakfast, and Cassie succumbed to them the moment her muscles protested lifting the first box.

Lily began her day with two phone calls, informing Amber and Chloe they had each been hired for the position of shop assistant. She waved her crossed fingers as she slipped into the backroom to place the calls. Amber Peterson, a local college student, who hoped to have a career in design, would be a fantastic addition to the shop. She had wonderful ideas for a chalk easel outside to draw customers in. All she needed was an idea to draw.

To complement her skills, Chloe Parker, had a mind for business. She'd outlined several sales and events she felt could add to their business. On top of those ideas, she was a local artisan and jewelry maker. Lily realized she also hoped to capitalize on a position there to sell her own wares, but with the young woman's ideas, she didn't mind the trade-off. They'd even discussed offering Chloe a space to display her jewelry and craftwork and naming it Chloe's Corner.

The line trilled after she dialed Amber's number. After three rings, Lily resigned herself to leaving a message, mentally preparing her speech as Amber's perky recorded voice yammered through the usual "I'm not here right now" message.

Lily cleared her throat as the beep sounded and launched into her message. "Hi Amber, it's Lily from *Buy the Sea*. I wanted to call you as soon as I…"

"Hello!" a breathless Amber answered her mid-statement.

"Oh, hi, Amber!" Lily said, after she recovered from the surprise. "It's Lily from *Buy the Sea*. I wanted to call you about the shop assistant position."

"Oh," Amber said, sounding deflated, "I didn't get it, did I?"

"Quite the opposite, actually," Lily answered. "You *did* get it and I wanted to let you know right away so you could get started. Cassie and I are trying for a weekend opening. It's a rush, I know, but we think we can pull it off and..."

"I can start today. Now, in fact! Well, as soon as I change clothes," she admitted.

"There's no rush..." Lily began, before being interrupted by Amber.

"I can be there in thirty minutes. Maybe forty-five. Between thirty and forty-five," Amber babbled excitedly. "If it's okay with you, I'd like to discuss the chalkboard design ideas. We can do an entire grand opening spread on it, and maybe get a big sign, possibly one of those skydancers! I can stop by the craft store on my way in."

Lily chuckled at the girl's exuberance. "Why don't you stop by the shop first, and we can take a field trip after we discuss our options."

"Okay," Amber agreed, "that sounds like a plan."

They said their goodbyes and Lily ended the call. With one call finished, she dialed Chloe's number, hoping she could make it two-for-two this morning.

Chloe answered on the second ring. Lily offered her the position which she readily accepted. She, too, offered to start today and said she would be in around noon. She'd stop by the cafe and order them all lunch before coming.

With her phone calls finished, Lily rejoined Cassie in the retail space.

"Well?" Cassie said.

"Two-for-two and they are both starting today!" Lily announced.

"Oh, great!" Cassie said. "That just leaves one more spot to fill."

"I'm hoping my interview this afternoon does it."

"Who is this with?"

"A young man by the name of Tom Murphy. A business major at the Hideaway U."

Cassie waved her crossed fingers as she continued to stock wooden lighthouses on the shelf.

Within thirty minutes, Amber arrived with her ruby red hair pulled into a high ponytail, and her blue eyes sparkling with excitement. With her, she brought Meghan and a carafe of hot chocolate.

"I stopped at *High Grounds* on my way in. I had an idea I thought we could discuss with Meghan," she said.

"Thanks for the refreshments," Cassie answered, as she sipped at the warm, chocolatey liquid.

Meghan outlined her plan to serve refreshments at the grand opening on Saturday, provided, of course, by the *High Grounds* coffee shop. After agreeing on a plan, Meghan perused the shop, while Lily and Amber stepped out to make a few purchases for advertising.

"This place is looking great," Meghan said.

"It's really coming together," Cassie answered, with a nod. "Thanks for helping with the grand opening."

"My pleasure. It's always great to help out another shop owner." She paused for a moment. "So, how's the house?"

"Oh, uh, it's fine," Cassie said, with a shrug and a smile.

Meghan raised her eyebrows.

"No ghosts yet," Cassie added.

"Ah, well, that's good." She offered Cassie a glance that suggested she didn't think the trend would last.

"I can't believe so many people really believe it's haunted."

"When you've been in this town your whole life, that's about all you ever hear," Meghan said. "That and the treasure."

Cassie finished with her box of items and slid the box

toward the back of the store. She slung her dust rag over her shoulder and refreshed her hot chocolate, joining Meghan at the register.

"I can see why it's got a reputation," Cassie admitted.

"Really? Why? What happened?" Meghan questioned, her voice eager with anticipation.

"Nothing happened, per se. But while cleaning, my mom found a hidden cubby."

"Oooooh, hidden secrets! What was in it?"

"A scrapbook with photos from the Davies family, filled with newspaper articles and a beautiful little carousel. It's really pretty. I have it in my room, but I'm thinking of bringing it into the shop to display it. Though I don't want anyone to try to buy it. I'm in love with the thing! It's so cute with tiny little horses that ride up and down as it spins."

"Newspaper articles about the disappearance?"

Cassie nodded as she took a sip of hot chocolate. "Yeah. What a strange story."

"Yeah," Meghan admitted. "That was before I was born, but her disappearance really rocked the town from what I understand. My parents still talk about it."

"Really?" Cassie asked, as she plopped onto a stool.

"Yep. It's one of those stories. And always a warning." Meghan made a stern face and lowered her voice an octave. "Don't want to end up like that Davies girl."

Cassie nodded. "So, did most people think she was kidnapped?"

"Kidnapped, murdered, ran away with her secret boyfriend, committed suicide..." Meghan listed. "You name it, people have said it. Right down to the theory that her own parents killed her."

Cassie's eyebrows shot skyward. "What? Really?"

"Yeah," Meghan answered. "I mean, I don't think they did,

but people have said it." Meghan rolled her eyes. "Especially after the father killed his wife and himself."

"What a terrible tragedy," Cassie said, with a shake of her head.

"It was. Especially in a small town like this. Honestly, the last time there was a murder here, before the whole Davies debacle, was probably in the nineteen-thirties or something."

Cassie considered it. She had no idea what the murder rate had been in her former residence, but she imagined it would be much higher than a small town like Hideaway Bay. That it remain unsolved probably set many people on edge. Part of the story probably came from people trying to rationalize and dismiss their fear of danger.

"Well, I guess I should let you get back to it," Meghan said, as Cassie remained silent.

"Sorry, didn't mean to send the wrong signal. I was just thinking about what you said about how rare murder is here. I suppose, despite the disturbing details of the Davies case, one of them being that we live in their house, it's comforting to know we moved to a charming small town where murder is rare!"

"Well, I hope you and your mom are the family that changes the bad luck that house has!"

Cassie smiled at the statement and offered a nod as Meghan ambled to the door. She spun to face Cassie before she pushed outside. "Hey, at least this place will always have the police's attention."

Cassie furrowed her brow as she rose from her stool.

"You hired Chloe–the sheriff's niece."

"Ohhh, good to know. Thanks!"

Meghan offered one last smile before disappearing through the door and across the street toward *High Grounds*. The smile slipped from Cassie's lips and her brow creased again. How did Meghan know they hired Chloe? It hadn't happened more than two hours ago. News really did travel fast in a small town!

Lily and Amber returned to the shop shortly before noon with materials to decorate for the grand opening. Amber went straight to work on her chalkboard sign.

"Wow, did they have anything left?" Cassie asked with a chuckle.

"I'm getting almost as good as you at spending money," Lily said, with a wink. "Amber had some great ideas for decorating for the grand opening, and we selected things we can transition into the fall events with."

Cassie raised her eyebrows. "Fall events? Sounds like you two have been busy!"

"Amber is a wealth of knowledge on all the events this town usually celebrates. She said fall is a pretty big season for shops here, and then there's the Christmas rush shortly after. If we can capitalize on that, we may not be in the red for long!"

"Sounds like a plan. Oh, speaking of knowledge, Meghan already knew you hired Chloe."

"News travels fast," Lily said, as she unpacked some of the new decor items.

"And she told me Chloe is Sheriff Cooper's niece."

Lily opened her mouth to respond, but the jingling bell of the front door interrupted her. Genny strolled in and waved. She held a notebook and pen in her hand.

"Hi, ladies!" she called.

"Hey, Genny!" Cassie called. "Come on in!"

"I'm here to discuss the order for the grand opening."

"Oh!" Cassie exclaimed. "Thanks for stopping by. I planned to call you this afternoon as soon as…"

Genny waved her comment away. "No problem! Meghan told me the plan. I just want to see what type of cookies you'd like to have out. Once we decide on that, I'll give you a few suggestions on numbers, and we'll get everything settled!"

Cassie smiled at her. "Thanks, Genny."

"I'll leave you to pick the cookies, Miss Sweet Tooth. I'll be in the back with Amber. Send Chloe back when she gets here."

"Okay," Cassie said, before turning her attention to Genny. She found the cookie choice harder than she expected. "They all look delicious," she mentioned several times, before she finally settled on a variety of four different cookies. She went with the order size Genny suggested and they wrapped up the conversation.

"So, heard you found a secret passage or whatever in ye old manor," Genny said as she made her final notes.

"Wow, news really does travel fast around here."

"Honey, you can't look sideways at someone without the whole town knowing about it," Genny informed her. "I hope you didn't value your privacy because there isn't much of it around here. By the way, I'd love to see the carousel some time. I just love that kind of vintage stuff."

"I'll bring it in one day," Cassie promised, still reeling from how quickly even the tiniest bits of gossip raced around the town. "But only if you promise not to steal it from me! I just love it."

"No promises. But if there's a theft, you can tell Sheriff Cooper I'm the prime suspect."

"I'll keep that in mind," Cassie said with a chuckle.

Genny strolled from the shop, holding the door open for two individuals entering. Chloe strode in, her hands filled with a drink caddy. A man Cassie had never seen before carried two bags with the local cafe's name stamped on them. His brown curly hair hung across his forehead, framing his thick eyebrows and deep-set brown eyes. The soft wrinkles around his full lips suggested he was in his late thirties.

Cassie wondered if this was Lily's last candidate for shop assistant.

Chloe marched to the register and set the drinks down. "Hey, Cassie!"

"Hi, Chloe. Thanks for grabbing lunch." Cassie eyed the man next to Chloe as he set the bags on the counter and smiled at her.

"No problem. It's easy for me to hit up the local cafe and even wrangle some help into carrying the lunch over. I have an in with the chef." She winked.

Cassie cocked her head at the statement.

"Cassie, meet my cousin, Ben Parker, owner and head chef of *Seaside Cafe*!" She thumbed toward the curly-mopped man next to her.

Cassie stuck her hand out. "Nice to meet you. We stopped for lunch at the cafe on one of our first days in town."

"I hope you enjoyed it," he said.

"We did! The chicken salad croissant was excellent."

"Oh, great," Ben answered. "That was always one of my mom's favorites. She insisted I offer a few lighter fare items beyond salad because she said some people, ladies in particular, like a lighter lunch or dinner."

"She was right!"

He chuckled. "I've found that she usually is."

Ben glanced around the shop. "It looks great in here. And you plan to open this weekend?"

"We do. We've made great progress with stocking and hiring," Cassie answered, motioning toward Chloe. "So, we think we'll be ready!"

"Cool," he said. "Well, I hope you enjoy the lunch. I'm glad you liked the chicken salad because…"

"That's what you brought?" Cassie answered.

He nodded and grinned. "Yep."

"Fantastic! And I know my mom will be thrilled with it."

Ben didn't move. Instead, he stood glancing around the shop, drumming his hands on his thighs.

"Are you staying for lunch?" Cassie inquired, as she pulled the takeout containers from the bags.

"Oh, no," he said. "I need to get back. The lunch rush will be hitting right about now. I just..."

Cassie raised her eyebrows at him as his voice trailed off. He leaned closer to her and lowered his voice.

"What's it like living... you know, there?"

Cassie's lower lip bobbed up and down as she formulated a response. She glanced between Ben and Chloe, both of whom stared at her wide-eyed awaiting her answer. She shrugged. "It's a very lovely house."

"What, that's it?" Chloe questioned.

"Pretty much," Cassie said. "No ghosts or anything, if that's what you mean."

Ben raised his eyebrows and glanced at Chloe. She gave him a shrug. "At least not yet," he said.

Chloe began, "You know it's..."

"Haunted, yes," Cassie finished. "So, we've heard. But, honestly, nothing's happened there to make us believe it is."

"Oh well, hope your streak of luck holds out," Ben answered. "And hope you enjoy the lunch!" He began backing toward the door, and disappeared with a wave after they said their goodbyes.

Lily and Amber joined Chloe and Cassie, and the four ladies used their lunch to plan the rest of the week. After an afternoon filled with stocking, and one additional interview in which Lily hired twenty-something Tom Murphy on the spot, Lily and Cassie piled into Cassie's Wrangler to return home. By the time they'd turned the key to lock the shop, the sun was already hanging low on the horizon.

They stopped for a quick dinner out at the local seafood restaurant before driving the short distance to Whispering

Manor. The women chattered exuberantly as they turned onto their street. Cassie flicked on the car's turn signal and swung into the home's gravel driveway, as Lily dug her keys from her purse.

"Hey! What the heck!" Lily shouted, as Cassie hopped on the brake and she lurched forward. The car came to an abrupt stop.

Cassie stared out of the windshield, her mouth agape. Lily followed her gaze, her eyes widening. A dim light shone from the windows, bobbling around as it moved from room to room. There was no mistaking the movement of a person, living or otherwise, in the house.

"This time, I think we should call the police," she whispered.

CHAPTER 12

Cassie nodded as she stared ahead at the bobbling light beam. She reached for her cell phone in the car's cup holder. She dialed 9-1-1 and waited for the operator to respond.

Within minutes, Wyatt Cooper pulled up in his own vehicle along with another officer in a marked police cruiser. Red and blue lights flashed across the darkening shadows.

"Are they still inside the house?" Sheriff Cooper asked, as he popped out of his car.

"We're not sure," Lily answered. "We haven't seen any light but they could be in the rear of the house now."

Cassie's eyes widened as Deputy Whittaker drew his weapon, before flicking on his flashlight and approaching the house with caution. Sheriff Cooper followed him with Lily's keys in hand.

Cassie wrapped her arms around herself as wind gusted past them, blowing her hair wildly. She shifted her weight as she watched the front door swing open. Deputy Whittaker shouted something before he moved into the house, Sheriff Cooper close behind him.

"I hope Willy's okay," Cassie murmured.

Lily put her arm around Cassie's shoulders. "He probably hid when he heard someone other than us." She understood her daughter's concern and hoped her words rang true. She wasn't sure they could take another loss, even of a cat.

Cassie nodded and bit her lower lip as she followed the officers' flashlights moving through the house. A shout carried across the wind from inside. Both women stiffened as they waited for any news.

Moments later, the two officers strode from the home.

"Anything?" Lily shouted as they approached.

Sheriff Cooper shook his head. "Nothing. We located no one on the premises."

"We did see the lights," Cassie insisted.

Sheriff Cooper nodded. "I'm sure you did, Mrs. McGuire…"

"Cassie, please."

"I'm sure you did, Cassie. I'm not saying you didn't. But neither of us found any signs of a trespasser."

Cassie clutched at her sweater, pulling it closed under her neck. "I'd like to have you both come in the house and see if anything is missing or disturbed. Whenever you're ready. No rush," Sheriff Cooper continued.

"I'd like to go in now," Cassie said. "I want to make sure Willy is okay."

"Willy?" the sheriff questioned.

"My cat," Cassie murmured, as she hurried toward the house.

"Oh," the sheriff mumbled, as he followed Cassie and Lily inside.

Cassie flicked the switch next to the door. Light bloomed from the chandelier overhead. Everyone squinted against the bright light. As Cassie's eyes opened to slits, she feared what she may find. She expected to see the home trashed, furniture on its side, their belongings strewn, books discarded on the library floor. Instead, she found nothing. The house appeared as they left it.

Cassie craned her neck to peer into the living room, then the library. They looked undisturbed.

"Doesn't seem like anything is missing, or even moved," Cassie said.

Lily agreed. She stepped into the living room. "Nothing's out of place, TV is still here. At a glance, seems everything's still here."

"We saw the lights upstairs, though," Cassie informed Sheriff Cooper.

He nodded. "If you wouldn't mind checking up there, Deputy Whittaker and I will do one last sweep of the entire house with the lights on to be sure."

"Thanks," Lily said. The two women climbed the stairs while the men checked the first floor again.

They split up to check their rooms first, then the other second-floor spaces. After a brief inspection, they again found nothing had been disturbed. No windows were open, no items missing, no belongings disrupted. Lily and Cassie met at the top of the stairs.

Lily shrugged as she spotted Cassie. "Nothing on my end," she said.

"Me either," Cassie answered. "But I haven't found Willy yet." She shoved her hands into her back pockets and glanced around. "You didn't see him, did you?"

"No, sorry. I'm sure he's here, though."

"Willy!" Cassie called. "Willy!"

"Crack a can of food, I'm sure he'll come running," Lily suggested.

Cassie nodded in response. "If I haven't found him by the time Sheriff Cooper and Deputy Whittaker leave, I will."

Cassie skipped down the stairs, her head on a swivel. Lily

followed behind her. Cassie continued her search, calling for the cat as Sheriff Cooper and Deputy Whittaker double-checked the upstairs.

As the men returned downstairs, meeting Lily in the foyer, Cassie trekked back through the living room. She called again to the cat. A quiet mew answered her.

"Willy?" she called again. "Willy, where are you, buddy?"

Another quiet meow. Cassie located the source of the sound. She dropped to the floor and peered under the couch. Flicking on her cell phone's flashlight, she shined it underneath. Willy's solitary eye squinted at the bright light.

"Hey, buddy, come on out," she coaxed. "It's okay."

She doused the flashlight's beam and reached her hand toward Willy. She gave his head a soft rub. His purr reverberated. He inched closer to her. "That's it, buddy. Come on out."

The cat crawled from under the couch and rubbed against Cassie. She scooped him up in her arms and stood.

"Ah, you found him!" Lily said, as she and Sheriff Cooper entered the room.

"I did," Cassie said with a smile. "Hiding under the couch. Something spooked him."

Sheriff Cooper glanced between the cat and Cassie. "I'm glad you found him and he's okay." Willy stiffened in Cassie's arms as the sheriff's voice filled the room.

"Thanks. It's okay, Willy," Cassie cooed. "He's a friend."

"On the note of being okay, Ted and I didn't find anything. No evidence of anyone in the house and no evidence of any forced entry."

"I suppose that's a good thing," Lily said.

"Except we saw lights in here. Moving lights," Cassie contended.

The sheriff nodded but didn't respond.

"We saw them!" Cassie insisted.

"I believe you," Sheriff Cooper answered.

"And obviously someone frightened Willy. He was hiding under the couch."

"Maybe he fell asleep there while you were out," Sheriff Cooper offered.

Cassie opened her mouth to argue, then thought better of it. She shrugged and offered a meek, "Maybe."

"In any case, everything seems secure. If you have any trouble, don't hesitate to call us again. But for the moment, everything seems fine."

"Thanks, sheriff," Lily said.

"Anytime," he answered. "I can see myself out, but perhaps you'd like to lock up after me?"

"Oh, yes," Lily said. "I'll walk you to the door and lock it right after you've gone out."

He smiled and nodded. "You have a nice rest of your evening," he said, as he stepped onto the porch.

They offered their thank yous and swung the door closed, latching the deadbolt. Lily pulled against it to ensure it held.

"Well, that was an exciting evening," Lily said.

Cassie nodded in response.

"I'm exhausted," Lily said.

"Guess we should head to bed," Cassie murmured.

Lily pushed a lock of hair behind Cassie's ear. "Cass," she said softly. "They didn't find anything."

"But we saw the lights."

"Even if we did, no one is here now."

"What if they come back?"

"After the sheriff was here? They might think twice."

Cassie returned her attention to Willy. She stroked the black fur on his back as he snuggled against her.

Tell you what," Lily said. "If you can't sleep, sneak into my room. We'll bunk together."

Cassie offered a half-smile. "Okay," she said. "I just might take you up on that."

Lily smiled at her. "No problem. Now let's head up. I don't know about you, but my body is ready to stretch out in my nice warm bed."

Cassie pushed the excitement from her mind and focused on Lily's statement. Stretching out in bed appealed to her tired muscles, too. With Willy cuddled in her arms, she ascended the stairs after Lily. They parted ways again, heading to their bedrooms for the second time tonight.

Cassie settled the cat on her bed as she completed her nightly routine. Before changing, she wound the carousel. Tinkling music filled the air as the object twirled around, its tiny horses bobbing up and down.

Cassie smiled at it, humming along with its tune while she readied herself for bed. As she pulled her pajama top over her head, the music slowed and stopped. She tugged the shirt down and whipped her head in the direction of the device on her dresser. Her brow furrowed as it stood frozen.

With a sigh, she trudged toward it. "Really? Can this night get any better?" she fumed.

Cassie picked up the carousel and studied it. She glanced underneath and wound it again. It didn't budge. Setting it down on the dresser, she stooped to stare at it. A frown formed on her lips and she poked at the carousel. It shifted on the axle but didn't move. After another poke, the carousel sprang to life. The platform whirled in a circle with the little horses seesawing up and down, and the jaunty music filling the room.

Cassie wound it again before crawling into bed. The carousel played in the dark as she settled back in the pillows. Pain relievers, coupled with a long day of work, allowed her to drift off to sleep, despite the excitement of the trespasser.

* * *

Lily stretched out in the dark, feeling the cool softness of her Egyptian cotton sheets. Silence filled the room as she closed her eyes and drew in a deep breath. After a moment, her eyes popped open. She stared around the darkened room, lit only by the moonlight streaming through the far window.

Her foot tapped the air as she ticked the moments by. Despite what she told Cassie, she couldn't sleep. And while her sore body appreciated her firm but forgiving mattress, her mind could not shut down.

With a sigh, Lily reached up and flicked on her bedside lamp. She slid up to sitting, propping three pillows behind her. The brown leather journal belonging to Henrietta Blanchard sat on the night table. Her eyes slid sideways to it. With a shrug, she pulled it onto her lap. "Maybe this will help," she murmured, as she flicked it open to the page she'd last read.

December 24, 1797

Mother, Father and Carolina arrived only yesterday. I had hoped to have more time between the holiday and their arrival. Alas, it was not to be. Still, I am making the best of it. We sat down for our first family dinner in my home this evening. I had hoped William would return home in a grand Christmas surprise, but this was also not to be. I received word that his ship is still miles off the coast far south of us.

To worsen matters, Mother brought up you-know-who as we sipped hot cocoa and decorated the Christmas tree. At the mention of his name, I nearly spat the warm liquid out of my mouth. After

I'd swallowed (burning my throat with it), a litany of less-than-ladylike words escaped my mouth. Mother scolded me over it and Father attempted to smooth my ruffled feathers. Carolina hid her face in her hands like a child. Honestly, she never seems to grow up. Yet, the conversation was thrust upon me in my own home while we decorated my first Christmas tree and I was expected to endure it.

Well, I did not. Mother attempted to discuss him again. I threw the porcelain cup on the floor, smashing it to bits. I screamed at them to stop ruining my holiday before I fled from the room. I raced up the staircase and to my room and flung myself across the bed. No one followed me. I sobbed there for an hour and still, no one came.

After I dried my own tears, I dragged myself to my writing desk to vent through this journal. Rage still heats my belly. I do hope Mother has learned her lesson about bringing up his name in my house. I will not tolerate it.

If I hear the name of my shameful brother, Clifton Nichols, uttered again in this house, I will burn it to the ground.

Lily grimaced as she read the last line. Henrietta's behavior seemed to be getting worse. She could understand why she had thrown herself off the balcony. She seemed unstable at best. Who threatened to burn their home down if their brother's name was mentioned?

Lily pondered the entry as she closed the journal and turned off the light. Tiredness finally washed over her, and she settled back in the pillows. Her mind wandered over what Clifton Nichols could have done to Henrietta to warrant such a strong response before she drifted off to sleep over an hour later.

CHAPTER 13

*C*assie poured steaming water into two mugs and bobbed tea bags in both. She set the mugs down on the table as Lily appeared in the kitchen.

"You're up early this morning," Lily said, as she sipped the sweet liquid.

"Couldn't sleep," Cassie answered.

"Did you get any sleep last night?"

"I did. After my carousel decided to stop working."

"Oh, no. Did it die on you? Maybe someone in town can look at it."

Cassie waved her comment away as she smeared strawberry jelly on two pieces of toast, and delivered the slices along with yogurt and granola to the table.

"I got it working last night. Must have just been a hiccup. I gave it a poke and it started up again." Cassie shrugged. "Seems to be working fine now."

Lily's eyebrows wiggled up and down. "Well, I guess all's well that ends well."

"You look like you had a rough night."

"Wasn't my best night's sleep. Despite what I said, after all that excitement, I couldn't get to sleep. I read more of that journal and then *that* kept me awake for a while."

"Ooooh, gossip! Is Henrietta still a brat?"

"Oh ho, and then some. We've skipped ahead to Christmas and now she's mad because her mother brought up her brother's name. She pitched a fit, and *then* she got upset that no one came after her to resolve the issue when she stormed to her bedroom."

"She sounds quite dramatic. What was the issue with her brother?"

It was Lily's turn to shrug. "I'm not sure. I might try to look him up on the Google," she said.

Cassie chuckled. "The Google? Really, mom? You're savvier than that."

"Well, whatever. I'd like to search his name and see if there's any info out there."

"I could ask around at the library," Cassie said. "I was going to stop by there today when I ran out for lunch and ask around about Susan. See if they have any additional articles on her."

"Okay," Lily agreed. She passed along his name to Cassie, who saved it in a memo on her phone for later.

After breakfast, they dressed and left for the shop for another long day of preparation. They planned to finish the final stocking today, and begin decorating for the grand opening. If all went to plan, they'd have the decorating finished tomorrow, leaving Friday for last-minute items and a final cleaning.

The bell tinkled as the door swung shut behind Cassie just before noon. She strode down the sidewalk, enjoying the September weather, still warm but not hot. The town's library was two blocks away, and she headed in its direction.

As Cassie turned the corner onto its street, she stared up at the tan stone building. Two columns supported a vaulted gable covering the stone steps leading upward to the door. LIBRARY was spelled out in large iron letters above the roof.

Cassie bounced up the steps, her ponytail bobbing up and down as she climbed, and pushed through the door and into the library. It took a moment for her eyes to adjust to the dimmer light from the sunny day outside. She took a deep inhale, appreciating the smell of the books inside. Memories of her former career flooded back to her and, for a moment, she recalled her former life.

With a shake of her head, she pushed back the tears that threatened, and crossed the lobby to the circulation desk. An older woman sat there, fiddling with something on her computer screen. Her glasses were perched on the edge of her nose, a gold chain dangling from each side. Her gray-brown hair was pulled neatly into a bun at the nape of her neck. Cassie couldn't help but be amused by the stereotypical librarian look.

She approached the desk and offered the woman a smile. The woman tilted her head down and peered over her glasses. "Can I help you, dear?"

"I hope so," Cassie said. She waved her hand around. "What a lovely library this is. I was a librarian before I moved here."

"Are you looking for a position? I'm sorry, we aren't hiring at the moment, but we do have a vacancy on the library board and we're always looking for volunteers!"

"Oh, I'm not looking for a job," Cassie explained. "I'm Cassandra McGuire, Cassie for short." She stuck her hand out toward the woman. "I'm new in town and was hoping to gather some information from you."

"Oh," the woman answered, her eyebrows shooting toward her graying hairline, "you bought Whispering Manor."

Cassie was again stunned by how quickly news traveled, and how far. "Yes, that's right."

"I'm Pearl Booker, the head librarian here. Now, you mentioned wanting some information?"

"Yes. We just learned about the misfortune of the last family who owned the manor."

"Ah, yes, the Davies family. Such a terrible tragedy." Pearl shook her head and frowned.

"I was wondering if you had any information, newspaper articles and the like, about the story."

"Yes, we do. Oh, it'll take a bit to pull them all together. Do you have time to wait?"

"Actually, could I collect the materials this weekend? Would that be okay?"

"Oh, yes, of course. That gives me plenty of time to gather everything we have on it."

"I imagine you have several local articles?" Cassie prodded.

"Oh, yes. The case was widely publicized here. Everyone knew about it."

Cassie glanced around again. "She disappeared from this very library."

Pearl nodded. "I was the last person who saw her alive."

Cassie's eyebrows raised higher. "Really? You were the librarian who saw her?"

Pearl's head bobbed up and down slowly as she eyed Cassie. "She sat right back there in that cubby." Pearl pointed toward the back corner of the large area. "Had her materials spread out all over the desk. I was shelving and walked past her. She was engrossed in taking notes. Had her shoes off and sat cross-legged on the chair, completely lost in her work." Pearl leaned closer to Cassie and lowered her voice. "You know those shoes were still there when I showed the police where she was."

"Really?" Cassie inquired. She hadn't come across that detail in any of the articles she'd read.

Pearl gave another slow nod and a cat-who-caught-the-canary smile. "It was one of those surreal moments I'll never forget. I showed the two officers back to her cubby. Her purse still hung from the chair, her materials were spread everywhere, and those little scuffed saddle shoes sat under the table. Very sad, but also eerie."

"I'll bet," Cassie answered. "Do you happen to know what she was researching?"

"Oh, yes!" Pearl confirmed. "She was researching the infamous pirate with ties to the area. Clifton Nichols."

* * *

Lily dragged her mouse around as she moved a sketch of a necklace on the laptop's screen. She narrowed her eyes at the screen as she considered the current design. Satisfied, she clicked the save button and spun the laptop around to face the shop's main floor.

"What do you think?" she called to Chloe, who was decorating a table display with fall leaf garland and ceramic pumpkins.

Chloe straightened and twisted to view the screen. In playful, colorful letters, the words CHLOE'S CORNER beamed from the screen. A necklace hung from the first C and a ring formed the apostrophe. The "o" in "corner" was formed by a bath bomb.

A smile lit Chloe's face. "Oh! I love it! Is that one of my bath bombs? And my necklace?"

Lily nodded. I snapped a few pictures of your work earlier and used them to create your logo."

Chloe approached the register and studied the laptop closer. "I love it. Thank you!"

"You're welcome," Lily said. "We can get it printed tomorrow and hang it Friday over the corner shelf with your items."

"That sounds perfect," Chloe agreed.

Lily shifted her gaze to the table. "That's coming along well."

Chloe glanced back and thanked her. "I'm moving on to the windows next. I'd like to get at least one finished before we leave tonight. I'd better get back to it. I've got a really involved idea. I hope I can pull it off."

"If you need help, let me know," Lily offered, as she spun her laptop to face her. She sent the logo file off to the printer as the front door's bell jangled. Lily pulled off her readers and glanced at the woman entering the shop.

"Meghan, hi!" she said with a smile.

"Hi, Lily!" Meghan answered. "Hope you don't mind me waiting here for lunch."

"Not at all. Cassie's not back yet. I think she was stopping at the library before picking up the food."

"No problem. We're in a lunchtime lull, so I figured I'd save her a stop at my place. I texted her to let her know I'd be here."

Lily smiled at her as her eyes wandered around the shop.

"It really looks great in here."

"Thanks. We're excited to open."

"I'm excited, too. I've got my eye on a few things in here," Meghan said with a giggle. She pointed to a set of sea glass earrings. "What's Cassie stopping at the library for?"

"Oh, we found a series of articles about the disappearance of Susan Davies and then subsequent deaths of her parents. She's been interested in the story. She stopped to see if they had any other articles on it."

Meghan's eyes shot up. "Now there's one ghost I *didn't* come in contact with in that house."

"Oh? Does she haunt the place, too?"

Meghan nodded. "Some people think so."

"She didn't die there."

"No, but they say she returns there, searching for her lost things. She's always accompanied by the scent of lilacs, her favorite flower. People have reported hearing her clawing at the walls on stormy nights as she tries to find her belongings!" Meghan's eyes grew wide as she recounted the story.

Chloe had ceased working at the mention of ghosts, and wandered toward Meghan and Lily.

Meghan continued her tale. "The last renter at the house swears on one black, stormy night, she heard the unmistakable clawing just outside her door. She tried to ignore it, but it grew so loud, she couldn't. As she rose from her bed, the scraping turned to sobbing. She eased her door open a slit and peered into the hallway."

"And?" Chloe asked with a gulp.

"And there she was. She wore a tattered pair of jeans, a dirty pink blouse and her black and white saddle shoes. Her red hair was pulled into a high ponytail. Her shoulders shook as she cried.

"The renter didn't know who she was and assumed she was real! She called to her and that's when she realized her mistake.

"Susan spun to face her. Her eyes burned red. The woman said she'd never been so terrified in her entire life."

"Did she ever see the ghost again?" Chloe asked.

Meghan shook her head. "No, she packed up her things that night and never came back."

Lily's eyebrows shot up. "She left that night?"

"Middle of the night, yep. Sheriff found a note taped to the door with a check for that month's rent. Said she'd left and didn't plan to return. She didn't even care that she paid for a month's rent she'd never use!"

"How did you hear the tale if she left town?" Lily questioned.

"Lucy Clifford," Meghan answered. "She called the woman to ask about sending a few items she left behind in her frenzy to flee. That's when she admitted what drove her off."

"That's scary!" Chloe said.

Meghan offered a slow nod. "Now you'll know. If you ever hear a scraping in the middle of the night, it's probably the ghost of Susan Davies."

* * *

Cassie's eyebrows raised at the name. "Did you say Clifton Nichols?"

"Yes," Pearl answered.

"The brother of Henrietta Blanchard?"

"You've done your homework," Pearl answered with a chuckle. "Yes, Clifton was Henrietta's brother. Although he didn't use this real name as a pirate, you know. But still, people eventually caught on that she was related. Oh, she tried to hide it, but it wasn't easy. He turned up now and again. She absolutely detested that, but it didn't stop him."

Cassie's mind reeled. Henrietta Blanchard's brother was a pirate? No wonder she detested the mention of his name. She wondered if he had impugned her husband's reputation in some way. Guilt by association, perhaps, Cassie pondered.

"And you said he was an infamous pirate?" Cassie repeated. "But he didn't use his real name. What did he go by?"

Pearl's green eyes sparkled as she leaned forward with a grin on her pale lips. She lifted an eyebrow. "Black Jack."

Cassie raised her eyebrows at the name. It sounded vaguely familiar, as though she'd heard it before. Then again, wasn't that the point of pirate names, she reflected? To sound familiar and ominous, so they could more easily strike fear into their opponents' hearts? An idea crossed her mind.

"Would you happen to have any information on Black Jack?"

"Oh, loads of it, dear," Pearl said.

Cassie winced at the woman. "Would it be possible to…"

"I'll have it ready with the other information you requested on Saturday. I won't be in, but I'll leave it here at the desk with your name, Cassie, marked on it." The woman offered a wide smile and a nod.

"Thank you," Cassie said.

Pearl held a finger in the air. "As long as you promise not to disappear like poor Susan did."

"I'm not planning on it, Pearl," Cassie said with a broad smile.

The two women chatted a moment longer, before Cassie thanked her and said her goodbyes. Armed with the new information, she couldn't wait to retrieve their lunch and pass her find on to her mother.

* * *

Work at the shop kept both Lily and Cassie occupied for the afternoon. As they settled at the dinner table with their meal, they discussed their day. Lily shared the information about their other resident ghost, while Cassie spilled the beans about Henrietta's brother.

"I found out the reason your bratty southern belle is so sensitive about her brother," Cassie said.

"Oh?"

"He was a pirate," Cassie said, with a gleam of mischief in her eye.

"What?!" Lily exclaimed, as she munched on a chip with her grilled cheese sandwich.

"The librarian dropped the story on me. She said that's who Susan was researching the day she disappeared from the library. He went by the name Black Jack. I asked her to pull some information on him for you. I'll grab it when I pick up the articles she's copying about Susan."

"That should make for interesting reading."

Cassie nodded as she chewed her pickle. "Pearl was the librarian working the day Susan went missing, speaking of interesting stories."

"Really? Did she have any insight?"

"Well, I'd say Susan didn't leave of her own free will after hearing Pearl's version. She said the girl's purse and saddle shoes were left behind. Who leaves without their shoes?"

"Funny you mention that, Meghan told me the 'ghost' supposedly roaming here wears saddle shoes."

"You'd think the poor ghost would be missing them," Cassie said. "Since she left the library without them."

"And since she's here searching for her things."

"I guess she found her shoes at the library," Cassie quipped.

"So what's Black Jack famous for? Or infamous for?" Lily inquired.

Cassie began to answer when their conversation was interrupted. The whispering sound they had grown accustomed to swept through the house. It was the other sound that accompanied it that hushed them both to silence. Footsteps fell on the floorboards above them.

Cassie's eyes slowly floated upward. She gulped before she shifted her focus to her mother. Lily froze mid-bite. With a frown, she set her halved potato chip down and wiped her hands.

The floorboards creaked and groaned as the unidentified

trespasser roamed the floor above. Willy peered out from under the table. His single eye stared at the ceiling. He narrowed it, letting out a hiss.

"This is getting old," Lily said.

"Should I call Sheriff Cooper?" Cassie asked.

"No one could be up there," Lily answered.

"Perhaps someone got in while we were out."

"The doors were locked when we got home. And I locked them after we came in."

"Sounds like they are in your bedroom," Cassie said.

The footsteps ceased. A new sound floated from above. Cassie's eyes widened as a scratching noise filtered through the ceiling.

She swallowed hard. "You don't think…"

"That it's a ghost? Certainly not, Cass," Lily answered. "I wonder if it's a wild animal. Raccoon or something."

"You want to go find out? I'll wait here," Cassie joked.

"I'm taking the bat," Lily said.

"I'll come with you."

"You can wait here, 'fraidy cat," Lily said.

Cassie offered her a wry glance. "I'm not letting my mother go upstairs with a wild animal, ghost or trespasser alone."

"Oh, goodness, Cassie, you act like I'm eighty. I could probably take them down easier than you could."

Cassie ignored the remark as she crept behind her mother to the foyer. Besides, her mother may have a point.

Lily grabbed the bat from the umbrella holder and peered up the main staircase. To the left of the railing, her bedroom door stood ajar as she'd left it.

"I don't hear any scratching now," Cassie whispered, as Lily mounted the first step.

Lily shook her head in response. "Me either," she breathed.

They crept up the steps. Lily frowned as she trod across the squeaky stair halfway up, despite her best efforts to remain noise-free. Lily sucked in air as she continued up the steps.

They froze again after two more stairs. A loud bang echoed throughout the entryway. Cool air swept past them. The hairs on the back of Cassie's neck stood up. They hurried up the remaining stairs to the second floor.

Lily dashed into her room. She pushed the door open further and scanned the space, bat at the ready. She saw no one inside, but her eyes focused on a new addition to the room. Her brows knit and she tilted her head as she stared at it.

Cassie stopped before entering the room. Another sharp bang sounded. She snapped her head in the direction of the noise. The door to the widow's walk gaped open before swinging shut. That explained the burst of outdoor air they'd felt moments ago, Cassie surmised. Was it also the escape route of the intruder?

She hurried up the steep staircase to the small balcony overlooking the sea. Cassie flung the door open and burst onto the walk. No signs of anyone, living or dead. She scanned the property and beach beyond. She saw nothing.

With a huff, she hurried back down to her mother's room. As she entered, she noted her mother, bat now hanging at her side, staring straight ahead. Cassie followed her mother's gaze. Her jaw unhinged as she spotted the object of her mother's attention across the room.

On the large mirror above the dresser, in dripping red blood was the word LEAVE.

CHAPTER 14

lashing blue and red lights reflected inside the old seaside manor's interior. Lily stood with Sheriff Cooper in the living room. She pulled her sweater tighter around her. "I'm sorry to bring you out here again, Sheriff," she said.

Two other officers were upstairs with Cassie in Lily's bedroom, photographing the message, which they now knew was painted with tinted Karo syrup, not blood. The officers also were checking for prints around the ominous message.

"No problem, Lily. And please, call me Wyatt."

"Well, Wyatt," Lily said, "I'm still sorry to have pulled you away from your family yet again."

"No problem. You only pulled me away from my TV," Wyatt admitted.

Lily offered a half-smile as he continued. He spun his hat in his hands as he spoke. "My wife left a few years ago. Took off with a tourist from Florida." He gave a half-frown accompanied by a sheepish expression.

"Oh, I'm sorry to hear that," Lily said. "I didn't mean to pry, though I guess I stuck my foot in my mouth."

Wyatt waved his hand at her. "You'd have heard it from someone else. I'm surprised you didn't know already, to be honest. Anyway, you're only pulling me away from my TV dinner and *The Walking Dead*."

Lily chuckled at the admission. "I'm a fan, too."

They stood for a few moments in silence before Wyatt spoke again. "Did you ladies have the locks changed after you moved in?"

"No," Lily answered. "I'm regretting that now."

Wyatt nodded. "I'd recommend it. Given the latest events."

"We'll call first thing in the morning," Lily stated, as Cassie rejoined them.

"They're almost finished up there," Cassie said.

Footsteps bounded down the stairs and a female officer, her brunette hair pulled into a severe bun, rounded the bend into the living room. "Do you have glass cleaner and paper towels, ma'am?"

"Oh, don't worry about that," Lily said, with a wave of her hand. "I'll get it."

"We'd like to take care of it, ma'am."

"I'll grab it for you," Cassie offered, gesturing for the woman to follow her.

"I'll send the locksmith in the morning," Wyatt offered. "He's a friend. He'll fix you up."

Lily smiled and nodded. "Thanks, Wyatt."

The police wrapped up their work and left the two women in a clean, but uneasy home. Cassie opted to bring Willy and bunk with Lily for the night, both of them too jittery to stay alone.

Moonlight streamed through the lace curtains on the windows as the night wore on. Cassie shifted in the bed, attempting to get comfortable. She squeezed her eyes shut, as though the action would force her to fall asleep. It didn't work.

After two hours of tossing and turning, Cassie's eyes slid sideways. "Are you awake?" she whispered.

"Yep," Lily said, her eyes still closed as she lay on her back.

Cassie flopped onto her side. She propped her head up with one hand and stroked Willy's fur with the other. The cat never stirred, but a soft purring emanated from him.

"You don't suppose whoever did this will come back, do you?"

Lily's eyes fluttered open. "I hope not."

"Do you imagine it was the same person we saw wandering around earlier in the week?"

"I'm not certain," Lily answered. "Though I guess that theory makes sense."

Cassie paused a moment, before she continued with her questions. "You do think it was a person, right?"

Lily's brow furrowed and she turned onto her side to face Cassie. "What do you mean?"

Cassie frowned and offered a shrug. "Maybe we do have ghosts," she suggested.

"Oh, Cassie," Lily said with a chuckle. "We don't have ghosts."

"I'm not sure which explanation I prefer, honestly."

"What? You'd prefer ghosts as the explanation?"

"It's preferable in some ways to a real person lurking around our house while we're in it!"

"But?"

"But the idea of an angry spirit skulking around the house might make me even more uncomfortable."

"How do you know the spirit is angry?"

"Well, she scrawled the word 'leave' across your mirror. It seems threatening."

"In dyed Karo. Do you think the ghosts have access to pantry items? And how do you know it's a she?"

"Point taken," Cassie said,, as she collapsed back onto the bed. "Okay, okay, there are no such things as ghosts."

"Which, I agree, doesn't make this any easier."

Cassie shook her head. "Nope."

"Perhaps once the locks are changed, this will die down."

"Gosh, I hope so."

Lily slid her arm across the bed and grasped Cassie's hand. "It'll be okay, Cass," she assured her.

Cassie squeezed her mother's hand in answer.

* * *

The alarm went off far too early for either woman's taste. They dragged themselves from the bed to begin their day. With the shop set to open tomorrow, Cassie headed in to oversee the final preparations, along with Tom's first day on the job. She'd also train all three of the assistants on using the register, credit card machine and inventory system.

Lily stayed behind for the morning hours to meet with the locksmith Sheriff Cooper arranged. She hoped to join everyone for lunch. She sat in the library on the window seat with Willy curled next to her. She had a view of the front driveway to watch for the locksmith. After an early morning call from Wyatt, who informed her his preferred locksmith would swing by this morning, Lily waited impatiently for his arrival.

She sighed after a glance out the window. Nothing so far. She shoved her annoyance aside, trying to focus on being grateful the man could fit them in immediately. Still, with a long to-do list, she regretted the time away from *Buy the Sea*.

Thirty minutes passed after Cassie left. Lily drummed her

fingers against her arm. Willy shot her an annoyed glance. "Sorry!" she exclaimed.

The tuxedo cat nestled his head against a pillow as Lily returned her gaze outside. After another moment, she gave up on willing the man to appear. With a huff, she pushed herself off the window seat and trudged up the stairs to her bedroom.

A chill swept up her spine as she stood on the threshold. She swallowed hard as she recalled the message scrawled across her mirror. A feeling of dread washed over her as she suddenly regretted sending Cassie to the shop and staying here alone.

"You're being ridiculous, Lily," she murmured to herself, as she forced a foot into the room.

She hurried across the room to her night table and snatched the journal from it. With a nervous glance around, she hastened to the door and left the room behind. After settling on what was left of the window seat after Willy stretched himself across it, she glanced out the window again. With the locksmith nowhere in sight, Lily pulled open the journal.

January 4, 1798

Mother, Father and Carolina departed earlier today. I have not written in this journal since prior to the holidays. I have remained far too stressed over their stay to write. My evenings have been filled with tedious, tiresome conversations which left me too drained to pen my thoughts.

On several occasions, Mother mentioned Clifton's name. She is blind to his wicked ways. She continues to treat him with a moth-

er's love, of which he is quite undeserving. I refuse to believe Mother has not caught wind of the tales of Clifton's so-called adventures on the sea. She believes him a legitimate ship captain. Though I know better. I cannot believe she does not.

When one mentions it to her, she waves her hand in the air and dismisses the talk immediately. It has become increasingly frustrating to deal with. I personally am glad they are gone. Father is not much better than Mother. He pretends to doze in his chair rather than discuss the subject. It is a lame attempt to escape an argument with Mother.

And Carolina is quite useless in the matter. The silly girl sits with a book in her lap almost every evening. On several occasions, I prompted her to take to town or the beach for a walk and she refused. She acts like a child would, clinging to her reading rather than searching for a husband. She claims she does not care. She will regret that when she is an old maid. And I certainly shall not bring her into my home after Mother and Father pass to become my ward. No, perhaps she can seek shelter aboard Clifton's magnificent ship since she finds his adventures "fanciful and exciting." What a ridiculous girl.

For weeks, I have pondered if I may have slipped into a realm where madness prevails. Such talk about piracy is nonsense. William has spoken much on the subject at dinner parties. The notion that pirates are somehow romantic is absurd. They are no better than common thieves and should be shot on sight. Clifton included.

Lily raised her eyebrows at the entry and blew out a long breath. Henrietta had very unyielding views of her pirate brother. And she'd not softened at all toward her family. Lily glanced out the window again. No vehicles approached, so she returned to her reading.

January 11, 1798

I have fallen into a depression. The bleak winter landscape in this forsaken place has driven me nearly to madness. I have received new correspondence from William regarding his return. It has again been delayed. As such, I have written to Mother and requested that she receive me for an extended visit until the winter months have passed. I shall pass the time as I await her response readying for the trip as I cannot imagine she will not oblige me.

January 26, 1798

I am outraged. I received a letter from Mother encouraging me to stay in Hideaway Bay for the remaining winter months. My child-hood home is closed to me!

Apparently, my outburst over the Christmas holiday is the source of the denial. Mother stated in her letter it is best for me to stay here given my animosity toward Clifton. Mother has once again opened her home to the louse and, therefore, finds it best that I stay away, lest my temper overcome me.

I have written a return message expressing my indignation over the slap in my face. And I informed Mother she should throw Clifton out on the street. Though I doubt she will heed my warning. Instead, she shall become the laughing stock of Savannah.

February 4, 1798

My beloved has returned home. I had hoped our reunion would make the remaining winter months bearable. Instead, our reunion has been tainted. First, William stated he shall return to the sea in two weeks. In truth, his return to the locker will not happen for one month, but he will travel to Raleigh in two weeks and depart from there where his ship has docked.

I am heartsick. Two weeks together only to be left alone again for months on end.

To add insult to injury, I have received another letter from Mother. She stands by her decision that I should stay away while Clifton remains at our family home.

My mother has chosen a hooligan over her own firstborn child.

June 1, 1798

My heart is broken. Tears stain these pages as I write.

A ringing startled Lily from her reading. Bells chimed loudly from the foyer. Willy's head snapped up. A knocking sounded against the wooden door. Lily inhaled deeply as she forced her heart to return to normal speed. A glance out the window showed a full-sized white van parked in the drive-way. Large block lettering on the van's side read VAN NESS LOCKS: Quick, fast, reliable!

Lily rose from the cushioned seat and hurried to the front door. Willy leapt down from the perch and slinked into the foyer and up the stairs, seeking a hiding spot.

Lily pulled the front door open to a short, balding but pleasant-faced man. He glanced up from his note-taking on his clipboard. "Mrs. Bennett?" he inquired.

"Yes," Lily said, extending her hand for a shake. "Please come in." She stepped aside and gestured for him to enter the foyer. "Thank you for coming on such short notice."

"No problem, ma'am, Wyatt's a good friend. I'm Carl VanNess."

"Hi, Carl. Please, call me Lily."

Carl smiled. "Wyatt said you're having some trouble with unwanted visitors, huh?" He eyed the lock on the front door.

"Yes," Lily answered, raising her eyebrows and emitting a sigh. "It started with a cat. We've since upgraded to the human variety of surprise visitors."

"A cat, huh?" Carl said with a chuckle. "Well, I doubt he tampered with the locks, so I can't help there. But I can help with the human problem." He bent to study the lock again. After a moment, he straightened. "I'll need to see all the doors."

"Sure."

As Lily led him to the door in the kitchen, he said, "Given the problems you've been having, I can also recommend a security system to monitor the house in addition to the lock upgrade."

"How long will that take?" Lily asked.

"I can have it installed in a few hours. You'll have access to the system via an app on your phone as well as a keypad at the front door. You can monitor doors and windows. We can even install a camera or two in a strategic location to monitor the premises."

Lily's brow crinkled as she considered the idea. Was he trying to upsell her because of the trouble, or merely attempting to offer the best assistance he could?

"There's no need to decide right now," Carl said, noting her hesitation. "I can always pop back in to install it. No problem."

Lily nodded in response as they reached the kitchen. "Thanks, I'll discuss it with my daughter, too. Here's our back door. We also have a slider through there that leads to a deck and down to the beach."

The doorbell chimed before Carl could answer. "Go ahead," he said in response. "I'll check out both these doors."

"Thanks," Lily said, as she darted toward the foyer. A figure moved on the opposite side of the privacy glass in the door. Lily pulled the door open to find Sheriff Wyatt Cooper on the opposite side.

"Oh, Wyatt, good morning."

"Morning," Wyatt answered with a nod. He held two coffee cups in his hand. "I brought you a tea from *High Grounds*. I checked with Cassie to see what you drank."

"Oh, you didn't have to do that," Lily said, accepting the cup.

"My pleasure. Meghan makes a nice house blend–I thought you might be interested in trying."

Lily popped open the top and took a whiff. "Smells delicious. Please, come in."

Wyatt stepped into the foyer. "I see Carl's here already."

"Mmm, yes," Lily said, after a sip. "Hey, this is tasty!"

"I don't drink tea much, I'm a coffee man myself but I've heard other people rave about it."

Carl emerged into the foyer. A smile lit up his ruddy face. "Wyatt!" he said, thrusting his hand out, then pulling the younger man into a hug.

"Hey, Carl. Already hard at work, I see."

"Yep. We'll get these locks switched out for you right away. You mentioned your daughter lives here, too, right?"

"Yes," Lily said with a nod.

"So, we'll get you three keys. One for each of you and a spare."

"That sounds great. And I'll text Cassie in just a moment about that security system."

"Okay, like I said, no rush on that decision. I can always pop in to install it later." Carl skirted past the two of them and headed out the door.

"Thinking of having a security system installed?" Wyatt questioned.

"Carl mentioned it this morning. I'll confess, I wasn't expecting that question, so I'm not sure what we're getting into here with cost and operating it and so on. I don't want to get into something I may regret."

Wyatt nodded as he sipped his coffee. "Well, Carl won't steer you wrong on whatever he recommends. He'll make sure you get a system that fits your needs and is easy for you to use."

"So, I can trust him, huh?" Lily said with a chuckle.

Wyatt laughed along with her and nodded. "Yeah, he's not just trying to upsell you because you had a bit of trouble. I honestly think it'll settle down but…"

"But?" Lily prompted.

"But you are two ladies on the outskirts of town. I don't mean to sound sexist," he added quickly, waving his hand in the air. "But some folks might take advantage of that."

"And those sort of folks live in this area?" Lily inquired.

"Those sort of folks live in every area," Wyatt answered. "We're a safe neighborhood and, like I said, I think this trouble will settle down, but you never know when a grifter may pass through town. Better safe than sorry."

"That's very true. Well, maybe I'll see what he has to say about the full security system. I'm certain it'll set Cassie's mind at ease."

Wyatt pursed his lips and bobbed his head up and down. "Was she upset after the incident last night?"

"She was. We both were," Lily admitted. "Even if someone was just hoping to frighten us and not do us any harm, it is worrisome."

"Hey, maybe it wasn't a person!" Wyatt said with a laugh.

Lily chuckled. "A ghost? Now you sound like Cassie."

"Starting to believe the legends, huh?"

"Well, everyone seems to agree this house is haunted by multiple ghosts."

"Not you, though?"

Lily shook her head with a frown. "Nah. I don't believe in ghosts."

Wyatt cocked his head and gave her a pensive look. With narrowed eyes, he said, "You soon might."

"Well, I suppose that's one plus of the security system. Maybe we can identify if the person is a person or a ghost."

"You mean if they pass right through the locked door?"

"Something like that, yeah," Lily said.

Carl pushed back through the front door, laden with a number of tools in two overflowing toolboxes.

"Well, I'll get out of your hair," Wyatt said. "Let Carl finish his work and get you all set."

"All right. Thanks for stopping by! And thanks for the tea!" Lily said, waving her coffee cup in the air.

"You're welcome. Take care, Carl," Wyatt said, offering the man a slap on the back.

After Wyatt ducked through the open front door, Lily said, "About those security systems…"

Carl spent thirty minutes outlining the options for security systems. After a few questions and a quick demonstration, Lily settled on a monitoring system that included door and window monitoring and two cameras.

Certain Cassie would agree, she moved forward with the installation, which Carl informed her would take the better part of the morning. With a second cup of tea in hand, she settled on the deck to enjoy the warm fall day.

Henrietta's journal lay on the table in front of her, but Lily found herself distracted by the glistening water gently ebbing and flowing on the beach. Content to sip her tea and study the sea, she slouched in her chair and let her mind wander.

CHAPTER 15

⁓

The installation of the security system lingered into the afternoon hours. Lily texted Cassie about the delay, learning they were making good progress at the shop. Cassie estimated they would finish early for the day, and offered to bring back take-out, before they settled for an early night prior to the big opening tomorrow.

While Lily felt a twinge of guilt about missing the work-day, it was unavoidable. Cassie assured her that, despite missing her at the shop, they were perfectly fine putting the final touches on the grand opening decorations. She sent a few snapshots of the shop's decor.

Silk leaves in red, orange and yellow enhanced one of the quaint window displays of ships, lighthouses and seashell jewelry. The words "GRAND OPENING" were painted in fall colors around the *Buy the Sea* logo. The second window read "FALL IN LOVE WITH OUR GIFTS." The word "fall" was painted in block letters with autumn colors.

A colorful chalkboard street sign detailed items within the shop on one side. On the other was a welcome message, with phrases detailing the grand opening offerings such as free hot chocolate and cookies.

The place looked fantastic. Lily couldn't wait to see it in person the following morning. Until then, she'd settle for the amazing fall view over the water.

As the sun cast long shadows across the deck overlooking the water, Carl popped his head out the door. "Okay! All set!"

"Great!" Lily answered. She'd just settled back in her chaise with the journal after a beach walk. She snapped the book shut, eager to finish the process with Carl.

"I'll show you how to use the system, and get you set up with the app on your phone. Sorry this took longer than expected; I've wasted your entire day."

"No problem. While I did miss being at the shop for the finishing touches, I won't complain about having a day to enjoy this gorgeous view."

"I can't argue with you there."

"Today's the first time I've gotten to take a leisurely stroll on the beach since we moved in!" Lily answered, as she ducked through the sliding glass door.

"Let's start here," Carl said, as he slid the door closed. He tapped the silver lock poking above the handle. "New locks here. Key matches the front and back doors. He stepped back and signaled toward the floor. Also installed a foot lock here. Just step down on it to engage and kick here to disengage."

"Got it, okay."

"Give it a try," he encouraged.

Lily stepped down on the lock, hearing a click sound as it engaged. She tapped the front and the lock popped up. "Easy enough!"

Carl showed her the new locks on the back and front doors. They then moved on to the security system. Carl demonstrated how to activate and deactivate the system from the keypad, keyfobs and the security app for Lily's phone.

"Now, I'll leave a list of instructions, so you can set this up for your daughter's phone, too."

"Great. Oh!" Lily exclaimed, as he shoved several tools into his toolbox. "What about the door upstairs?"

Carl's brow wrinkled. "Door upstairs?" he repeated.

"Yes, to the widow's walk."

"Ohhhh, yeah." He shrugged. "I don't have a lock on it nor did I alarm it. If anyone's coming in that door, it must be one of your ghosts." He burst into laughter as he shoved a few more tools into his toolbox.

Lily offered a nervous chuckle as she glanced up the stairs, recalling the incident last night. "I don't mean to sound like a pain, but would you mind putting a latch or something on that? It was banging open the other night. And while I don't think it was the point of entry for our visitor, I'd prefer it not to bang open and closed with every wind gust."

Carl's eyes slid upwards toward the door. "Oh, ah, sure," he said, as he retrieved a few tools. "I'll just put an eyehook on it for you. No problem."

"Thanks, I appreciate that."

After another thirty minutes, they had a latch on the upstairs door. After settling the bill, Lily collapsed on the couch, as the crunch of gravel announced the departing van. Silence settled over the house and she glanced at her watch. Cassie would be home soon. Her eyes slid sideways to the journal she'd laid on the side table next to the couch. No time to read the reason for Henrietta's heartbreak now.

She pulled herself off the couch to ready plates and cutlery for their take-out meal. As she bustled around the kitchen making lemonade for their dinner, she entertained reasons for Henrietta's tear-stained entry.

"What bothered you this time, Henrietta?" she mused aloud. "Spring came too late? New dress was the wrong color? Hangnail?"

Lily chuckled over her laundry list of items that may be the cause of Henrietta's grief. As she stirred sugar into the lemonade, a warm, furry creature rubbed against her legs. "Hello, Willy. Ventured out, did you?"

The little cat trilled and reversed his course, tossing his body against her legs. "Hungry?" This inquiry was met with a meow.

"Your mom should be home soon to feed you." Another meow. "No, I'm not going to take her job away from her. You can wait a few more minutes."

A door slammed in the distance. "Mom?" Cassie called. "I'm home." Willy raced from the kitchen toward the front door.

"Coming!" Lily hollered.

"Hey, buddy!" Cassie said, as Lily entered the foyer. She'd dropped the takeout bag in favor of scooping up the cat. Cassie raised her eyebrows at Lily. "New locks and security system, and you leave the front door unlocked, huh?" she joked.

"Since you don't have a key, I didn't want you locked out."

"I figured you'd let me in. I do have the food, after all," Cassie said with a wink.

"Speaking of–here is your new key and alarm system keyfob," Lily said. "And we'll have to program your phone for the security system."

Cassie picked up the instruction card and studied it. "I'll work on this while we eat."

After they finished their take-out meals from a local Italian eatery, and with the new security system app loaded on Cassie's phone, the two women collapsed on the couch for a quiet evening before their grand opening the next day.

They settled in with a movie, before turning in for the night.

* * *

Bright sunshine sparkled off the water as Lily and Cassie climbed into the car.

"Ready?" Cassie said, as she slid on her sunglasses.

"Too late now if I'm not," Lily joked.

Cassie grinned at her, pulling out past the Whispering Manor sign that now hung correctly from the light post.

Cassie pulled the car into the rear of the shop and they pushed into the storeroom. Lily marveled at the fall wonderland in the retail space, as she and Cassie unlocked the front door and dragged two tables onto the sidewalk out front.

Meghan met them outside as they set up the first table and pulled an orange tablecloth over it. She set a carafe of hot chocolate on the fluttering tablecloth. "Good morning, ladies. Ready?"

"I think so!" Cassie said.

Amber arrived next as Meghan set out cups, napkins, a covered bowl of marshmallows and a few canisters of whipped cream before trudging back to *High Grounds* to retrieve more refreshments.

Chloe, Tom and Genny arrived next, all toting boxes of cookies and pastries. They set them down on the neighboring table and Genny began to set out a selection.

Chloe dashed inside the store to retrieve the remaining decorations for the tables out front. As the opening hour approached, Tinsley Thompson hurried down the sidewalk toward them. She pushed through the already-building crowd toward Lily and Cassie.

"Ladies! Oh, ladies, yoo-hoo!" She waved her bedecked hand in the air to catch their attention.

"Mayor Thompson," Lily greeted her. "How nice of you to stop by for our opening!"

"Stop by?" Tinsley breathlessly exclaimed. Her eyes went wide. "No, no, no. When I heard through the grapevine you were planning to open this morning, I threw myself into overdrive to rearrange my schedule!" She hurried to the door and affixed a large yellow ribbon to one side, before drawing it across to the other. "If this is going to be a grand opening, it should be GRAND!"

"Oh," Lily stammered, as she watched the scene unfold. "Well, thank you, though I didn't think to call and put a demand on your time. I'm sure you're very busy!"

Tinsley shoved a large pair of golden scissors into Lily's hands. She made a face and waved her hand in the air. "Please—never a bother to help two smart ladies open their business in MY town!" She grinned widely as she scanned the crowd. "Oh, hi, Gloria!" she called, waving at another woman.

"Well, we certainly are glad to have you here," Cassie chimed in.

"I think it's important! Not only for me, as mayor, to show interest in my town's businesses, but to give a little… oomph to the opening. Some class and style! Some pomp and circumstance." She lifted a shoulder and raised an eyebrow as though she was stating the obvious.

Cassie swallowed hard and shot Lily a glance. Lily shrugged and offered an amused smile. At the dot of nine, Tinsley waved her arms in the air. Meghan approached with a sturdy wooden box and dropped it next to Tinsley. With her assistance, the navy-clad mayor climbed aboard and waved her arms again. "Folks! Folks!" she called.

A hush came over the crowd, and Tinsley adjusted her navy and red scarf, before she clasped her hands in front of her. A wide smile crossed her face as she surveyed the quiet crowd.

"Neighbors. Friends. Visitors to our lovely little harbor town. Welcome." She paused as a few applause broke out. "I'm so pleased to be here on this lovely fall day for such a momentous occasion!"

Meghan sidled up to Lily and Cassie who stood near the door. "I didn't know we were supposed to call the mayor," Cassie whispered.

Meghan held in a chuckle. "She does this all the time. That's why I had the box ready."

Mayor Thompson continued, "In my time as mayor of our gorgeous little seaside hamlet, I've seen a number of businesses open along Main Street. And now, I am so pleased to welcome yet another.

"Featuring local artisans and craftspeople, Lily Bennett and her daughter, Cassie McGuire, though new to our town, embody what it means to be a true citizen of Hideaway Bay. So, without further ado, I give you... *BUY THE SEA!*" She showcased the shop front with a broad gesture that looked as though she'd practiced it in front of the mirror several times. "Ladies, if you'll do the honors!"

"Oh!" Lily exclaimed, raising her eyebrows as she glanced down at the scissors. Cassie hurried to the opposite side of the door. Each woman took one side of the scissors and, after a misstep, they snapped them shut, and the yellow ribbon broke away.

Drums sounded and instruments played as customers streamed toward the entrance.

"Come on in, everyone!" Cassie said, smiling as she searched the crowd. "She brought a band?" she breathed to Meghan.

"Every time," Meghan said. Cassie spotted the marching band stomping down Main Street in full uniform. "They're from the local high school. I think they love the chance to perform."

Mayor Thompson climbed down from the makeshift step stool and greeted customers. Cassie fought through the throng of first customers and grabbed Tinsley's elbow. "Thank you!"

"Oh, you're welcome! Oh, hi, Teresa, how are the kids? Gary! Love that green on you!" Tinsley was in her element, and after passing along her thanks, Cassie hurried inside the store. Tom had stationed himself at the cash register, already ringing out the first few customers. Chloe and Amber filtered among the others who were browsing, checking to see if anyone needed help.

Penny Whitlock approached Lily and Cassie as they greeted people at the door. "Hi, ladies! Fantastic opening."

"Thank you," Lily said. "We couldn't have picked a better day weather-wise."

"Absolutely," Penny agreed. "And how is the house?"

"We love it," Lily said.

"Had a few disturbances, I heard? I hope that's all behind you."

"Oh," Lily hedged, unsure how the information had gotten to Penny.

"Wyatt's my nephew," she filled in.

"Ah," Lily said, as understanding filled her. "Yes, nothing serious, just a few harmless pranks. I expect they'll die down once people realize we're staying."

"Good for you," Penny said, as she patted Lily's arm. "Now if you'll excuse me, there's a pair of sea glass earrings I've been admiring from the window for days."

The morning hours were filled with customers, conversations and cookies. In the late morning, Pearl Booker wandered through the shop's door. She spent a few moments glancing at various items, before she spotted Cassie near the shop's rear, assisting a customer with handmade photo albums. As the woman headed for the register, Pearl patted Cassie's shoulder.

"Hello, dear," she said. Her light pink lips formed a grin, and she clutched something to her chest.

"Oh, Pearl! Hello!" Cassie said.

"What a lovely store." Pearl's eyes panned the space.

"Thank you! And thanks so much for stopping by for our first day!"

"You're welcome! Well, I had a reason."

"Oh?"

"I figured you'd be quite busy with the shop opening, but I didn't forget your request. I've got everything you asked for right here," she said, patting the stack of folders she held.

"Oh, thank you," Cassie exclaimed. "You didn't have to bring them over, but I appreciate that."

"I didn't want you to have to run to the library after an exhausting day. Now, I've got all the articles on Susan here, all the articles Susan was studying and anything else we had on our local pirate legend."

Cassie eyed the folders as Pearl held them out. In primary colors, she must have sorted the materials into three separate folders. Cassie extended her hands to accept them. "Thank you so much. This was so kind of you. If you have a moment, I'd love to introduce you to my mom. She's the one interested in Clifton."

"Of course, dear! Lead the way."

Cassie located Lily near the register with Tinsley and a group of women. She stowed the folders behind the counter before she approached them.

"Oh, Pearl!" Tinsley called. "Venturing out of the library? Never thought I'd see the day!" She gave that cackling laugh.

"I do occasionally pry myself from the warm embrace of

the books there, Tinsley," Pearl said, seeming unfazed by the joke at her expense.

"Oh, you know I'm only joking. I know you're an avid supporter of our local businesses!"

"Particularly when they are run by librarians," Pearl said, patting Cassie's arm.

"Mom," Cassie interjected, "this is Pearl Booker, the librarian here. She brought the articles we requested, so we didn't have to stop by after closing up here. Pearl, this is my mom, Lily Bennett."

Lily shook the older librarian's hand. "How thoughtful of you."

"And what articles are you two ladies reading up on?" Tinsley prodded.

"We learned about the tragic history of the last family who owned the house," Cassie said. "What a sad story. I was interested in learning more about the case."

Tinsley nodded. "Yes, a terrible story. I was a young councilperson at the time. Such a shame when a young life is lost like that. And in a safe town like this. Though there's no proof of foul play. The girl may have simply run off."

"My interest lies a bit further in the past," Lily admitted. She turned to address Pearl. "Cassie found a journal at the house from Henrietta Blanchard. I've been using it for some light nighttime reading. She mentioned her brother, Clifton Nichols. I was shocked when Cassie filled me in on the details you shared with her."

Pearl nodded, an amused smile on her face. "How interesting. I'd love to look at it. Once you're finished, of course. An item like that would be a lovely addition to our history display in the library. And yes, Clifton is quite a legend around here."

"Well, thank you for the articles," Lily said. "I look forward to learning more about him!"

"Oh, come on, Pearl," Tinsley teased. "You can't leave it hanging like that! You simply *must* tell the story. I've never heard anyone tell it so well as you!"

"Perhaps another time," Pearl said, as she eyed the busy shop.

"Oh, please, feel free to share your story," Lily encouraged. "I'd love to hear it."

"Well," Pearl said, hesitating for a moment before continuing, "I suppose I could."

"Come on, Pearl, don't be shy!" Tinsley encouraged.

Pearl glanced at the floor, her eyebrows raised. "Well, as I told your daughter, Cassie, Clifton Nichols was the brother of Henrietta Blanchard. Poor woman detested that her brother was a pirate. She tried to hide it at every turn.

"Her husband was a ship captain–a legitimate one–if you believe Henrietta. But rumors abounded about a connection between Captain William Blanchard and the infamous pirate, Black Jack. Of course, everyone assumed the tie existed through Henrietta. Some even hypothesized the marriage solidified the partnership.

"Henrietta denied this to her dying day, which came much earlier than anyone could have anticipated."

"She threw herself from the house's widow's walk, didn't she?" Cassie inquired.

Pearl's eyebrows raised again. "Well, that's the story."

"Story? Is it fact or fiction?" A shop-goer inquired from behind Tinsley. Cassie glanced around, realizing a crowd had gathered to listen to Pearl's story.

"Well, that depends entirely on how much of the legend you believe."

"What's the legend?" another person shouted.

"Yeah, tell us the legend!"

Pearl chuckled for a moment. "All right, all right." She smiled at the crowd before she continued. "Captain William

Blanchard died at sea. News of his death reached Henrietta who was devastated. The young bride hadn't even been married for a year when she lost her husband. Most assumed she became so distraught that she lost her mind. Her behavior turned erratic. Rumors flew that she wandered the widow's walk in search of her lost husband. Her family tried to convince her he was dead but she insisted he was not. She waited and waited for his return, until she became so despondent that she flung herself from the widow's walk."

"What? That's it?" someone called.

Pearl offered a lopsided smile. "That's what some people believe."

"Is there another side of the story?" Lily asked. She surmised there was, based on the coy smirk on Tinsley's face. She fingered the string of pearls around her neck with one eyebrow raised as she watched the scene unfold.

"She was murdered," Pearl said.

CHAPTER 16

A hush fell over the crowd at Pearl's latest piece of the twisted tale.

"Who murdered her?" a red-haired man inquired.

"That remains a mystery."

"Why was she murdered?" another asked.

"Now *there* is where the legend of Black Jack comes in," Pearl said, raising her finger in the air. "Black Jack was an infamous pirate. And a very successful one, too. He raided ships considered too secure to raid, and amassed a fortune because of it. He took risks no one else would and the reward was immense."

"Was he brutal?"

Pearl gave a coy glance at the crowd. "Very. He had a reputation of leaving only one person alive."

"Why one person?"

She raised her eyebrows as she responded. "To warn his future victims not to fight."

"What happened to his fortune?"

"What, indeed!" Pearl answered. "The legend says it's hidden right here, in Hideaway Bay."

A few gasps came from the crowd along with a few chuckles from the locals. Pearl continued, "The legend says Black Jack got himself embroiled in a war with another pirate, the fearsome Redbeard, named for his red hair and bloody history.

"He sailed from the Caribbean with his treasure loaded onto his black-sailed ship. He barely made it into port, the ship was so laden with his bounty. He consulted his sister, Henrietta, and she hid the treasure for him."

"I thought his ship sank before it made it here?"

"Oh, no!" Pearl corrected. "No, no. *Neptune's Servant* definitely made port here in Hideaway Bay. And with it, supposedly untold treasure. Jewels the size of goose eggs, gold bars and coins, silver pieces.

"All smuggled ashore in the dead of the night. And all put in a location only known to Black Jack and Henrietta.

"But that didn't stop Redbeard. He wanted that treasure, and he wanted it badly. And for that reason, Black Jack cursed the treasure. Anyone who tried to claim the treasure would pay a terrible price.

"That still didn't stop Redbeard, though. He and his men came to town in search of the treasure. He never found it, but his son continued the search and vowed vengeance long after his father was killed by Black Jack. And before long, Henrietta was shoved from the widow's walk to her death." Pearl shoved her hands forward.

"Did anyone ever find it?"

Pearl shook her head. "No. At least… no one's admitted to finding it."

"Isn't that what Susan Davies was researching when she disappeared?" the red-haired man asked.

Pearl nodded. "Yes, she was studying the legend of Black Jack and his missing treasure. Was she getting close to an answer? Is that why her young life was snuffed out? Or was she just another victim of Black Jack's curse?" Pearl shrugged. "Who knows?"

Silence filled the shop as everyone mulled the fantastic pirate story. Complete with a missing treasure and a curse, it certainly entertained the crowd. A slow clap began. Cassie spotted Tinsley's hands slapping together. The applause spread as Tinsley smiled and nodded.

"Thoroughly entertaining as always, Pearl!" she shouted. "And now, please, everyone, enjoy the shopping! There's plenty of pirate-themed items here and all over town! And these ones aren't cursed!"

Laughter rose through the crowd as it broke up. "Thanks, Pearl," Cassie said. "I look forward to learning more about Black Jack and Susan. Thank you for the articles you brought!"

"Oh, anytime, dear. Just don't let the curse get you!" The woman chuckled, before she wandered away to speak with a few other people.

The afternoon brought a slower, but steady, stream of people. As Cassie rang out an elderly couple, she noted Frida meander through the door. She wandered around for a few moments, before she picked up a wooden lighthouse.

Frida stalked to the register and slammed the lighthouse onto the counter. "Find everything you were looking for?"

Frida grunted. "Sister's birthday's coming up. She likes lighthouses."

"Well, this one is very nice. I love the weathered blue paint. I'm sure she'll love it, too."

Frida shrugged, as though she didn't care if her sister liked the gift or not. "Would you like a box?" Cassie asked.

"Nah, I'll have them pack it up at the post office. Use their box."

"Okay," Cassie said with a smile, and gave the total.

Frida pulled cash from her wallet and shoved it toward

Cassie. "How's the cat?" she asked, as the register drawer popped open and Cassie made change.

"He's doing great! He wasn't pleased about his first vet visit but he seems to be settling into the house well! Thank you for asking."

Frida offered another grunting response as Cassie passed the bagged item to her. "Have a nice day and thanks for stopping by *Buy the Sea*!"

Frida took the bag, letting it dangle from her fingertips. She hovered for a moment before taking a step toward the door. She hesitated another second before she leaned back toward Cassie. "I'd be careful about digging too deep into the past," she said, "you might end up regretting it." With that, Frida spun on her heel and strode out the door.

Cassie stood staring after her, with her jaw agape. Did Frida just threaten her?

* * *

Cassie and Lily climbed from the car, exhausted and sore from the long but successful day. Cassie pulled the folders from Pearl from the backseat, before they trudged up the steps to the house.

Lily fiddled with her keychain fob in the orange-red light of the setting sun behind them. "Which is unlock?" she asked, squinting down at it.

"On the left," Cassie said. "No, wait, right."

Lily dropped her arm to her side and rolled her eyes. "Which one, Cass? Left or right?"

Cassie glanced at the keyfob again, as she juggled the folders and their takeout meal. "Right."

Lily pressed the button. A muffled voice announced the alarm was disarmed in a crisp British accent. Lily shoved her key into the lock and pushed the door open for Cassie.

"Whew, I'm glad to be home," Lily announced, as they stepped through the door. Willy threaded through their legs. Lily relieved Cassie of the folders, tossing them on the desk in the library before she gave Willy's head a rub.

"What do you say we get your dinner, and then curl up on the couch with ours?" Cassie asked the purring kitty.

"After we change, of course," Lily stated.

"Of course," Cassie said with a grin.

Within twenty minutes, the women were curled on the couch in robes and pajamas, with buttered gnocchi and side salads. Willy curled between them, his belly full of his Sea Captain's Choice pate.

"Seemed like a successful day," Cassie said.

"Yes," Lily agreed. "We got a lot of support from the community. And the mayor."

"And the marching band."

"I did not see that one coming!" Lily said with a chuckle.

"Neither did I. Meghan said she does it all the time."

"I suppose it is important to have a thriving town to brag about."

Cassie nodded as she slid her potato dumpling around in the butter, before skewering it and popping it into her mouth.

"Is it terrible that I'm already looking forward to my day off on Tuesday?" Lily inquired.

"No," Cassie answered. "This is why we hired assistants! So we'd have some time off to spend together."

"And they seem to have it together. They did great today."

"Mmm-hmm," Cassie agreed. "You chose well."

"We'll test their mettle on Tuesday. First day alone for them."

"I think they'll be fine, but we'll be right here if they need us."

"How about that story Pearl told?" Cassie asked.

Lily raised her eyebrows. "Quite interesting. That's another reason I can't wait until Tuesday. I'd love to dive into those materials. I'm way too tired to do it tonight, though."

"And it is a school night," Cassie mentioned.

Lily chuckled. "Yes, it is. At least we have a late start tomorrow." She referenced the 10 a.m. Sunday opening time.

"Thank goodness for small miracles," Cassie answered.

"I hope I can sleep after all of today's excitement. If not, I may be up perusing those files anyway."

"Me too. Especially with the extra bit I got."

"Holding out on me?"

Cassie sighed. "Not really. It's probably nothing but…"

"Well, are you going to make me guess or tell me?"

"Frida stopped in to buy a lighthouse for her sister's birthday. Before she left, she said something kind of strange to me."

"Oh?"

"Yeah, something about not digging into the past, or we might regret it."

Lily puckered her lips and narrowed her eyes.

"Yeah, same thing I thought," Cassie said, in response to her expression. "It almost sounds like a threat, don't you think?"

Lily shrugged. "Maybe it's her odd way of being friendly?"

"Friendly?" Cassie guffawed. "How can you construe that as friendly?"

"I don't. But she is an oddball. Her version of friendly may be completely different from ours."

"I'll say," Cassie answered.

"I'm just saying that perhaps she wasn't meaning it as a threat, but rather a piece of neighborly advice. People don't like 'outsiders' poking around their small town business."

Cassie considered it as she munched on a leaf of Romaine. "Maybe," she concluded.

They finished their meal discussing a few additional highlights of the day. Ten minutes after they'd collapsed back onto the couch after cleaning up, they both dozed off.

"Well," Lily said, patting Cassie on the leg, "I'm heading up, kid."

"I'm right behind you," Cassie said, with a yawn.

They climbed the stairs and parted ways. Cassie and Willy headed to Cassie's room. Soft light filled the space from her bedside lamp. Cassie wound the pint-sized carousel and listened to the tinkling music as she peeled off her robe and laid it at the foot of her bed. She slathered lotion on her hands, perching on the edge of the bed.

The music tinkled away as she pulled her covers back before climbing between the sheets. Willy spun in a circle and he curled into a ball on Cassie's plush robe. As he settled, the music ceased without warning.

Cassie frowned at the carousel. She glanced at it. Its horses stood frozen ready to leap forward, but held at bay by some unseen force. Cassie crossed the room and poked at the miniature merry-go-round. It didn't budge. She wound it again and gave it a shimmy. After another poke, she gave up. "Guess I'm not going to be so lucky this time," she said with a sigh.

She trudged back to bed and climbed in. She pulled the covers up around her and reached for the light on her night table. Before she could pull the chain and welcome the darkness, a noise crashed through the relative silence.

Cassie instinctively ducked at the sound. Her heart pounded and her pulse raced. Despite her eyes being squeezed shut, she identified the sound as breaking glass. She wondered for a brief moment if the carousel had broken. A loud bang followed by clattering, pushed the thought from her mind.

When the noise died down, she risked a glance around

the room. Across from her, a curtain fluttered in the breeze. Jagged glass still edged the window but a gaping hole sat in the middle. Shards of broken glass scattered across the hardwood. Following its path, Cassie saw a round object wrapped in paper.

She swallowed hard as her heart pounded. Willy flattened his ears and body as he clamored up the bed toward Cassie. "It's okay, buddy," she soothed as she stroked his fur. He remained spooked, his one eye glancing warily around the room.

Before she could climb from her bed, Lily pounded against the door. Cassie jumped at the noise, letting out a deep sigh as she realized it was her mother's voice calling to her.

"I'm okay, but don't come in. There's glass all over the floor!"

The door swung open, and Lily scanned the room. "What happened? Are you okay?"

Cassie pointed to the paper-covered object on the floor. "Yeah. Someone lobbed that through my window!"

CHAPTER 17

*L*ily's eyes went wide at the sight of the broken window and the fist-sized rock on the floor. "Did you call the police?"

"Not yet," Cassie said, swiping her phone from her night table. "I was just about to when you knocked."

"I'll grab my shoes and head downstairs. Careful when you follow me. And bring Willy; I don't want him to try to walk across that glass."

Cassie nodded as she typed 9-1-1 on her keypad. She spoke with the emergency dispatcher, explaining the situation. Afterward, she scooped the cat into her arms and picked her way through the glass after sliding into her soled slippers.

Lily waited for her in the living room. "Are you okay?" she inquired again.

Cassie nodded. "Yeah, just... startled."

Lily shook her head. "I can't believe someone threw a rock through your window. This is becoming dangerous. First, they lurk around the house, now this?"

"Probably a high school kid on a dare."

"Well, a high school kid should know better than to destroy someone's property. Someone could have been hurt!"

Blue and red flashing lights painted the inside of the living room, punctuating the end of Lily's statement. Cassie leapt from her seat on the couch and hurried toward the door. As she swung it open, Wyatt peered inside.

He winced. "Hey, Cassie."

"I'm so sorry to call again, Wyatt," Cassie said, as she backed up and gestured for him to enter.

"No problem. Dispatcher said you had a rock thrown through a window?"

Cassie nodded as Lily joined them. "Lily," Wyatt greeted her with a nod.

"Hi, Wyatt," Lily said, as she leaned against the door jamb. "Sorry to bother you again."

"No bother at all, Lily. Sorry we keep meeting under these circumstances."

"I'll show you the scene of the crime," Cassie said, pointing upstairs.

Wyatt glanced upstairs and nodded. Cassie led him to her bedroom. Crumbled glass pieces lay scattered across the dresser near the window and the floor. Wyatt frowned at the scene, and glanced out the window.

"Did you see anyone?"

"No," Cassie admitted. "I was in bed when the rock came through. I hadn't seen anyone before that–though, I wasn't looking out the window."

"They had to be close, I'd reckon."

Cassie sighed. "Maybe the alarm system and new locks deterred them from getting into the house. So, we got this instead."

"Can't say that's much of an improvement."

"No," Cassie agreed. "Though I suppose it's better than them lurking around in the house."

Glass crunched under Wyatt's feet as he stepped toward the object laying on the floor. He cocked his head and stared at it for a moment, then squatted down.

He pulled gloves from his back pocket and snapped them on before lifting the object. Cassie stretched her neck from the doorway to peer over his shoulder. "I saw the paper earlier, but didn't want to disturb the scene. Does it say anything?"

Wyatt stood and joined Cassie at the door. As he approached, she noted a rubber band holding a white paper onto the fist-sized object. He peeled the rubber band off and unwrapped the object. A large tan stone lay underneath. Both he and Cassie spotted something scrawled on the inside of the paper. Wyatt unfurled it further, flattening the paper. Cassie peered over his arm at it.

In bold, red letters, the paper held one simple message:

LEAVE THE PAST ALONE

Cassie snapped her eyes to Wyatt's face, studying his reaction.

"Well," he said, with a twist of his head, "this changes everything."

Cassie gulped. "What do you mean?"

"We may have chalked this up to a neighborhood prank. In bad taste of course, but nothing more than that. But this looks like a threat. Especially coupled with the tale told at your opening today."

"Oh, you heard about that?"

"I'm sure the whole town did. I snuck in the back while Pearl was telling her story. You and your mom's interest in a few of the more lurid town legends is no secret."

"We don't mean to pry, but…"

Wyatt waved his hand at her. "No, I don't mean to say this

is your fault. It's natural curiosity, especially when everyone's feeding you stories about the tragedies within this house and how the house is haunted. It's natural to want to know the history of one's home. No one wants to listen to tales about their house constantly. But it's no secret you're both exploring the past, and that bothers some people."

"Anyone in particular?"

Wyatt shrugged. "No one that I'd pin this on. I'd like to think there's no one in this town who would be this hostile. Of course, that's a pipe dream, since someone was."

"Someone was what?" Lily inquired as she joined them.

"There was a note wrapped around the rock," Cassie explained, "warning me or us to leave the past alone."

"So, this wasn't some random prank?"

"Afraid not," Wyatt said. He glanced back into the room. "I don't think we'll get any information from the scene. If you have any plywood, I'll fix the window and help you clean up."

"Umm, there may be some in the shed," Cassie said.

"I'll get it," Wyatt offered. "Do you have any nails and a hammer?"

Cassie nodded. "I'll grab those if you'll get the plywood. Mom, can you make sure Willy doesn't get in here?"

"Sure."

Cassie led Wyatt to the shed next to the house, and they retrieved the items to patch up the window. When they returned to the room, Lily had already begun to clean up the glass.

As Wyatt worked to board up the open window, and Lily and Cassie removed the glass bits, Wyatt asked a few additional questions.

"Has anyone been openly hostile to you since you arrived?"

"No," Cassie answered. "Mom?"

"I can't think of anyone who's been openly hostile, no," Lily agreed.

Wyatt twisted to face them, a nail clenched between his teeth. "Subtlety hostile?" he said, with a tight jaw.

"Everyone's been pretty friendly and helpful," Cassie informed him.

"I'd agree," Lily added.

"Well except…" Cassie said.

Wyatt spun again and eyed Cassie. "Except who?"

"It might be nothing," Cassie said with a shrug.

"Let me be the judge of that," Wyatt answered.

Cassie swallowed hard and glanced at Lily, who sat back on her haunches. "Well," she said, rubbing her hands against her pajama pants, "earlier today Frida stopped by the shop. Maybe it was nothing but before she left, she said something similar to this note."

"Frida Friedman from the pet store?"

Cassie nodded.

"Do you remember what she said exactly?" Wyatt questioned.

Cassie wrinkled her forehead in thought. "Umm, something like I might regret digging into the past. It may be nothing, but I remember wondering what she meant by it. And now with this…" Cassie shrugged as she motioned to the window.

Wyatt wiggled his eyebrows and raised one shoulder. "I'm not surprised that your digging in the past bothered her. What with her ties to the Nichols clan."

"Wait a minute," Lily interjected. "Did you say Nichols clan?"

Wyatt pounded the last nail into the plywood and jimmied it. "That should hold for now." He spun to face them and dusted off his hands. "And yes, Frida is a descendent of the Nichols."

"Any relation to…"

"To Clifton Nichols?" Wyatt nodded. "She's descended from his sister. Not the one who lived here. His younger sister, Carolina. Apparently, Carolina thought the world of her older brother."

Cassie climbed to her feet after gathering the last of the larger glass pieces on the floor. "It bothers her when people bad-mouth Clifton," Wyatt continued. "She's almost like the black sheep of this town. She thinks everyone thinks of him as a villain, and by extension her, too. She's really sensitive about it."

"Do you think this could have been her?" Lily asked.

"I'll talk to her. See if I can get any information."

"You didn't answer the question," Lily noted.

Wyatt offered a chuckle. He raised his eyebrows and said, "Honestly, no. I don't see Frida doing this. As gruff as she is, I can't see her destroying someone's property."

"Which means whoever did this is still a big question mark," Cassie said with a sigh.

"Try not to sweat it. We'll find them."

Cassie nodded, but a frown formed on her lips. She hugged her arms to her chest as Lily wrapped her arm around her. "Looks like you're bunking in with me again tonight."

"That sounds like a great idea," Wyatt said. "And I'm going to have a car out here patrolling every hour. Hopefully, that'll keep trouble away from you."

"Thanks, Wyatt," Lily said.

Wyatt smiled at her as he gathered the rock and note he'd placed into a baggie earlier. "We'll see if we get anything off this, though I wouldn't get my hopes up. And I'll send someone out first thing Monday for the window."

"Thanks," Cassie said.

"All right, ladies. Well, try to have a good night."

They followed Wyatt downstairs and said their goodbyes. As the red and blue lights went dark and the car pulled away, Cassie scooped Willy from his perch on the window seat and carried him to Lily's room. They settled in for a sleepless night. Cassie jumped with every small noise. Lily paced the floor on and off. They eventually both dozed off in the wee hours and slept in until after the sun rose.

With a yawn, Cassie stretched and climbed from the bed. She shoved her feet into her slippers and shuffled downstairs. Lily had already set a kettle on the stove and was frying eggs. "Thought I'd surprise you with your favorite!"

A smile crossed Cassie's face as she pulled orange juice from the refrigerator and poured two glasses. "Did you get any sleep?"

"Some," Lily answered.

A knock on the door almost caused Cassie to drop the glasses of orange juice on her way to the table. Lily dished the eggs onto two plates and set them on the table. She patted Cassie's shoulder. "Eat, honey, I'll get the door."

Lily strode from the room. Cassie considered slumping in the chair but she decided against it. She inched her way toward the foyer and peeked around the corner. Wyatt stood in the foyer.

"I came past a few times last night. I didn't see anyone. Did you get any sleep?"

"A little," Lily answered. Cassie stepped into the foyer.

"Good morning, Cassie," Wyatt called with a wave. "Just checking in. I patrolled past here a few times last night. All quiet."

"Thanks. I'm still a little on edge, but hopefully getting back to the store today will help."

"I'll have the deputies continue to check the house all day. Make sure you lock up and use the alarm."

"We will," Lily said. "Can I offer you some coffee?"

"No, thanks. I am about to head home and collapse into bed."

Lily offered a chuckle. "We've been keeping you busy lately."

Wyatt laughed. "Yeah, my job wasn't nearly this hard before you came to town."

"Sorry about that," Lily said, with a wince.

"No problem. Though as nice as it is to feel needed, I'll be glad when things settle for you. Have a great day, ladies."

The women trudged back to the kitchen to finish their breakfast before heading to the shop. Both of them spent the day on pins and needles waiting for any news from Wyatt. They received none.

On Monday morning, the window repair orchestrated by the sheriff was completed. Cassie headed in to the shop late after overseeing the work.

"Got it all taken care of?" Amber said, as she dumped her bag in the storeroom before heading toward the register.

"Yep. I have a front window again in my room."

"What was the damage?" Lily inquired.

"Not too bad," Cassie said, as she passed the total along.

"Neither was the time," Lily answered. "You got the better end of the deal with servicemen."

"Hey, speaking of windows," Cassie said to her, as Amber busied herself dusting the shelves. "I noticed a window on the side of the house when I was with the repairman outside."

"And? Oh, don't tell me it's broken, too," Lily groaned.

"No," Cassie said. "I can't figure out where it is in the house."

Lily screwed up her face. "Huh?"

"I'll show you when we get home. The window on the outside isn't on the inside."

"Oh, maybe one of those fake windows," Chloe chimed in, as she finished rearranging a few items in Chloe's Corner.

"Fake windows?" Cassie replied with a wrinkled nose.

"Yeah. You know, to balance the house, but, for whatever reason, the window was covered on the inside. Like it's in a closet or something. And it would be dumb to have a big window in a dusty old closet."

"Ohhhh," Cassie said, realization hitting her, "I can't say I've ever come across one of those, but maybe."

Cassie bit her lower lip as she considered the location. She didn't recall a closet being there, but perhaps she was incorrect. Was there a window behind the large wardrobe in the hall? Willy had been pawing at the furniture item a few days ago. Perhaps he smelled air from the outside.

The tinkling bell above the front door broke her train of thought. Wyatt strolled through the door, his hat in his hands.

"Hey, Uncle Wyatt," Chloe called. She sauntered over for a hug.

"Hey, ladies," he said as he searched the store. "And Tom?" He ended his last statement with a questioning tone, unsure of Tom's whereabouts.

"It's Tom's day off," Lily said.

"Oh," Wyatt said, "then I was okay with just ladies." He grinned, flashing his white teeth. "How's it going?" He directed the question to Lily and Cassie.

"Good," Cassie said. "All's quiet on the western front, as they say. And your window guy came by this morning, so we're all patched up."

"Great."

"Any news on the culprit?"

"Culprit?" Amber asked, as she emerged from between two shelves.

"We had another incident at the house," Lily explained.

163

"Someone threw a rock through Cassie's bedroom window with a menacing note."

"Oh my goodness! When?"

"Saturday night."

Amber and Chloe's faces blanched. "Why didn't you say something? Why did you two come in yesterday? We could have handled the store!" Amber said.

"We weren't hurt," Lily said, "and the distraction was nice!"

"Anyway, the long and short of it is, no, we haven't found the culprit."

"What about Frida?" Cassie inquired.

"Frida Friedman? From the pet store?" Chloe asked, her face a mask of confusion.

Cassie nodded. "Yes, I mean, I don't think she did it. But she said something odd to me on Saturday. And the note secured to the stone was similar to what she said."

"What did she say?" Chloe asked.

"To stop digging in the past or I might regret it." Chloe raised her eyebrows at the comment. Cassie flicked her gaze to Wyatt. "Did you speak with her?"

"Yes, I did."

"And?" Lily prodded.

"And she says she was at home watching a movie with her dog and cat. Of course, no one can corroborate that, but according to her she didn't do it."

"A likely story. And you're just going to take her word for it, Uncle Wyatt?" Chloe crossed her arms and pouted her lips at him.

Wyatt shrugged before responding. Cassie beat him to it. "If it's worth anything, I'd be surprised if it was her, too. I just couldn't think of anyone else."

"I'd tend to agree with Cassie. Frida's an old grouch..." Wyatt began.

"Hey, age has nothing to do with it," Lily interjected.

Wyatt chuckled before rephrasing. "Frida's a sourpuss, but dangerous? I wouldn't say so. And destroying someone's property isn't her style. She'd just complain about them."

"Any other leads?" Cassie asked.

Wyatt shook his head. "Sorry, no."

Cassie pinched her lips and nodded. "But we're not giving up," Wyatt assured her. "We're monitoring your property and if there's any further trouble, we'll get 'em."

"Hopefully there isn't any more trouble," Lily said as she slid off her stool. "As much as I'd like to know who did this, I'd prefer the drama to die down."

Wyatt nodded. "Well, I'll keep the patrols on your house for at least another week. And if anything else happens, no matter how small, call us."

"Will do," Lily promised.

The day finished without any additional news. Lily and Cassie made their way home and, after fiddling with the alarm system, entered the dark house.

"Should have left a light on," Lily grumbled, as she bumped into a table before flicking the light on.

"I didn't think we'd be back this late," Cassie admitted as light flared through the house. Willy zoomed down the steps to greet them.

"We wouldn't have been if you hadn't gotten us roped into eating out."

Cassie held out her hands, palms up and shrugged. "Sorry," she said with a half-frown, "I didn't know Penny meant she wanted to have dinner with us tonight!"

Lily rolled her eyes. "Oh well. At least we didn't have to cook."

"There's the spirit!" Cassie cheered. "I've just got to get this little guy fed and then we can curl up on the couch.

There's a new season of *Dynasty* posted if you want to watch it."

"Ohhh," Lily cooed, "I'll race you to the couch!"

The women concluded their Monday binge-watching a few episodes of a favorite show, before turning in.

CHAPTER 18

The sun shone into Lily's window early the next morning. With no clouds on the horizon, bright light streamed freely through her east-facing window. "I need a blind," she lamented, as she crawled from her bed earlier than she'd hoped.

She pulled on her robe and headed downstairs. Before she stepped out of her room, she backtracked and grabbed the journal from her night table. After boiling a kettle of water, she sat down on the deck in the bright morning light, and popped open the journal to where she had left off.

June 1, 1798

My heart is broken. Tears stain these pages as I write. I have received word the Captain is missing at sea. His entire vessel and crew along with him have disappeared off the coast of some God-forsaken Caribbean island. They are missing presumed dead. I refuse to accept it. William will return to me.

Those who tell me differently are merely attempting to upset me. He cannot be dead. He cannot be!

Again, I find myself weeping in despair. I must remind myself that he will return. These tears are wasted, I am certain.

June 15, 1798

I have received another blow. A letter arrived from one of William's sea-faring friends. No sign of his ship has been found. He has been missing for over one month now. They have told me to prepare myself. But I refuse to do so. Missing is not dead. I shall wait for my beloved to return.

June 25, 1798

Mother and Father arrived earlier today with Carolina in tow. I did not understand the reasoning for their surprise visit, but now I know. They have come to agitate me further regarding the situation of my missing husband. There is still no word on the Captain's whereabouts.

Mother and Father insist otherwise. They told me a tale that I cannot believe. Wreckage was found. Pieces of wood floated in the ocean off the coast of one of those God-forsaken islands. One piece bore the letters "ueen." It is presumed these floating remnants are from The Atlantic Queen. The supposition has been made that the ship smashed against a rocky shoal during a storm. No survivors were found in the water or on the nearby island.

Mother felt it best to deliver this disturbing news in person so as to soften the blow. It did little to mitigate the news that my husband has been presumed dead. I collapsed to the floor when Father imparted those words to me. Carolina rushed to retrieve tea, as though tea could solve any issue. Silly girl. This is why she will never marry.

When I recovered my senses, I demanded to know the source of this story. I nearly collapsed for a second time when Mother admitted, after prodding on my part, the tale's origin. My dear brother,

Clifton, made the discovery. How fortuitous for him to have stum-
bled upon news that might crush me in this way.

I do not believe it. Clifton is, once again, as is his nature, stir-
ring trouble. For what reason, I do not yet know. However, I am
convinced he is lying about the discovery of the ship. Oh, perhaps
he discovered wreckage, but I doubt it contained a piece of drift-
wood with part of the ship's name painted upon it.

No, Clifton has concocted this story for a reason. Most likely
one that will benefit him. I do not understand why yet, but I shall
find out. Once William returns, everyone will know Clifton for the
liar he is!

Lily sipped her tea and pondered the journal entries. Was Henrietta clinging to any thread because she could not accept that her husband had died? Or was there some truth to the idea that Clifton would invent a tale like this?

The morning sun glistened on the calm water. The red and pink traces were almost gone as the fiery ball rose higher in the sky. Lily rose from her chair and ducked into the house. She squinted in the dim light as her eyes adjusted before she darted to the library. She glanced upstairs through the banister, noting Cassie's closed door. Cassie must be taking advantage of her day off with a luxurious sleep-in, she figured. More time to read, Lily told herself.

She grabbed the colorful array of folders from the library desk. After peeking into each, she grabbed the yellow and red folders containing articles about Clifton Nichols and local pirate lore, leaving the other behind for Cassie.

Lily stepped out into the bright morning sunshine, squinting against it and shielding her eyes as she inched forward and collapsed in the deck chair. After sliding her sunglasses on, she flicked open the first folder and scanned the array of articles.

They began with the local newspaper reporting the death

of Captain William Blanchard. Lily raised her eyebrows as she scanned the few articles detailing the major announcement. The article reported the news came from a reputable sea captain and friend of the Captain.

He'd spoken with the newspaper after passing along the tragic news to Henrietta. A service was held, in which an empty casket was buried, since his remains were not recovered. Henrietta had an outburst at the funeral before storming out of the church. Lily fluttered her eyelids as she read the accounting. After reading the woman's journal, she could easily see this happening. Though, being a widow herself, she understood the urge to hope for a better result than life had dealt you.

Lily pulled the journal closer to read the next entry.

June 28, 1798

Captain Reginald Adams arrived in town today. He brought with him dire news. He repeated the story my parents carried with them days earlier. My bottom lip trembled as he rehashed the tale of finding the shipwreck. His evidence, though, proved more damning than Clifton's. He claims to have found wreckage confirming the entire name.

Mother and Father suggested a funeral service. I cannot think of it now. I have retreated to my bedroom to consider the matter further. My beloved William... dead. No, I cannot accept it.

July 1, 1798

Against my wishes, a funeral service was held today for William. Mother and Father convinced me to attend, and though I did not agree, I dressed in black and went to the church. They paraded an empty casket down the aisle. As the pastor spoke of William's life, a giggle escaped my lips. Mother attempted to shush me, but it erupted into a full laugh.

Gasps rang out in the church as tears streamed down my face as I doubled over in laughter. Father suggested he remove me until I could calm myself. "No!" I shouted. My holler echoed off the stone walls and a hush fell over the church.

"No, I will not be quiet!" I exclaimed as I rose from my seat. "Here you all sit, crying and praying over an empty casket. William is not here! You don't know he is dead. None of you! So willing to accept it and why? You vultures come to my doorstep to offer condolences when what you seek is a death declaration and a claim on his fortune.

Shame on you. All of you! You sit here and mourn a man who isn't dead so you can profit from his death! I will no longer be party to this!"

I shoved the coffin and it toppled from the bier, crashing to the floor below and falling open to reveal its empty interior. As gasps rang out again, I stormed down the aisle and into the bright sunshine beyond.

As I emerged into the day's light, a figure stood from a nearby bench. I halted, my jaw unhinging and my muscles tensing.

"Hello, Ri," he said.

I stared at the tall, muscled man in front of me. His dark hair, painted golden from the sun framed his dark brown eyes. His square jaw tightened and released as he awaited my response.

"Good morning, mom," Cassie's voice interrupted.

Lily jumped and pressed her hand over her heart. "You startled me, sneaking up on me like that."

"Sorry," Cassie said, settling into a chair with her teacup in hand. She set a fresh steaming mug down in front of Lily before she stretched with a groan. "You should have woken me!"

"I figured you needed the sleep. Besides, I've had some interesting reading."

"Apparently," Cassie said with an eyebrow arched. "You were really engrossed in that."

Lily nodded. "I was."

"I see you've even dug into the research from Pearl."

"I wanted to confirm the story about the Captain's death," Lily said. "Henrietta is a bit hard to read sometimes. I can't tell if she's being dramatic or if there was a conspiracy to convince her he was dead."

"And?"

"And it looks like she was just being dramatic. There seemed to be overwhelming evidence of his death. She just didn't want to see it. She even pitched a fit at his funeral. Knocked the casket over and everything."

"Oh, wow," Cassie said.

"Yeah. And now she's shocked to see someone outside."

"Who?"

Lily shrugged. "I don't know, some bumble-head inter-rupted my reading."

"Sorry," Cassie said, with a penitent expression. "You can get back to it later. I'm going to make pancakes!"

"I'll read it now then," Lily said with a smile, as she settled back in her chair.

Cassie frowned. "I thought you'd help me."

Lily chuckled. "Oh, did you now? All right then."

As Lily poured the first circles of batter onto the griddle, her brow furrowed in thought. "Hey, where is that phantom window you mentioned yesterday?"

Cassie pointed toward the opposite side of the house. "Opposite side, second story," Cassie said, as she licked batter off her finger.

"Hey, stop eating that raw! Funny, I never noticed that."

"Yeah," Cassie said. "I want to check it out today. "It's where the hall ends, I think."

"So, is it in the bedroom off the hall there?" Lily questioned.

"No," Cassie said. "That bedroom has a window in it. There's a second window on that side, though."

"Hmm, we'll have to check it out later."

The ladies ate their pancakes and cleaned up their breakfast. "Whew, I'm stuffed," Cassie said as she rinsed syrup from her plate, before stacking it in the dishwasher.

"Me too," Lily answered. "Perfect time to curl up with a good book."

"I'm tempted, but I think I'll check out that phantom window first."

Lily puckered her lips. "All right, I'll go with you. I want to see what you're talking about."

Cassie fiddled with her phone for a moment. "What are you doing?" Lily asked.

"Oh, just checking for a message from Tom or Amber. I thought maybe we'd have heard something by now."

"Cassie, they just opened an hour ago!"

"Well…"

"They're fine," Lily assured her. "Come on."

Cassie left the phone on the counter and followed Lily to the deck outside. Together, they rounded the side of the house. Lily shielded her eyes as she glanced upwards.

"See the window there?" Cassie said, pointing to a window near the back of the house.

"Yeah."

"That window," Cassie said, "is in the bedroom off the hall. This window is nowhere!"

"Isn't the closet of that bedroom behind the hall wall?"

Cassie shook her head. "It can't be. It's nowhere near that

deep. This is almost at the corner of the house! The closet would be the size of an entire room!"

Lily glanced at her. "What?" Cassie asked.

"Maybe it is an entire room."

Cassie raised her eyebrows. "Seriously? Like hidden in the wall?"

Lily shrugged. "What else explains it? Now that I'm thinking about it, that hall seems short. It ends just after the door to the bedroom, but shouldn't it continue further down? I figured it didn't because it went nowhere but…"

Fifteen minutes later, the two women stood in their upstairs hall. With narrowed eyes and crossed arms, they considered the wall. A large mahogany linen cabinet filled most of the space. Cassie had seen Willie sticking his paw behind the wardrobe on several occasions.

Cassie cocked her head and pursed her lips. Lily approached the cabinet. She tried to peer behind it, before she rapped her knuckles against the plaster beside it.

"Well?" Cassie inquired.

"Turn on your flashlight."

"I need to run down and grab my phone."

Lily shook her head. "I'm surprised you left it all alone down there!"

"Very funny, mom!" Cassie called as she darted down the steps. When she returned, Willy sat next to Lily's feet. He stared at the cabinet. "Yeah, this is the spot you found so intriguing a few days ago."

"Maybe he was on to something," Lily said.

Cassie tapped around on her phone's screen until her flashlight bloomed to life. She pointed it behind the large furniture piece. With her head squashed against the wall, she struggled to see behind the massive cabinet.

Lily peered from the opposite side. Cassie pulled away

with a sigh. "I can't see anything." She stuck her hand behind, but couldn't get further than her wrist.

"We're going to have to move it."

Cassie grimaced. "It's huge."

"Maybe we can slide it."

Cassie pushed against it a few times. "We should empty it out first," Lily said.

"Oh, right. Good idea."

They spent a few minutes emptying the wooden cabinet of its contents. With blankets and sheets piled around the top floor landing, they tackled the cabinet again. Both women squeezed on one side and leveraged themselves against the wall behind them.

"On three," Lily said. "Ready?" After a nod from Cassie, she counted and they both pushed. The massive cabinet inched toward the opposite wall. They tried again. After three pushes, the cabinet slid several feet.

Lily wiped her brow as they stepped back to survey the wall behind the cabinet.

"Oh, wow!" Cassie said with raised eyebrows.

"Guess the cat was on to something," Lily answered.

They exchanged a glance before returning their gazes to what was revealed.

Covered in cobwebs, a large wooden door peeked from behind the cabinet.

CHAPTER 19

*C*assie reached for the brass doorknob, swatting away a web or two, before she grasped it. She held her breath as she spun the knob on the hidden door. "Locked," she said with a frown, her shoulders slumping.

"You didn't think it would be that easy, did you? Someone hid this door for a reason."

"I'll grab the keys Lucy gave us. Maybe one will fit," Cassie said. She hurried down the stairs again to the pantry and snatched the extra set of keys from the keyring.

When she returned upstairs, she shoved a few into the lock with no luck. On her fourth attempt, the lock clicked. With a grin, Cassie stood and twisted the doorknob again. This time, the door swung open. A burst of cool, dusty air floated out. Cassie coughed and waved the dust away. She peered in through the open door.

A cotton candy pink room met her gaze. With white furniture and rose accents, it appeared to be a girl's room. A fluffy rose-colored comforter and pink and white pillows dotted a daybed. Posters decorated the walls; Cassie recognized a few heartthrobs from several decades ago. Several trophies decorated the top of a dresser. Stuffed animals sat on white shelves, and papers lay sprawled across the stick-legged desk.

Willy slinked through the small opening and began to explore the room.

"Let's pull this forward a bit more so we can squeeze in there," Lily suggested, motioning toward the cabinet.

Cassie nodded in agreement, and with a little work, they angled the cabinet enough to pass through the opened door into the room beyond.

"I can't believe we found a secret room!" Cassie exclaimed, as she studied the dusty area.

Willy leapt onto the bed and sniffed around, before issuing a few high-pitched sneezes. He hopped off the bed and after one final glance around, he stalked from the room and disappeared down the stairs.

Cassie studied the notes sprawled across the desk. She pushed a few papers around. Under a wadded ball of light pink notepaper, she found a stack of lined paper. She scanned the top of the page.

Finding Black Jack's Treasure
By Susan Davies
English Composition II
Mrs. Fields

Cassie raised an eyebrow. "I think this was Susan's room!"

Lily joined her and glanced at the paper. She squinted at one of the trophies on the dresser's top. "Yep," she confirmed, pointing at the gold plaque at the bottom. "Susan Davies, Top Tapper, Dawn Bee's School of Dance."

Cassie ran a finger along the desk lamp's plastic shade. A thick layer of dust covered it. "I'd say it's been closed off for quite a while."

"Probably since her disappearance or death," Lily surmised. "I'm guessing her mother closed it off. She probably wasn't able to deal with removing her things.

"When I found the secret panel in my room, it had a teddy bear and the carousel."

Cassie nodded. "She took two things of hers and nothing else."

"I should really check out those articles Pearl sent over."

"And we probably should clean in here," Lily added.

"I suppose you're right," Cassie said with a sigh. "It's very sad, though. Her things have been here for decades. I feel bad throwing them out."

"We could close it back up, but I don't see the point."

"No, you're right. With some cleaning, all this could be donated."

"Good idea," Lily answered. "I'll get the sheets and comforter and toss them in the wash, if you want to gather up her personal items. I wonder if there's anyone in the family left who would want them."

"I guess we can ask Lucy. I'll text her. In the meantime, we still have boxes from our move; I'll stow the stuff in there."

Cassie fired off a text to Lucy. She retrieved a few boxes as her mother pulled the bedding off for a wash. Lucy responded telling Cassie the family did not want anything from within the house. Anything they found could be donated or thrown away.

Cassie boxed up her personal things before filling several trash bags with her clothing for donation. As she cleared off the desk's top, she found a pink notebook hiding under several papers and a teen magazine.

Cassie flipped open the front cover. In bubbly letters, it read, "Susie's Journal PRIVATE KEEP OUT!"

Cassie chuckled at the teen's warning. She thumbed through a few pages. Bubbly pink-inked writing filled it.

Cassie set it in the box with the trophies. She continued to clean out the desk's drawers. After a moment, she slid her eyes over to the journal. She stalked toward the box and retrieved the pink-bound book. She studied it for a moment before she decided to keep it. She dropped it off on her night table before she returned to the room.

Within a few hours, they had the room cleared. After ninety minutes spent wiping the furniture down, they had most tasks finished. Lily called a local donation center to arrange for a furniture pick up.

Over a sandwich lunch, they decided to place their office furniture in the room. Currently left in storage, their furniture would fill the space and create a nice home office for their small business. They discussed a color scheme over the meal.

Cassie dragged Susan's personal items onto the porch after lunch, before settling in the library's armchair. Lily lounged on the window seat with Willy curled at her side.

"Time to curl up with some good reading," Cassie said. She flashed the folders from Pearl and Susan's journal.

"Oh, you found a journal, too, huh?"

"Yep," Cassie said with a grin, "though I doubt this will be as juicy as your reading. Come on, buddy, you can cuddle with me." Cassie motioned for the cat to join her.

His one eye opened a slit and glanced at her, before he readjusted himself next to Lily and closed his eye.

"Traitor," Cassie groused as she pulled open the folder filled with articles about Susan's disappearance.

Cassie shuffled through the articles, some of which she'd read, and some of which were new to her. Pearl had them ordered chronologically. Cassie pulled the ones she hadn't yet read from the folder.

The first article detailed the investigation into the missing girl. It confirmed police suspected she may not have disappeared by her own volition. Several of her friends had been questioned, but none provided any reason to believe she would run away. According to the sheriff at the time, the fact that her purse and shoes were left behind at the library was the largest piece of evidence pointing to an outside party.

Cassie flipped to the next article. A picture of a young Pearl Booker graced the page. She stood near a carrel desk in the library, her hands clasped behind her back. The article reported Pearl's involvement, albeit limited, in the case. She had been the last known person to see Susan alive. She recalled assisting the teen in finding articles related to Black Jack, and the legend that he'd hidden treasure in the region.

"She was very interested in Black Jack since his sister had lived in her house," Pearl was quoted as saying. "She asked me a lot of questions about the treasure supposedly hidden in the area, whether anyone had found it, and all about the local legends.

"I helped her comb through all the resources we had. She was writing a school paper, you know, and she needed sources. She had them all laid out on the desk, and she was making notes when I saw her last.

"When I passed the table again while I was shelving books, she was gone. I assumed she'd gone in search of another book because her shoes were there."

The article detailed Pearl's obvious upset as she spoke of the incident and uttered, "I don't think I'll ever get the sad image of those little saddle shoes out of my mind."

Pearl's haunting words were the last statement in the article. Chills ran up Cassie's spine. She skimmed the rest of the articles. They discussed the investigation, turning from intriguing, to desperate, then to morbid. The Davies family pleaded with anyone who had information to come forward.

Finally, the last few articles detailed the grisly find of the girl's body.

Cassie snapped the folder closed, suddenly disinterested in reading the articles. The sad story disturbed her. With her recent experience with death, Cassie understood the emotions the family experienced all too well.

What had happened to the girl? Had she been abducted? Why? Was it a crime of opportunity or something more?

With no answers, Cassie glanced down at the little pink journal in her lap. Perhaps this would provide lighter reading. She ran her fingers along the cover. Was it an invasion of privacy? Perhaps, but Susan intrigued her. She'd just read a few entries. If there was anything too private, she'd stop.

* * *

Lily's hand found the warm furball next to her. She stroked his back. The cat stretched a paw out in front of him before he commenced purring. She smiled down at him as she popped open Henrietta's journal. Time to find out who the mystery man is, she thought. She re-read the last few paragraphs again.

As I emerged into the day's light, a figure stood from a nearby bench. I halted, my jaw unhinging and my muscles tensing.

"Hello, Ri," he said.

I stared at the tall, muscled man in front of me. His dark hair, painted golden from the sun framed his dark brown eyes. His square jaw tightened and released as he awaited my response.

I narrowed my dark eyes at him. My muscles tightened and my lips formed a grimace. "How dare you show your face here," I spat at him.

I stormed down the few steps from the church to the path below. He sidestepped into my path. "Ri, wait," he said, his hat clutched in his hand. He gazed at me with a softened expression. I understood why mother gave in to him so easily. Clifton had a way about him, able to disarm someone with only a glance.

"For?" I questioned, attempting to hold firm in my resolve. "For you to lie to me? For you to tell me my husband is dead? I will not believe it! I..."

Suddenly, my knees buckled. Emotion overcame me and I swooned forward. Clifton caught hold of me before I could fall. "Oh, Riri," he cooed at me, "let me help you, please."

"I... I do not need your help," I choked out, as I struggled to right myself.

My legs wobbled and I stumbled a step before I grasped Clifton's arm. "No one should see us together. The rumors..." I stammered.

"To hell with the rumors, Ri," he said as he steadied me. "You are my sister. I had no desire to tell you of your husband's death. Truly, when I set sail, I hoped to find him alive. Please let me help you get through this."

I gazed into those cocoa brown eyes. "There is nothing to get through," I said, my lower lip trembling as I held back the tears brimming in my eyes. "I do not accept it." My last statement was barely above a whisper.

"Ri..."

"No!" I shouted. "No, he cannot be dead!" My knees gave way a second time as tears spilled to my cheeks.

Clifton reached for me, sweeping me upward as I wept. He carried me the short distance to Whispering Manor, instructing the housemaid to prepare a toddy for me and deliver it posthaste. I groaned as the maid set the warm drink on my table and asked if I preferred to sit in my chair. I shook my head as I sniffled.

Clifton reappeared in the room as the maid departed. He knelt at my bedside and wiped a tear away. "Leave," I insisted.

"No," he said. He paused a moment before continuing. "You can have your tantrum, but I am your brother. I am not leaving you in your time of need."

"He is not dead," I whispered.

"If it helps you to hold on to that hope, then do so, Ri."

My fingers closed around his large hand. My eyes shut and I drifted away at his words.

When I awoke, Clifton sat near the fireplace. "You're awake. How do you feel?"

I sniffled and rubbed at my puffy, sore eyes. "Terrible," I moaned.

"Mother, Father and Carolina returned from the funeral. I sent them to town. There are some Independence Day events taking place."

I swung my legs over the bed's side. My head pounded with every movement. I swayed with wooziness and squeezed my eyes shut as I attempted to steady myself. "You should have gone with them."

Clifton stood and paced the floor. "I had reason to stay back."

"And what, praytell, is that?" I pressed my hand against my forehead as my temples pounded.

Clifton approached and knelt in front of me. "Brace yourself, sister, you have more bad news coming."

CHAPTER 20

*C*assie's eyelids drooped and her chin dropped toward her chest. As the journal clattered to the floor, she snapped her head upward.

"For goodness sake, Cass, what are you doing over there?" Lily said. "You startled both me and Willy!"

"Sorry, must have dozed off. I can't believe it after that extra-long sleep-in I had this morning."

"Reading's that interesting, huh?"

Cassie chuckled as she retrieved the little pink book from the floor. "She's not as interesting as your gal."

"No? She hasn't pitched a fit yet over Christmas dinner or anything?"

Cassie shook her head. "No, so far she's discussed the carousel she got for her birthday, how much she likes her new classes this year and plans to go to a sleepover with a few friends. How's Henrietta? Any more tantrums?"

Lily arched an eyebrow. "I have a feeling another one is coming on. Her brother has just shown up and he says he has bad news for her."

"Uh-oh, that sounds ominous."

Lily nodded. "I was about to find out what that news was, when a certain someone caused a ruckus."

"Sorry," Cassie said, with a sheepish grin. "How about some food first? I'm hungry!"

"Sure, but let's order something. I don't feel like making anything. Who delivers?"

Cassie glanced at the clock ticking away on the desk. "By the time we order, it should be late afternoon. Late lunch, early dinner?"

"Sounds perfect."

After retrieving their take-out menus, they selected a restaurant on the edge of town called *Nacho Average Restaurant*. They placed an order for loaded nachos, tacos and sopapillas. At least this place didn't bemoan delivering to their house when she gave the address.

"Okay," Cassie said as she clicked off her phone's display. "They said about thirty minutes."

"Wow, that's quick!"

"Yep, though I suppose you can find out the terrible news awaiting Henrietta before we chow down."

"I plan to. Try not to fall asleep reading yours though."

Cassie offered her a wry glance, before she pulled open the pink journal to read the next entry.

We got a new assignment today in Mrs. Fields's English class that I'm kind of excited about! We're supposed to write an essay about something in history that's important to us and we're connected to in some way. At first, I couldn't think of a good topic. Lots of things in history are important, but I don't have any connections to any of them. I mentioned it to Mom and Dad. I asked them if they had any idea of a historical event we were connected to. After a minute of thinking, Dad told me a really cool story!

He said a pirate used to live in this house! Well, only sort of. Actually, the pirate's sister lived here. But Black Jack (that's the pirate) came here a lot! AND he not only was a pirate, but he had a treasure. His treasure has never been found. The legend is it's buried around here somewhere. It would be so cool if I found it.

So, for my project, I'm going to research the legend of Black Jack's treasure. Not only that, I'm going to find it! He has to have left clues to it. Maybe I'll find a treasure map with a big X marking the spot. I wonder if he buried it somewhere on the property or if it's hidden in a cave or something like that. Well, I'll probably find out more when I start researching. I bet Pearl at the library can help me. This is going to be so fun!

So, Cassie thought, as she stared down at the light pink paper, Susan was not only studying the legend of the local pirate, but she also hoped to find the treasure. Had she stumbled upon something that led to her death?

The ringing doorbell interrupted Cassie's musings. She set the book aside and leapt from her chair, hurrying to the door. She returned with two bags of food.

"Ohhhh, tacos, tacos, tacos," Lily cheered.

"Looks like they put everything we need in here. Do you want me to grab plates?"

"Nah, we'll just eat it out of the containers. I'm heading for the couch though!"

"I'll grab us a few Ginger sodas and meet you there!"

Cassie handed the two bags to Lily as she headed for the living room. The two women made short work of the delicious Mexican cuisine.

"Did your reading get better?" Lily inquired, as she dunked a sugar-covered donut into chocolate sauce.

"Yeah," Cassie said between bites. "She's talking about working on a class assignment. She's researching Black Jack and his treasure for an essay assignment. She is hoping to find the treasure. And I started wondering if this contributed to her death."

"Really? Do you think she got that close?"

Cassie shrugged. "I don't know. Seems odd, though. How about your reading? Did you find out the bad news?"

Lily shook her head. "I checked out a few of the articles on Clifton instead."

"What? You left Henrietta on a cliffhanger?"

"I did. I figured it would be good reading before bed."

"You heading up after we eat, or do you want to watch a movie?"

"It's still early. Let's go for the movie!"

* * *

Lily settled under the comforter. Cassie opted for her own bedroom after a quiet few days. The clock ticked away the time as the moon rose in the sky. Lily pulled the journal onto her lap.

"Okay, Henrietta, what tragedy is about to befall you now?" As she paged to where she left off, Lily ruminated about Henrietta Blanchard. Despite the jokes she made with Cassie, the woman did seem to have a tragic life.

As I pen these words, I find myself still reeling from Clifton's tale. It is as if my heart is broken all over again. As though I am not hurt enough, the revelation poured salt into my open wounds. He is lying. He must be! It cannot be true. Though if it is...

The entry ended. Lily tossed her head back into the pillows. "Oh, Henrietta! Did you have to be so coy?!"

As if on cue, a noise sounded outside Lily's door. She glanced toward the closed door. What was that, she wondered? It sounded like a scratching sound. She wondered if it might be Willy, seeking a new bed to sleep in, though she was surprised Cassie hadn't taken him into her room.

She shoved the journal aside and slid her feet into her slippers. The scraping noise filled the air again. "Okay, okay, I'm coming," she called.

Lily reached the door and pulled it open. Her brow furrowed as she found no cat outside it. She stuck her head into the hall and searched for the source of the noise. Her eyes focused on the open door across the hall. Was there something they'd disturbed in Susan's bedroom?

Lily grabbed her robe from the hook on the door and wrapped it around her. She stepped into the hallway as she cinched the robe tie. Silence greeted her. She waited another moment and listened, before padding across the landing and into Susan's room.

She flicked on the light and studied the space. Nothing seemed amiss. She pulled the handle on the bifold closet door and glanced inside. Empty. She hadn't heard any additional noises. Perhaps it was another branch scraping against the house, she surmised, as she flipped off the lights and pulled the door partway closed.

As she padded past the staircase leading down to the foyer, a screeching noise filled the air again. Lily stopped in her tracks. The sound seemed to be coming from in front of her. In the direction of her room. She hurried across the hall and peered through her open door.

The room looked undisturbed. A loud clap and another screech sounded, and she spun in the direction of the noise. Her eyes slowly drifted up the narrow staircase leading to the widow's walk. At the top, a sliver of light caught her attention. It disappeared as the metal door banged against the frame. The screech sounded again as the light reappeared.

Was someone trying to open the door? Who? Lily hurried up the creaky wooden staircase, cursing the tall rise of each step. She released the lock and flung the door open. She found an empty walkway. Pulling her robe tighter around her, she stepped out onto the narrow walkway situated against the house's roof.

The view was amazing. Moonlight glittered off the calm waters below. Must have been the wind, Lily concluded. Though, as she stood staring over the gently swaying ocean, she realized there wasn't much wind. In fact, there was barely a breeze. Before she could overthink the situation, she spun to reenter the house. Movement caught her eye.

Gauzy white fabric fluttered, caught on the edge of the railing. Lily yanked it free and stared at it. "Henrietta?" she questioned. She stuffed it in her pocket and ducked through the doorway.

Cassie stood at the bottom, hands on her hips. "What are you doing out there?" she demanded, in her best parent tone.

"Sneaking out–sorry, mom," Lily said with a chuckle.

"Planned to climb down the side of the house, huh?"

"Yep, I was going to hop over onto the rungs, and then shimmy down the trellis for the beach roses."

Cassie laughed. "And all in your pajamas."

"Yeah. I was planning a real wild night on the town in my flannels."

"So, seriously, what were you doing out there? Couldn't sleep?"

Lily shook her head before responding. "I was reading more of the journal when I heard a racket out here. I thought maybe we disturbed something in Susan's room when we opened it up. I got up to check but I couldn't find anything. On my way back to my bedroom, I heard it again. The door up here was opening and closing. Well, opening and closing a sliver. I went up to check it out."

Concern crossed Cassie's face. "Did you find anything?"

"Not really. Though I don't know what I expected to find. We may want to consider a better lock on that door."

Cassie's eyes darted around as she considered it. "Do you think someone could climb up there?"

Lily shrugged. "That's a pretty good climb. I didn't see anyone running away or shimmying down our drain pipe. The only thing I found was this." Lily pulled the scrap of fabric from her pocket.

Cassie grabbed it and studied the material. "Where did you find this?"

"Stuck on the railing."

Cassie's eyebrows raised. "Do you think someone *was* up there, and this ripped off their clothes while they were making a getaway?"

Lily shrugged again. "It seems farfetched. Maybe the fabric just blew up there."

"I guess stranger things have happened."

"Anyway, I don't think it's anything to worry about. I'm going to head back to bed."

"Okay," Cassie agreed. "Oh, by the way, what was the bad news?"

"Huh?"

"Henrietta's bad news. What was it?"

"Oh, she didn't say. She says she's reeling from it and it can't be true, but never said what the brother told her."

"Bummer," Cassie said. "Well, don't stay up too late trying to find out."

"Yes, mom," Lily said with a coy grin, as Cassie ambled down the hall to her bedroom.

Cassie eased the door shut to her bedroom. Willy's one eye peered at her from the middle of her bed. "I see you made yourself comfortable." She crawled into bed and inched him over. "Nothing going on, buddy, go back to sleep." His eye closed as he sighed.

Cassie flicked off the light and lay back in her pillows. Within minutes, she reached for the light again. As much as she didn't want to admit it, the incident with the scrap of fabric left her disturbed. Was someone climbing around on their widow's walk in an attempt to enter the house? With the locks changed, that could be the case.

Or was this not a real person, her mind pondered? She attempted to shove the thought aside as she scanned her room. No ghosts here. She closed her eyes, wondering if she could fall asleep with the light on. After a few moments, she popped them open again. She sighed. Sleep wasn't coming anytime soon. She was wide awake.

Her gaze fell to the journal on her night table. Cassie scooted up to sitting and pulled it onto her lap.

"Okay, Susan," she muttered, "maybe you can chase my nerves away."

Cassie pulled the journal open to where she left off, hoping the bubbly pink writing could alleviate her mind.

I started researching Black Jack. There are all sorts of stories about him! He was a ruthless pirate, known for lying in wait in coves then attacking merchant ships. He even raided military ships for weapons and munitions.

Whenever he raided a ship, he'd take no prisoners. Instead, he'd make everyone walk the plank except one person. That one person he would chain to the center mast and leave them on the ship. He did it so that the lone survivor could tell everyone what a terrible pirate he was and build his reputation. Sometimes those people would float on the ocean for days before someone found them. They'd be almost half dead when they uttered their tale about the frightening encounter with the dreaded pirate, Black Jack.

I can't wait to learn more about him. That's what I read from an encyclopedia entry about him. I'm going to go to the library soon and see if Pearl can help me find out more.

Cassie turned the page and read another entry detailing a

sleepover with two friends. Susan discussed eating s'mores and telling scary stories.

When it was my turn, I told a story about Bloody Mary. My friends booed me and said the story wasn't that scary and wasn't real, so I dared them to try it. They all said no. Chickens. Then they said I should do it because I lived in a haunted house anyway. I rolled my eyes and told them the house was NOT haunted. Marissa insisted it was and said she'd go next with her story. She swiped the flashlight and held it under her chin.

She said the original owner of Whispering Manor was a sea captain who brought home a beautiful young wife from the south. His name was William but everyone called him The Captain. Then he went back to sea. He came home once more to visit her before he left again. He would never return.

His ship wrecked, smashed to bits on rocks in the Caribbean. When word reached his young wife, she refused to believe it. She insisted he'd come back and she watched for him every night on the widow's walk. She'd paced back and forth waiting for her husband to return. And when she finally realized he wouldn't, she threw herself from the roof.

But, Marissa said, her voice growing low and thick, she never really left. To this day, she continues to roam the widow's walk in search of her lost husband. Sometimes you'll see her there staring out across the sea. People can spot her from far away because she's wearing a gauzy white dress that blows around in the breeze. And people hear her weeping all night long.

Sarah started to say "OOOOOOOOH" and wave her hands at me. "Have you ever seen the ghost of Henrietta, Susie?" she asked me.

"No," I said. "My house isn't haunted."

"I think it is," Marissa said.

I threw a piece of popcorn at her. "There are no ghosts at Whispering Manor. The noise people hear is the wind blowing."

"Or a ghost!" Sarah said.

"No, you guys are all wrong," Cassidy spoke up.

"Oh, yeah?" Marissa said. *"How do you figure that?"*

Cassidy swiped the flashlight and held it under her chin. *"After her husband disappeared, Henrietta might have gone crazy if her brother, the dreaded pirate Black Jack, hadn't shown up.*

"See, HE killed her husband. He attacked and raided The Captain's ship, not knowing it was his sister's own husband. He forced The Captain to walk the plank. And before he stepped off to his doom, he said, 'Tell my wife, Henrietta, I loved her.'

"Then he stepped into the drink and a shark ATE HIM!"

Sarah screamed. Cassidy's blonde hair swung wildly while she made a shark bite motion with her jaws. *"Stop it, you weirdo!"* she shouted at her.

Cassidy giggled before turning serious again. *"When Black Jack realized he'd widowed his sister, he felt terrible. He sailed to Hideaway Bay with his treasure and offered it to her. She took it in repayment for her husband's death. But...*

"The treasure was CURSED by the pirate Redbeard. And Henrietta was driven to madness. And THAT is why she threw herself from the widow's walk."

"Nuh-uh," Marissa countered. *"He never brought the treasure here, that's just a myth."*

"No, it's not," Sarah argued. *"The treasure is buried here somewhere, no one's ever found it."*

"I'm going to find it!" I said, stuffing Reese's pieces in my mouth.

"Did you find a treasure map in your house or something?" Cassidy questioned.

I shook my head. *"Not yet, but I'm going to. I'm doing my report for Mrs. Fields's class on Black Jack. I'm going to research everything and use it to find his treasure."*

Marissa rolled her eyes. *"He never brought his treasure here.*

My grandpa said that's all fake. He said she just threw herself over the balcony because she was so sad. It's so romantic."

"Killing yourself is not romantic, dweeb," Sarah said. "Plus, how does that explain the coin?"

"What coin?" I asked.

"The legend is she had a gold coin in her dress pocket when she killed herself."

"She didn't kill herself—she was cursed," Cassidy retorted. "And you will be, too, if you start poking around for that treasure." She poked her finger at me with her eyes wide.

"There are no such things as curses. That's silly," I answered.

"Do what you want, but the past is best left in the past," Cassidy said with a shrug of her shoulders.

"Hey, let's braid hair!" Sarah said.

The conversation ended with that, but I put it in here as part of my research. So, did Black Jack bring his cursed treasure here or not? Most legends say he did, but Marissa says he didn't. And did Henrietta kill herself over her husband or the treasure? Maybe Black Jack changed his mind about giving her the treasure and killed her! My treasure hunt might be turning into a murder mystery!

Cassie yawned and stretched. She was getting sleepy, but the spooky tale about the ghost of Henrietta had her mind reeling about the scrap of white fabric her mom had found on the widow's walk. Was it a coincidence? She didn't want to ponder anything else. Maybe the next entry could distract her. She turned the page to read on.

I'm super frustrated. :(All this work I'm doing and nothing is getting done!!!!! I've read a few things about Black Jack and talked to a bunch of people and everyone has a different story! How am I supposed to know what is real and what isn't? Some people say he brought his treasure here, others say he didn't.

I'm so frustrated. I'll never find the treasure if it's even here! Sometimes I think all of this is just a stupid legend people made up to draw in tourists and sell stupid pirate hats and gold coins made of chocolate.

Maybe this is all just a big lie. I might have to change my topic. I'm going to talk to Mrs. Fields first thing tomorrow and ask her if I can switch it.

Cassie turned the page as her eyelids grew heavy. With a sigh, she nestled further into the pillows and began reading the next entry.

Mrs. Fields told me she'd allow me to switch my topic BUT only if I stuck with this one for another two weeks AND talked to Pearl Booker. She said she thought I could find much more information and that the point of the assignment was to use real sources. She said while talking to people can help, it's important to learn to sort fact from fiction. She also said she'd really prefer I stick with my topic. So, tomorrow after school I'm going to stop at the library and ask Pearl for some help. I'm still not convinced but maybe I can still make this work. My fingers are crossed!

Cassie turned the page to the next entry.

I might be on to something!

Cassie's eyelids slid closed as she drifted off to sleep.

CHAPTER 21

*L*ily settled back into her pillows with a sigh. Perhaps
the door was loose in the frame, so even the
slightest breeze rattled it. She pulled the white
fabric from her night table and stared at it. Her mind spun
out of control with possibilities.

With a roll of her eyes, she said aloud, "You, Lily Bennett,
are being ridiculous." She sighed and set the fabric aside. "If
Blake was here, he'd tell me how silly I'm being."

Still, she couldn't bring herself to switch off the light just
yet. The brown journal lay on the covers next to her, where
she'd discarded it after hearing the noise. With a half-frown,
Lily pulled it onto her lap and paged through it to where
she'd left off.

"Don't come to haunt me again, Henrietta," she mumbled
as she found the page. With a suspicious glance around, she
settled in and began to read.

*I have confirmed what I thought to be a lie from Clifton. I cannot
believe it. His words were true. This blow may be worse than the
news that my husband supposedly perished at sea. Though, given*

the news, he may prefer to have died at the hands of the Locker than return home, as I surely would have placed my hands around his neck and squeezed until the life left his body.

I am no stranger to anger, though I find it odd to direct it at William, my beloved. Though I suppose the point is moot. Everyone insists he has perished. Perhaps he has. Perhaps he has slunk away to some remote location where he can spend the remainder of his miserable life in anonymity rather than face the embarrassment of returning to Hideaway Bay.

In any case, the fact remains, I am left to deal with the mess. My grief has been replaced by rage, and I use my acrimony to fuel my will to live.

Clifton offered a solution. I was undecided on the course of action I should take. My antipathy toward Clifton's chosen profession suggests I should rebuff his offer. My desperation, though, dictates that I accept it. I suppose this is my downfall. My arrogant pride has brought me low and now, in an effort to dig myself from the hole William has placed me in, I must cast aside my haughtiness and accept Clifton's proposal.

Though, I cannot deny that I find the prospect somewhat exciting. I am busy planning which has helped with my grief. I shall record the conversation we had yesterday following the faux funeral to keep a record of the details.

"Finally!" Lily exclaimed to the empty room. "Let's get to the good stuff." She turned the page to continue the story.

"Brace yourself, sister, you have more bad news coming," he said, as he knelt in front of me with eyes full of concern.

"What could be worse than the tale you've already spread of my husband's demise?" I groaned.

He clutched my hand and squeezed it. I pulled it away from his grasp. "Do not dally with your dreadful announcement, brother. I am certain you are chomping at the bit to share it."

He drew his lips into a thin line and stared at me. "It gives me no pleasure to tell you this, Ri, despite what you may think of me."

I raised my eyebrows at him to prod him to continue.

"I am afraid your troubles are only just beginning with William's death." My shoulders slumped at the mention of my beloved's demise. "He's left you in rather a mess."

"Yes, quite. He has left me alone in the world." My voice cracked and I choked back my emotions.

"That is not true," Clifton countered. "Though it is quite a bit worse than only that."

"Quite a bit worse than widowing me at this age?!" I shouted, my voice incredulous. "What are you jabbering on about?"

"Simply put, Ri, he has left you destitute."

My jaw unhinged. "What?" I snapped.

Clifton nodded to confirm his statement.

"Impossible!" I shouted as I leapt from the bed and paced the floor.

"You may check with your agent at the bank. Though I am certain you will find your accounts quite low and several bad debts against them."

My stomach somersaulted and I struggled to form words. Penniless? Me? What would become of me? Would Mother and Father take me in? Could I stand to return to Georgia with them? Could I endure the shame? Would I be able to marry again with a good match after this? Not from Georgia, I concluded. I had barely gotten away the first time.

I collapsed onto the bed, grasping at the post to steady myself as thoughts raced through my head. "How?" I managed to choke out.

"The Captain was a drunkard. In his inebriated state, he'd often gamble. I'm afraid he wasn't very good at it. He racked up quite a series of debts with some rather dangerous people."

"You lie!" I shouted.

"I do not, Ri. No one wishes you to know this. Mother and Father expressly requested you be kept in the dark, in fact. Rather *salt in the wounds as they viewed it. But you must be made aware of your circumstances."*

"No," I said, my forehead wrinkling. "No, William was not a drunk. He did not gamble. He was an upstanding sea captain. Revered!"

Clifton set his eyes upon me, his jaw tensing. "I am sorry, Ri. We all have our vices." I studied his face, his eyes. He spoke the truth. My brother, however estranged I had made us, could not sneak a lie like this past me. He had only done so once in the past. But he did not on any other occasion. Not in the past and not now. This was no lie.

"But what of his trade business? Surely it can cover..."

Clifton gave a slight shake to his head.

"Oh," I groaned as my shoulders slumped again.

My gaze fell to the floor as I processed the dire news. Clifton's hand squeezed my shoulder. "What will become of me?" I whispered. Images of me wearing ragged clothes with a dirty face flashed through my mind. I would turn into a street urchin. Or I would be forced to return with Mother and Father. The idea turned my stomach.

Clifton tipped my chin up to meet his stare. A devilish grin crossed his face and his brown eyes sparkled. "I have a plan."

The alarm screamed through the silence. Lily awoke with a start. Her glasses sat askew on her face. Her bedside lamp still radiated light. The journal lay open on her chest. She groaned and slapped the clock before pulling herself up to sit. She wiggled her shoulders and yawned.

"Must have fallen asleep while reading," she mumbled. She placed the journal on her night table, as memories of the last entry she'd read flooded her mind.

"And I never found out the plan." She sighed, as she fastened her robe around her waist.

She slid her feet into her slippers and headed downstairs to begin her day.

* * *

Cool air caressed Cassie's skin as she stared into the abyss. Her brow furrowed and she rubbed her bare arms as she shivered. She stood in the library of Whispering Manor, which was also, oddly, attached to the mall she frequented as a teen.

"Hello?" she called into the darkness.

She grasped hold of a flashlight and flicked it on. Its weak beam did little to beat back the darkness. "Hello?" she shouted again.

Willy appeared at her feet. He rubbed against her legs before trotting into the darkness. "Willy! Wait!" she called.

Cassie glanced around the room for help. She found none. Not wanting to let the small animal get too far ahead, Cassie steeled her nerves and stepped into the darkness. Her bare feet swept across the dusty floor. Her lips formed a grimace as she padded across the cold stone.

The little flashlight she carried barely pierced the darkness ahead of her, but she pressed on. "Willy! Willy!"

The beam caught the little cat ahead of her. His one eye glowed against the light. With a shake of his tail, he turned and darted down another passage. "Wait!"

Cassie hurried to the spot in which he'd stood. She swung the flashlight's beam to the side and found the open passage.

A cobweb stuck to her face and hair as she stepped into the darkened corridor. Cassie swatted it away, shivering and brushing herself off in case any spiders came with the web.

"Willy!" Her voice echoed off the cold stone walls.

She continued her trek, winding through a series of

passageways. As she rounded a corner, warm light flickered from the hall's end.

Cassie continued toward it. Willy appeared in the lit chamber before scurrying further in. As he disappeared around the corner, Cassie hurried toward the light.

She stepped into the large chamber. Flaming torches were positioned on every wall, and wooden crates filled the space. She scanned the area in search of the one-eyed cat. Her eyes fell on another object. Propped against a wooden crate, facing Cassie, was a skeleton. An eye patch covered one eye socket. A black tricorn hat perched atop the skull's head. Its bony fingers curled around the trigger of a blunderbuss aimed directly at Cassie.

"Leave," a voice echoed throughout the chamber.

Cassie jumped, startled by the sound. Her head swiveled as she searched for the source. She failed to identify anyone else in the room.

"Leave or be cursed," the voice said again. The crease in Cassie's brow deepened as she attempted to locate the speaker. Her jaw fell open and her eyes went wide as the voice spoke again, issuing a similar warning, and she realized the statements emerged from the skeleton. Its jawbone snapped open and closed as words flowed from it.

Cassie stumbled back a step as she processed the information. Her lip trembled and her pulse raced. Willy stalked to the room's center. The small cat caught Cassie's eye. She had to rescue him before she fled.

She darted toward the furry creature. "Stop!" the pirate skeleton demanded.

"Willy!" Cassie called, as she scooped him up and spun to flee.

A deafening blast sounded. Cassie turned to see the muzzle of the pirate's weapon flare to life. Aimed at her, she'd never escape its volley. A scream formed in her throat and emerged through her mouth.

* * *

"AHHHHHHHHHH," Cassie shrieked, as she shot up to sit in her bed. Sweat covered her forehead and her heart pounded in her chest. She gasped for breath as she clutched at the comforter.

After a moment, she recognized her surroundings. Her breath slowed and her heart returned to normal speed. She glanced at her clock. Her alarm would go off in seven minutes. With a sigh, she decided to get up.

As she swung her legs over the side of the bed, Susan's journal clattered to the floor. Cassie leaned over and swiped the pink book from the floor. "No wonder I had nightmares," she muttered under her breath, as she set it on the night table. "All those pirate stories about hidden treasure."

After pulling on her robe and sliding her feet into her cozy cat slippers, she padded downstairs and set a kettle of water on for tea, before crafting two breakfast sandwiches in their hot sandwich press.

Lily padded in moments later. "Up already?"

"I had a bad dream, and decided I'd forego the extra seven minutes of sleep," Cassie said as the water began to boil.

With steaming mugs and warm sandwiches, they sat down for their breakfast.

"Nightmares, huh?" Lily questioned.

"Yes. I guess I read too much of Susan's journal before bed. I couldn't sleep after our ghostly scrap of fabric turned up. And then in her journal, Susan details a story told to her about how the ghost of Henrietta Blanchard is always seen wearing a white dress. So, then, I really couldn't sleep and I read on about her frustration separating fact from fiction, and must have dozed off reading. I think I was just getting to the good part, too." Cassie wrinkled her mouth into a frown. "What about you? Did you find out what other bad news Henrietta had coming?"

"I did," Lily said, between bites of her egg sandwich.

"And?"

"She's broke."

Cassie raised her eyebrows. "Really?"

Lily nodded again. "Yep. Completely destitute. Apparently, The Captain was not quite the catch Henrietta, or Ri as her brother calls her, assumed he was. He was a drunk and a degenerate gambler. He'd gambled away his entire fortune before his death."

"So, what's Ri going to do? And how did her brother get involved? I thought she hated him."

"There's a bit more to their relationship than just hate. I think she pretends to hate him because she thinks that's what's expected of a woman in her station. But deep down, they'll always have that sibling bond."

"Hmm, interesting. Being that I have no siblings, I'm not sure I can relate."

"It's a tricky thing," Lily admitted. "As mad as they can make you, you'll still always love them."

Cassie considered it and ended her thoughts with a shrug.

"Anyway," Lily continued, "Clifton is the one who told her about The Captain's gambling and her financial state. According to him, he's got a plan."

"Oooooh, sounds almost villainous. What's his plan?"

"I don't know. I fell asleep."

"Awww, come on! At the best part?"

"I know, I know. I'll keep going tonight if I'm not too tired."

"I'm dying to know this plan!" Cassie exclaimed.

"I'm dying to know what Susan's on to, but you fell asleep before you could find out, too."

Cassie bit her lower lip, her brows mashing together.

"What?" Lily questioned.

Cassie shrugged. "Nothing."

"I know that expression. That's not nothing."

With a shrug, Cassie said, "I can't shake the feeling that Susan's death resulted directly from her being on to something with her treasure hunt."

"Really? You think someone took her and killed her over the treasure?"

Cassie shook her head. "Sounds far-fetched, I know, but…" She hesitated before continuing. "Someone sure seems interested in spooking us. First the person in the house, then the rock through the window. And all after we started asking questions about the past. I just wonder if something similar happened to Susan."

"Perhaps you'll find out more from her journal," Lily suggested.

"That was a non-answer."

Lily shrugged. "I really don't know, Cass. It does seem far-fetched, but if there really is a treasure, there may be a lot of greedy people searching for it who could have been that ruthless."

Cassie inhaled a long breath and nodded. "Which means we should be careful with our digging," Lily added. "We may be unearthing skeletons people would rather have buried."

After finishing the final bites of breakfast, the women dispersed upstairs to dress before they headed into the shop.

Cassie sauntered into her bedroom. After a quick shower, she wandered to the carousel and wound it. It whirred and played a few notes before slowing to a stop. With a sigh, she continued to apply her makeup before slipping into her clothes. She grabbed the carousel on her way out the door along with her tote.

"Taking that with you?" Lily asked as she pulled her shoe on in the foyer.

"Yes. It's not working right. If we have any downtime, I'm going to take a look at it and see if I can fix it. I just need to grab the tool kit."

Cassie disappeared into the pantry, returning with her pink toolbox. She slid it into her oversized tote. "Ready!"

Lily offered a half-smile. "I remember when your dad bought that for you," she said with a wistful glance.

Cassie gave her a tight-lipped smile and squeezed her forearm. "Let's hope Dad brings me luck and it does the trick."

They filed out of the house and, after arming the alarm system, climbed into the SUV and headed for town.

Amber had the shop ready to open when they arrived. "Good morning!" she called as she adjusted a few items in the shop. "How was your day off?"

"Great," Lily answered.

"How did things go here?" Cassie questioned. "Any trouble or anything?"

"Nope! Everything was all good."

"Oh, good," Cassie said. "We didn't hear from you so…"

Amber twisted to face her. "Oh, was I supposed to text or call or something?"

"No," Lily said with a chuckle. "Cassie can be a little uptight. She was sure something went wrong yesterday."

"No, we didn't have any trouble at all. Here's the sales log. The wooden lighthouses are doing really well. We may want to order some more. Chloe came up with a great idea, too. She wondered if Sam could make them with seasonal themes. You know, pumpkins around the lighthouse with fall colors, snow on the ground with a cardinal, spring flowers, that kind of stuff."

"Oh, yeah, great idea!" Cassie answered. "I'll discuss it with him. I'll email him and mention it when I place another order."

"They are cute. I may need to buy a few for the manor," Lily said, as she eyed the few remaining on the shelf.

The women bustled about the shop for the morning hours, restocking, dusting, inventorying and assisting customers. Amber clocked out just after lunch, heading for her studio art course on the nearby campus.

As the customers lulled in the early afternoon hours, Cassie settled behind the register with her tool kit and the carousel. She examined the miniature merry-go-round from all angles. After finding several screws on the bottom, she removed the cover and stared at the mechanism powering the little musical item.

She wound the carousel as the front door's bell tinkled. She overheard Lily greet the customer. Cassie glanced up, spotting a man with shoulder-length, red hair stroll in and nod at Lily. He glanced around a few items, his hands stuffed into the pockets of his baggy tan pants.

Cassie returned to studying the carousel. She wound it again and watched the components attempt to move. Using the tip of her screwdriver, she poked around the gears to determine which was stuck.

She flicked her gaze upward when she felt eyes on her. "That's quite a carousel." The red-haired man grinned. His pearly white teeth contrasted starkly with red facial hair. His dark, deep-set eyes were fixed on the merry-go-round. Up close, Cassie pegged him to be a decade older than her, give or take.

Cassie smiled at him. "Yes, it is," she answered. "I've never seen another one like it."

"How much?" he asked.

"What?"

"How much for the carousel?" The man pulled his wallet from his pocket and unfolded it.

"Oh, I'm sorry, it's not for sale."

His eyebrows raised and his lips formed a pout. "Are you certain you can't part with it? I'd pay any amount you ask."

"I'm sure," Cassie answered. "Sorry, I'm in love with it. It's definitely not for sale."

"Having trouble with it?" he asked, motioning toward her tool kit.

"Yes," she admitted. "It doesn't want to play. I'm just poking around to try to find the problem."

"Perhaps I could help. I'm pretty good mechanically. I could take a look at it for you."

"Oh, thank you, but no. I'm pretty good mechanically, too. I'd like to fix it on my own so if it happens in the future, I know what to do."

"Fair enough," he said. "If you ever change your mind, let me know. I'd love to have it."

Cassie smiled and nodded.

"So are you from around here then, Mr...?" Lily inquired, letting the statement hang as she awaited his name.

"Baxter," he answered, shoving his wallet into his pocket and sticking his hand out. "Barney Baxter. And sort of. My family's been in and out of the area for years. I'm a bit of a rolling stone, but I'm in town frequently. It always feels like something draws me here." He offered a wide smile.

Lily shook his hand. "Well, Mr. Baxter, you'll be the first to know if Cassie decides to sell it, though I wouldn't hold my breath. She's quite smitten with that little carousel."

"Yes, it seems so. It is really an interesting item."

"Is there anything else I can help you find? Maybe one of these hand-made lighthouses? They're selling like hotcakes!"

He narrowed his eyes at the item as Lily showcased it. "I'll consider it. Thanks for your help. You ladies have a lovely day." He nodded to them both, before he strolled through the door, whistling a tune.

Chloe stood to the side to allow him to exit before ducking into the shop. "Him, again, huh?" she asked as she stowed her purse behind the register.

"Again?" Lily asked.

"Yeah, he was in here yesterday. Strange guy. He wanted to know which of us was the owner. When we told him neither, he just walked out without another word."

"That's weird," Cassie said, as she prodded the bottom of the carousel.

"Maybe he wanted to meet the new kids," Lily suggested. "What can you expect from a guy named after a cartoon pirate."

Chloe shrugged. "Maybe."

"He said his family was from around here," Cassie said.

"I've never seen him before yesterday. Oh wait, he was at the grand opening, too. Is this the famous carousel?"

"Yep, it is," Cassie answered.

Chloe asked why she'd dismantled it. Cassie explained about its problem as she reattached the bottom. An influx of customers interrupted any further conversation. Cassie set the rebuilt, but still inoperative, carousel on the shelf behind the register, and pitched in to assist the customers.

The late afternoon and early evening hours went quickly. They closed up the shop as the sun lowered in the sky. Cassie and Lily stopped for a chicken salad sandwich at the local cafe, before they hopped in the car to head home.

"Oh, shoot!" Cassie exclaimed as she fired the engine.

"What?"

"I left the carousel on the shelf behind the register."

"Eh, leave it until tomorrow," Lily suggested.

"We're off again tomorrow," Cassie reminded her.

"Oh, right. Well, leave it until Friday."

"If you don't mind, I'd rather grab it. Then I can look at it tomorrow. Something's causing it to hang up, but I can't see what it is."

"You're the one driving; I go where the car takes me."

"It'll only take a minute."

Cassie pulled the car onto the street, aiming away from the house and back toward the shop. She eased the car into the parking space behind the building. Leaving the engine running, she hopped out of the driver's seat and hurried into the shop. In the waning light, she spotted the carousel on the shelf behind the register. After a quick sprint across the shop, she swiped it from the shelf and returned to the car.

"Got it."

"Great, let's get home. Willy's probably starved."

Cassie chuckled. "Probably." She handed the musical carousel to Lily as she shifted into gear and headed for home.

CHAPTER 22

A shrill ring interrupted Cassie's sleep. She poked her head up from the pillow as she sought to grasp what was happening. Her cell phone jangled across the nightstand, buzzing and chirping. Its light illuminated the room.

Cassie squinted at the bright screen. She didn't recognize the number. As she swiped at the phone's display, she fought to shove her panic to the side. The last time she'd received a call in the middle of the night, she'd lost both her husband and her father.

With a lump in her throat and shaky hands, she raised the phone to her ear and answered it.

"Hey, Cassie." She recognized the deep voice of Sheriff Cooper.

"Yes?" she answered, her voice quavering with confusion. Her mind shot in a thousand different directions.

"Sheriff Cooper here. Sorry to disturb your night but we have a little situation. It's nothing to panic over, but I'm going to need you to come down to the shop as soon as you can."

"O-okay," Cassie mumbled, her brow furrowing at the conversation.

"You've had a break-in. We're on site, but we'd like to secure the premises and see if anything is missing."

"What?" Cassie said as she climbed out of bed. "Okay."

"Take your time. I'll be here."

Cassie nodded even though Wyatt couldn't see her. "I'll be there as soon as I can."

She ended the call and pulled on her robe. Cassie hurried from her room and eased open the door to her mother's room. "Mom!" she whispered.

She crept to Lily's bedside and gently rocked her. "Mom!"

"Huh, what?" Lily said, awakening with a start. "Cassie? What is it?"

"Wyatt called. Something happened at the shop. We need to head down there."

"Okay," Lily said, as she hurried from under the covers. "What happened? Is it a fire or a break-in or what?"

"Break-in," Cassie answered.

"Ugh, well at least it's not worse than that. I hope there's not too much damage. I'll meet you downstairs, I just need to throw on some clothes."

Cassie nodded and disappeared from the room. Both women trundled down the steps in sweats and ponytailed hair. Cassie slid into sneakers and Lily shoved her feet into her athletic clogs. They hurried out the door.

"Oh, wait," Lily said, waving her arms in the air as she sat in the car. "Forgot to put the alarm on."

She swung the car's door open and tried to exit. "Also forgot to take my seat belt off," she murmured as she pushed the orange button to release the restraint, before darting out of the car. Cassie spotted her waving her key fob in the direction of the front door and emphatically jamming a button before she hurried down the steps and back into the car.

"Okay," she said with a winded sigh. "Let's go."

Cassie threw the car into gear and they made the short trip into town. The red and blue flashing lights filled Main Street as Cassie pulled up next to the police cruiser. Wyatt met them at their car as both women slid their feet onto the pavement.

"Good morning, ladies. Sorry to roust you out of bed in the wee hours."

"No problem," Lily said. "What happened?"

Wyatt lifted the police tape as they ducked under. Cassie stared at the shop's front. Both windows were intact, but the shop's full-glass door was broken. Shattered glass dusted the shop's interior. A rock lay haphazardly near one of the front shelves.

"We left everything as we found it until you got here. We'll get this covered with plywood in a few minutes. Can you ladies step inside and take a quick inventory of what's in there? See if anything is missing. I don't need an exhaustive list, but generals will do for the initial report."

Cassie unlocked the door and pulled it open, feeling rather ridiculous when they could step through the mostly missing glass piece.

"Careful of the glass," Wyatt said. Cassie attempted to skirt around the mess, but her feet still crunched on a few wayward pieces. Lily circled the opposite way, also not able to escape all the fallen glass.

"It doesn't look like much is disturbed, to be honest," Lily said.

"I'll get the lights and we can do a more thorough inspection." Cassie flicked on the overhead lights, and everyone squinted as their eyes adjusted.

Lily wandered into the shelves while Cassie checked the register.

"Without doing a full inventory, I can't say for sure anything is missing, but from the looks of the shelves, there's not much taken, if anything," Lily said as she emerged from between two shelving units.

"Register's not disturbed and no cash is missing. Just this shelf behind it has a few things moved around on it. Nothing else."

"Moved around?" Wyatt asked.

"Yeah," Cassie said. "We have a few display items on here, but I didn't leave them in a jumble like this." Cassie motioned to the items that were squashed together on one side of the shelf.

"Anything missing?"

Cassie scanned the items and shook her head. "Nope. Everything's here, just shoved to the side."

"Okay," Wyatt said, as he flipped open his notebook. "So, no cash missing, no items missing that you can tell so far. The only thing you noticed at first blush is that a few items were moved around."

"Yep," Cassie confirmed. She stepped over to the mess scattered across the floor. "Is there a note on the rock?"

"No," Wyatt said. "I checked for that since you've had this happen at the house. Did you keep anything valuable here?"

"More valuable than the cash in the register? No," Cassie said with a shake of her head.

Lily chimed in, "And they didn't take any inventory. Not that it's valuable, but if they were looking for something that's worth money, wouldn't they take a few of the pricier items?"

Wyatt shrugged and pursed his lips. "The reason I asked is because it seems like they were looking for something. As you mentioned, nothing was taken from your inventory. The register is intact, it's not even tampered with."

Lily shrugged. "Perhaps this is just another 'welcome' message."

"Maybe," Wyatt answered. "But…"

"But?" Cassie prodded, when his voice trailed off.

"Why move the display items on the shelf around if they weren't looking for something?"

"I can't come up with what that could be," Cassie said.

"Well, if you think of anything, shoot me a text or give me a call. Ted's got the door almost secured with the plywood. As soon as he's finished, you ladies can get back home and go back to sleep."

"I doubt I'll sleep now," Lily said. "I didn't bargain for this much excitement when we moved to this sleepy hamlet."

Wyatt chuckled. "We really haven't given you a great impression, have we?"

Lily offered a smile. "We really do love the town and the house. I, for one, will love it more when people stop trying to scare us out of it, though."

"I know I keep promising this, but we'll get to the bottom of it," Wyatt said. "We're going to check some of the CCTV cameras and see if we can spot anyone coming or going."

"Let us know what you find," Cassie said. "Thanks."

"Will do. Looks like we're all set with the door, so you can lock up. We've finished our work, for now, so we'll get out of your hair."

After locking the shop with its new and unimproved door, the women stepped onto the sidewalk, intending to return home. Genny hovered near the door, her arms wrapped around her to ward off the night's chilly air.

"Hey, ladies," she said, her mouth forming a grimace. "So sorry this happened to you."

"Hi, Genny," Cassie said. "What in the world are you doing here at this hour?"

"Baking," she said. "I come in at four to start all the baked goods. I saw the broken window and called the police."

"Oh. Thanks for that," Lily said.

"Did you see anyone?" Cassie questioned.

Genny shook her head. "No. I already spoke with Wyatt. When I got here, the window was broken but no one was inside or anywhere around."

Cassie's shoulders sagged.

"Why don't you two come in and have a pastry and some tea? I could use the company while I bake!"

"I should try to get some more sleep, but I know that'll never happen," Cassie said as she glanced at Lily.

"I'll never sleep either."

"May as well keep me company then!" Genny said.

"Okay, deal," Cassie said. They followed Genny into her bakery and settled at the small table in the back.

Genny flitted around the kitchen, pulling muffins from the oven and shoving another batch in.

"Let me get the tea," Cassie offered.

"There's a Keurig there," Genny said, waving to a corner. "Just pop in whatever you'd like and press the button!"

Cassie set to work brewing three mugs of English tea. As she waddled over with three steaming mugs, Genny slid a plate of cookies onto the table. "Hot from the oven! My famous Spanish butter cookies!"

Lily eyed the thin biscuit. "Oooh, these look good!" She snagged one from the plate and took a bite as she waited for her tea to cool from scalding to drinkable.

"Do you need some help?" Cassie inquired, as Genny tossed some butter into the stand mixer and turned it on.

"Nope! I've got this place down to a science."

"I feel bad," Cassie said. "You're running around here

doing all this baking while we sit here."

"Hey, I'm used to it! Plus you just got some really awful news. Just take a minute to relax."

"Yeah," Cassie agreed. "So much for our day off. I'll text the girls later in the morning and let them know we'll be doing a cleanup first thing. I still can't figure out what they'd be looking for in the shop."

"They were looking for something?" Genny questioned, as she poured a cup of sugar into the creamed butter.

"That's what Sheriff Cooper assumed since nothing was taken. The register wasn't disturbed either."

"No, and it sounds like they had plenty of time to peruse the place. No one found the window broken until you, Genny, and you didn't see anyone," Lily said.

Genny shook her head as the mixer spun in circles. "No, I didn't. Whoever did it was probably long gone by the time I got here."

"Maybe it was just another 'welcome to the neighborhood' like you suggested," Cassie said.

Genny's brows knit and she glanced at the floor.

"What?" Cassie asked.

She shook her head and waved Cassie's question away. "Nothing," she said as she spun to add flour to the mixer.

"That look wasn't nothing," Cassie said, her eyes narrowed at the baker.

"I mean," Genny began, hesitating a moment before continuing, "this usually isn't the way people are welcomed to our town."

"I should hope not!" Lily said with a chuckle.

Genny finished scraping the bowl and set the mixer twirling again. "I'm being serious," she said. "No one else has had this happen."

"So, people just don't like us?" Cassie asked.

Genny shook her head again. "No, I'm not saying that. As

216

far as I can tell, everyone likes you just fine. But…"

"But?"

"You have a connection to *that* house," Genny said. "And people get weird about that whole haunted house, buried treasure story."

Cassie shot Lily a glance. "I hate to admit it but I've been wondering the same thing."

"Really?" Genny asked.

"I've been reading about Susan, the girl who disappeared all those years ago. She was researching the pirate treasure. Then she disappeared. Why? Was it connected somehow?"

Genny's eyes widened. "Oh, you think she stumbled on to something and ran into the wrong people?"

Cassie shrugged. "Maybe. What else explains it? Sure, she could have run away, but almost everyone says she wasn't that type of kid. Plus, why leave your purse and shoes? It doesn't make sense."

They talked for another few minutes about the possibility, but without more information, something they may never have, they couldn't draw any conclusions. They broke up as the sun peeked over the horizon. Cassie stretched as they strode onto the sidewalk to her car.

"Are you heading to bed when we get home?" she asked Lily.

"I won't sleep," Lily admitted.

"Me either," Cassie said, her hand lingering on her car door's handle.

Lily cocked her head. "Want to just start the clean-up now?"

Cassie nodded. "May as well. Maybe we can still salvage some of our day off."

They walked the few steps to their shop and entered the front door. Cleaning up all the glass took a little under an hour. They spent another hour doing a complete inventory of all items, including those in the back room. They found no items missing. Cassie rearranged the display items as Lily called a glass company about fixing the door.

She ended the call and reported that they'd be sending someone out in twenty minutes to discuss glass replacement.

"Should we close for the day?" Cassie inquired.

"I guess the door still works. Though if you don't want to leave Tom, Chloe and Amber alone here, we could close."

"I suppose in the light of day it should be safe," Cassie said. "I'll text them and see if they feel comfortable."

Cassie sent out her set of texts to each of them explaining the situation and asking if they preferred not to come in today, while Lily met the glass company's representative. With the door measured and order placed, he estimated they'd have it repaired by tomorrow afternoon. All three shop assistants also had no issue working after the incident, so Cassie and Lily left the store in Tom and Chloe's hands and headed home for the day.

They lumbered through the front door and staggered to the couch. Both women collapsed into the cushions.

"Ugh, I'm exhausted and it's not even noon yet," Cassie complained.

"Tell me about it. It'll be a quiet day for me."

"Me too," Cassie agreed. "I'm ready to kick off my shoes, settle down somewhere and try to relax."

"We've already had a day, we may as well. And grab another cup of tea."

"Sounds like a plan," Cassie said.

As early afternoon rolled around, Cassie and Lily settled in the library with a second cup of hot tea and their reading materials. Cassie took a few sips and stared out the window, the journal laying on her lap.

"I'm warning you ahead of time," she said to Lily, as she flicked the journal open, "I may fall asleep."

"Just don't let the book clatter to the floor again, in case I'm asleep."

Cassie offered a wry glance and a chuckle before she pulled the book closer.

I might be on to something! I found some things in the house belonging to Henrietta, Black Jack's sister! Specifically, I found a journal. It had some dried flowers stuffed in it that fell apart when I opened it. I need to read through everything but I hope it gives me some clue about his treasure. I'm really excited because this is a first-hand source!

I read through the first few entries in Henrietta's journal. So far, it doesn't look promising. She had a bunch of love letters stuffed in the front that had nothing to do with the treasure at all! And when I started to read what she wrote, it sounded like she hated her brother! So, then, why would she know where his treasure is? Maybe she blackmailed him to get it! I'll keep reading to find out.

I made more progress with Henrietta's journal. She's just found out her husband is dead. Poor Henrietta. She doesn't want to believe he's gone. I feel sorry for her. I'm starting to wonder if the treasure is real at all. No mention of it so far. Plus, she seems like she's off her rocker. Maybe she was just crazy and told people there was a treasure when there wasn't.

Cassie furrowed her brow. "Hey, Mom, were there love letters stuffed in that journal?"

Lily glanced up from her journal. "No?" she replied. She thumbed through the pages and turned the book upside-down, giving it a shake. "There's nothing here."

Cassie puckered her lips and narrowed her eyes as she glanced at her own book.

"Why?" Lily questioned.

"Susan says she was reading that journal, and she found

love letters and the remains of dried flowers."

"Maybe she kept them."

"I didn't see them in any of her stuff when we cleaned it out."

"Maybe we missed them."

"It's all still on the porch," Cassie said. "I'm going to go check it out."

"Have fun nosing through the trash. Willy and I will be hanging out here, won't we, sweet boy?" Lily cooed at the cat as she stroked his back.

Setting her journal aside, Cassie strolled out of the room, through the foyer and to the porch.

Lily returned her attention to the journal. She hadn't read much when Cassie had interrupted her. She scanned the few paragraphs she'd already read.

Clifton tipped my chin up to meet his stare. A devilish grin crossed his face and his brown eyes sparkled. "I have a plan."

"What possible plan could you have to undo all the poor choices I've made?" I inquired, my voice wavering as tears threatened again.

"Oh, Riri," he chided.

I stood and stalked to the window, my arms clutched around my middle. "It is the honest truth," I said. "You warned me. I did not listen." Ironic, I ruminated, my buccaneer brother attempted to stop my marriage to William. I ignored him. In the end, he was right. "You should be gloating!"

I twisted to glance at him. He said nothing. "Well, go on," I pressed. "Tell me you told me so. Tell me this is my fault. Tell me I should have listened..." My voice broke as tears began to flow. I covered my face with my hands and my shoulders shook as I wept.

Strong arms wrapped around me. I did not look up. Instead, I collapsed into my brother's arms further and continued to weep. When I pulled my hands away, I stared out the window as tears continued to flow. My head rested against his shoulder. After a time, my tears ceased. I sniffled and wiped at the stains on my cheeks.

"Are you quite finished now?" Clifton asked me.

I sniffled again and shook my head. "I am not certain you could have many tears left, sister," he added.

"Is this the extent of your plan?" I questioned. "To badger at me until I no longer grieve. You always excelled at it when we were children."

Clifton chuckled at me.

"Do not laugh at me," I cautioned, though his laughter proved contagious and I found myself giggling.

After several jovial moments, I pushed away from him and wandered to my bed. I plopped on it, my hand pressed to my forehead. "Oh, what will become of me now?"

"You will be better for it," Clifton said. "You will rally."

"Are you quite daft?" I questioned. "My husband is dead. He has left me no means to provide for myself until I may secure a new marriage. IF I can..."

"If? You're still a beautiful woman, Ri, though..."

"Though I am now damaged goods," I said. "A widow, not a beautiful young unmarried girl. My prospects have diminished."

"That's not what I meant."

"Isn't it? Well, dear brother, what insights have you to share?" I rearranged the folds of my dress as I inquired after his meaning.

"You should have no trouble attracting a new husband, Ri, if that's truly what you want."

"What other choices have I?"

"You have many, Riri. The world is at your feet."

I burst into laughter again. "Oh, dear brother," I choked out between giggles, "perhaps it is you who is the drunkard. How much liquor have you imbibed before this conversation?"

"You laugh, yet you shall soon see my meaning."

"Well, please, enlighten me."

CHAPTER 23

*C*assie slogged into the room and collapsed in the armchair.

Lily glanced over her reading glasses. "Well?"

"Nothing!" Cassie answered, flinging her arms into the air.

"Hmm. Oh well, you tried."

"It would be nice to find them." Cassie bounced from the chair. "Maybe there's another journal." She perused the shelves near where she found the first. Willy joined her, rubbing against her legs before turning his attention to the bookshelf. "See anything, Willy?"

In response, the tuxedo cat leapt onto his hind legs and batted at the bookcase. "What'd he find? A bug?" Lily murmured.

"No, I don't know what he's after. He was playing around over here the last time we were in here, too."

After a moment, she shook her head and flopped into the chair again. Willy stared at the bookshelf for another few moments, before stalking over and leaping onto the window seat next to Lily.

"That was fast."

"The entries she described are the same as what you told me about. So that's the journal she found them in. I wonder what she did with them. Oh well, guess I'll just keep going with this one."

Lily chuckled. "No torrid love letters for you."

"They were from the eighteenth century, I doubt they were torrid."

"Mmm, you never know. He may have suggested stealing a kiss from her under the stars."

"Shocking!" Cassie said with a laugh as she pulled the journal open.

Lily returned her attention to her own reading, hoping she would finally get to the heart of Clifton's plan.

Clifton settled into the armchair near the fireplace. "I have amassed a fairly large fortune from my excursions."

"You mean your pirating," I corrected.

He offered me a shrug, his eyes twinkling at me. "It's not much different than what your so-called beloved husband did, you realize."

"I beg to differ. He did not pillage and rob.'

Clifton smirked. "He did, just not to his own people. It's a moot point and I am not here to debate."

"Continue," I said.

"As I said, I have amassed quite a large fortune."

"I fail to see how your fortune sets the world at my feet."

He arched an eyebrow at me. "I need help," he said simply. "I need a hiding spot for my riches. With a keeper. Someone I can trust."

"I suppose the bank will not take stolen funds," I answered.

"I need you, Ri," he said.

"Me? To guard your stolen money? Surely you jest, brother."

"I do not."

"You have no trusted associates?"

"None I trust more than you."

"What are you proposing? I fail to see how this sets the world at my feet."

He raised his eyebrows. "I am proposing you oversee my bounty in return for a slice of the pie. A generous slice, I might add." He cocked his head and awaited my reaction.

My mind processed his request. The pieces of the puzzle fell into place. He meant to provide the means by which I could support myself. The offer intrigued me but several loose ends dangled in my mind.

"Would your generous offer be enough to cover William's debts?"

Clifton rose from the chair and paced the floor. "I have already paid down his debts, both to the more nefarious characters and at the bank."

I widened my eyes and hiked my eyebrows. "Call it an advanced payment for services to be rendered," he added.

"So, Whispering Manor..."

"Belongs to you. Well, technically to me, but for all intents and purposes, you, Riri."

"So, I have only swapped guardians. From husband to brother," I stated.

Clifton turned his gaze to me. He offered a half-frown. "I have no desire to play guardian to you. You are a capable woman. I do not mean to control you. Not that I could, anyway."

I arched an eyebrow. "Under the arrangement you propose, I am free to do as I wish then?"

"Absolutely."

"Travel?" I tested.

"Wherever you'd like, sister dear."

"Alone?"

He shrugged. "If you so desire. The world is your oyster.

Though Neptune's Servant remains at your disposal." He offered a slight bow and a sweeping hand gesture.

"Purchase lavish items?"

"Your choice."

"Write?"

"I sincerely hope you do. I have missed your stories."

"Marry?"

He narrowed his eyes at me. "Would you, Ri? Would you prefer to, really? Given the choice of your freedom versus a life tied to a husband, would you remarry?"

"I should think it to be expected of me."

"When have you ever preferred to do what is expected?"

"I learned long ago that what I prefer does not matter. It is what is expected that matters," I said wistfully.

"This mentality led you into your first marriage. And this disaster."

"Love led me there," I said, as I spun to face the window.

"Did it, really? You wept before Father paraded you down that aisle. Did you truly love him? Or did you merely love the life you expected him to give you? Or were you merely out of other suitable options?"

I considered his statements. I'd accepted William's proposal in the absence of others. After what had happened in my earlier life, I assumed my options to be limited. Marriage to a sea captain seemed a good match. Had I loved him? Or had I loved the freedom I expected would be provided to me as a married woman? In truth, I had been freer as a child than as Mrs. Blanchard.

A tear fell to my cheek and my lower lip trembled. I clutched at a handkerchief, twisting it until it was taut. Clifton's hand fell onto my shoulder. "You can be free now, Ri," he whispered.

I spun and flung my arms around him. Tears streamed down my cheeks, though, for the first time in weeks, they were from relief, not sadness. I pulled back and gazed at my brother. A tiny smile crept across my lips.

> *Clifton matched my expression. "Are we agreed then?"*
>
> *I nodded. "Bring the treasure!" He grinned at me. "Though I have several questions," I added.*
>
> *"I expect nothing less. This is why I've hired you."*

Lily's eyebrows raised and her jaw dropped open. She swung her legs off the window seat and leaned forward. "Cassie!" she exclaimed.

Cassie stared at the journal in front of her, a perplexed expression on her face. Her body was tense and her lips parted as her eyes widened. She raised her eyes from the page to her mother's face. "Mom!" Cassie answered.

"There is a treasure!" they both exclaimed at the same time.

"Susan just said Henrietta's journal talks about the treasure!"

Lily nodded her head. "Henrietta's brother just told her about the fortune he amassed, and told her he wants to bring it here."

"Does he?"

"I don't know. I stopped reading when she told him to bring the treasure. Didn't Susan say?"

"No, I must have read her entry about the entry you just read. She says, 'I found an entry about the treasure! Henrietta's brother asked her to guard it. They had a big discussion about her fate after her husband's death. He offered her enough money that she'd be able to be independent, and she accepted. I hope she tells me where they hid it!' Then she goes on to discuss how odd it is that Henrietta couldn't just live on her own at her age as a woman."

"Guess we need to keep reading."

"I guess," Cassie said with a sigh.

"What's with the sigh? We're on to something here! Maybe we'll find a pirate treasure!"

Cassie raised her eyebrows and lifted one shoulder. "If it was that easy, don't you think someone would have found it? Generations of people have lived in this house. No one found that journal and used it to find the treasure?"

Lily turned her palms up and lifted her hands. "If they did, no one said they found it."

"Well, I guess it doesn't hurt to try," Cassie said. "It's not like we've been searching all our lives."

"Yeah, maybe it'll be a nice puzzle."

"Guess we'll press on then, and maybe become famous!"

Before they could return to their reading, Cassie's phone jangled. She glanced at the display. "Uh-oh, it's Wyatt." She swiped at the display and answered the call.

"Hey, Cassie. Wyatt here. Got a second?"

"Yes, is this about the vandalism?"

"It is, we've got a few leads."

"You do!" Cassie wiggled her eyebrows at her mother.

"What?" Lily mouthed.

Cassie held up her finger. "Hey, my mom's with me. Do you mind if I put you on speaker?"

After receiving the all-clear from Wyatt, Cassie tapped at her phone and said, "Okay, go ahead."

"Hi, Lily," Wyatt said, before launching into his reason for calling.

"Hi, Wyatt!" Lily called.

"So, we reviewed the CCTV and checked the footage near your store. We caught someone on camera. We don't have eyes directly on your door, but we can see an individual coming and going. I wanted you to take a peek at the video, see if it triggers anything. Maybe someone who's been in the shop or you recognize."

"Okay, sure. Did you want us to come to the station?"

"At your convenience–no rush."

"Well, we're both off today," Lily said. "So we can stop in. Just give us a few minutes."

"Great. See you both soon." Wyatt clicked off the call.

"Guess our pirate treasure will have to wait," Cassie said.

"Guess so!"

CHAPTER 24

The two women pulled themselves from their comfy spots, grabbed their gear and headed for the car. "Guess we may as well grab something to eat while we're out."

"Wow, Mom, look at you turning into the out-to-eat connoisseur!"

Lily shrugged and said, "What can I say, I've never liked to cook and now I don't have to. Plus, the food in this town is close to homemade, it's not like we're dining in chain restaurants."

"We did pick a nice little town, didn't we?" Cassie said, as they pulled from the driveway.

"That we did," Lily agreed as she slid her sunglasses on.

They arrived a few minutes later at the police station. A three-story, red brick square of a building, the police station wasn't one of Hideaway Bay's most beautiful buildings, but it served its purpose.

Cassie and Lily found a parking spot in the side lot, and climbed the stairs entering the cool building. A blond with a pixie cut, painted red lips and large black-rimmed glasses sat at a desk facing the door. She glanced up at them as they entered.

"Can I help you?" she asked, a smile crossing her delicate facial features.

"Hi," Cassie greeted her. "Cassie McGuire and Lily Bennett to see Sheriff Cooper."

She nodded. "He's expecting you. Just a second." She pushed her wheeled chair back a few inches and leaned back. "HEY SHERIFF!" she shouted. "CASSIE AND LILY ARE HERE."

She offered another demure smile as she pulled herself back to the desk. "He'll be right out."

"Thanks," Cassie said, as she held in a chuckle.

Wyatt hurried down the hall with a few folders in his hands. "Thanks, Ruby. Also, can you file these?"

"Sure," she said, her dimples showing as she grabbed the stack of folders. "And I set out the tea like you asked."

Wyatt nodded and turned to face Cassie and Lily. "Come on back to the conference room." He motioned for them to follow him down a short hallway and into a small nondescript room with a table and chairs filling its center.

"Have a seat. Tea?" he offered, as he motioned to a Keurig.

"Thanks," Lily answered, as Cassie nodded in agreement.

Wyatt fiddled with the machine for a moment. He twisted to face them and offered a tight-lipped smile before he stepped into the hall. "Hey, Ruby!"

As if awaiting his call, Ruby swept into the room, followed by Wyatt. She flipped open the top as she spoke. "I've already got the water in here. Now just stick in a k-cup pod like this, press the lid down, and press this button," she said, showcasing the button with a ruby red nail. "Now when this one's done, just pour more water in, put in another k-cup pod, put the mug underneath and press the button again."

"Thanks," Wyatt said. She smiled and nodded as steaming water streamed into the waiting mug. "I'm not so good with these new-fangled things."

"I can get the next one going," Cassie offered, as Lily's tea finished brewing.

"Okay, thanks," Wyatt said as he crossed to the table. He seated himself in front of a closed laptop and a folder. Cassie settled at the table with her mug of tea as Wyatt flicked open the folder. "Thanks for coming in. Now we don't have much, but I wanted to go over what we caught on camera."

He spread a few papers out and slid them down the table in front of Cassie and Lily. The pictures contained a few grainy shots of Main Street. A hooded individual was captured as he or she made their way across the street toward the shop and then back.

"I know they're not great, and blowing them up really makes it hard to see them, but on the off-chance you recognize this person, I wanted to show you. Also, the video itself may help." He pulled open the laptop, and fiddled around for a moment.

Cassie and Lily studied the pictures. The person had kept their head down and out of the camera's eye for the most part. The streetlamp shed little light on the subject as he or she crossed back to wherever they'd come from.

"Sorry to say I don't think I can identify this person off-hand," Cassie said.

"No," Lily agreed, "though I would probably say we can safely rule out Frida. Her build doesn't really match this person's."

Wyatt nodded in agreement. "Yes, I would say this is a male. It may be easier to see that in the video." He tapped around on the laptop before a disgusting sigh escaped his lips. "Hey, Ruby!" he called out the open door.

Ruby flitted back into the room and headed straight for the

laptop. "I don't know what happened to it," Wyatt explained. "It was there when I opened the laptop and now it's gone."

"You just minimized it. It's down here, see?" She clicked a few times on the trackpad.

"Oh, there it is. Thanks." Ruby offered a nod before she scooted out the door again.

Wyatt shook his head at the two women. "When I became a cop, I thought I'd just have to catch criminals, not master all this technology. Anyway, here's the video," he said. He spun the laptop to face them. A video played showing Main Street. The hooded figure appeared in the bottom right corner. With hands shoved in his pockets, he hurried across the street at an angle and hopped onto the sidewalk. The presumed man disappeared off the camera.

Wyatt eyed the laptop and clicked a few spots after referencing a sticky note. The figure came back across the screen, his head down as though he was avoiding the camera.

"I agree the person moves like a male," Lily answered.

"Yeah and…" Cassie paused as the figure disappeared. "Sorry, can you play it again?"

"Sure." Wyatt tapped around and the video of the man crossing the street played again.

Cassie studied it, her forehead wrinkling. "Spot something?" Wyatt questioned.

Cassie shook her head and shrugged. "I'm not sure." She replayed the video again twice.

"What is it, Cass?" Lily asked.

"Maybe I'm way off base here, but don't these pants look like the ones the guy who asked about the carousel was wearing?"

Lily leaned in and squinted at the screen. "Possibly."

Wyatt retrieved his notebook and flipped it open. "Who is this?"

Cassie shrugged. "I don't know him. He stopped in the store yesterday and asked about buying my carousel."

"Chloe said he came in the day before and asked for the owners. He left when she said we weren't in."

"He introduced himself, what was his name? Barney?" Cassie said.

Lily pointed to her. "Barney, yes. Barney Baxter–like the cartoon pirate."

Wyatt jotted the name on the paper. "And do you have this guy's description?"

"Uh, he had red hair, longer, down to his shoulders," Cassie said. "Facial hair. Full beard and mustache, trimmed close to the face. Dark eyes."

Lily nodded and added, "He was about five foot ten, thin build. I'd peg him around early fifties for age."

Wyatt nodded as he jotted it all down. "Would you mind looking through some mugshots?"

"Not at all," Lily said.

"Okay, let me get the book." He disappeared from the room for a few moments, then hurried back carrying a large binder. "You check these, see if you recognize him."

"You don't know him?" Cassie asked.

Wyatt shrugged. "I don't recognize the name, that's for sure. If you don't find him in there, I'll speak with your shop assistants to see if I can get any additional information. For now, I'm going to run this name through our database and see if I get any hits. If you find anything, just holler. I'll be in my office."

"Okay," Cassie answered.

He scurried from the room and Cassie and Lily turned their attention to the large book in front of them. Seconds later, they overheard Wyatt's voice call to Ruby.

"He's really not good with technology, is he?" Lily said.

Cassie shook her head. "Uh-uh," she said, as they paged through the book.

They came to the end without spotting their mysterious store visitor and suspected vandal. Wyatt appeared a few moments after they finished. "Find anything?"

"Nope, sorry."

"It's okay. I didn't get any hits either," he admitted. "But I'll ask around. At least we have a direction to move in. I'll keep you updated but that's it for now. You're free to head back home."

"I had one other question," Cassie said.

"Shoot," Wyatt prompted.

"On the video, did I see the correct times? Did he approach the store around 2:30 a.m. and leave close to quarter after three?"

"Mmm-hmm, that's correct. He spent about forty-five minutes in the shop. Assuming this is our guy."

"Wow," Lily answered. "I suppose we should be thankful there was no real damage beyond the window, given how long he had access."

"Which is why I'm convinced he was looking for something."

"But what?" Cassie asked.

"Your guess is as good as mine. There's nothing valuable that you sometimes leave at the shop?"

Cassie shrugged and shook her head. "I can't think of anything. Certainly not anything behind the…" her voice trailed off as her brow crinkled.

"What is it?" Lily asked.

"You don't think… no," she said, shaking her head.

"Think what? Spit it out. We can't read your mind, Cass," Lily said.

"He asked about the carousel. You don't think he was looking for that, do you?"

"Really?" Lily questioned, her voice incredulous. "He broke into our shop for a toy carousel?"

"I said no," Cassie answered. "It couldn't be that."

"Carousel? Is this carousel valuable?" Wyatt questioned.

"I wouldn't think so," Lily answered. "It's a beautiful little piece, but I can't imagine it's rare or anything like that."

"Are you sure? Where did you get it?"

"No," Cassie answered. "But I can't imagine it is. It belonged to Susan Davies. My mom found it hidden in the house with a photo album."

Wyatt drew his lips into a thin line and narrowed his eyes.

"What is it?" Lily asked, noting his expression.

"Nothing, really," he answered. "I just... when you mention anything involving the Davies girl, I always think it's suspicious."

"How so?" Cassie asked.

"Well," Wyatt said with a shrug, "her case was odd. I was a rookie cop at the time. It was the first major case I worked."

Cassie nodded, offering a tight-lipped smile as he continued. "We never did find out what happened to her but there was something off about her case. And whenever her name comes up, it just makes me wonder what the people who took her were after."

"So you don't believe she ran away?" Lily inquired.

Wyatt shook his head. "No, I don't. There was no evidence of it. Who runs away and leaves her shoes? It just never sat right with me. I think someone took her. And the only reason I can come up with is because she was after that damned treasure."

"After all these centuries? Someone was still after it? Enough to kill a high school kid?" Cassie questioned.

"People do all sorts of strange things. Believe me, I've seen a lot working as a cop."

"What are you suggesting?" Cassie asked.

"I'm not certain I'm really suggesting anything," Wyatt answered. "But that kid went missing thirty years ago, then she wound up dead. The Davies had multiple intruders after Susan's disappearance. There have always been reports of trouble at Whispering Manor on and off. People wrote it off as ghosts, but it could have been break-ins searching for something. And right after you two show up, and take an interest in the house's history, you've had a slew of trouble."

"You think they're all connected. Susan's disappearance, her search for the treasure, and our disturbances," Lily said.

Wyatt nodded his head. "That's what I suspect, yes. I think someone thinks you may have stumbled on to something, and are after what they were after thirty years ago."

"Thirty years is a long time to wait," Lily said.

"It's not that long when it comes to a treasure the size of Black Jack's," he said. "Well, at least not according to the legends. Even if the treasure isn't the size people assume, it's still quite a discovery."

Cassie lifted her eyebrows.

"You don't agree?" Wyatt asked.

She shook her head. "I think it's a long time for a treasure to be missing and never found. So, to me, that suggests either the legend is just that, a legend; or it's been found at some point or simply was depleted by Black Jack within his lifetime."

"He died well before he could deplete his supposed fortune. Well, at least that's what the legend says."

"Can't believe everything you hear," Cassie said.

"Aww," Lily groaned. "He died young?"

Cassie shot her a glance, her face screwed up.

Lily shrugged. "I kind of liked him. And now you've ruined the end of my story."

Wyatt offered a half-frown. "Story?"

"Yeah. I'm reading Henrietta Blanchard's journal. She talks about her brother. I rather liked the guy."

Wyatt raised his eyebrows at the statement, but offered his apologies. "Sorry about that. Though I imagine it's half-ruined already, since you know Henrietta dies too."

"Yep. A real Bonnie and Clyde, those two."

"Well, sorry to have given away the ending, but at least you're prepared for it," Wyatt said. "You ladies have a nice rest of your day and I hope to have more information for you soon."

They thanked Wyatt, and offered their thanks to Ruby on their way out. She wiggled her fingers, her ruby red nails glittering in the light as they pushed through the doors and into the fall air.

"Where to for lunch?" Cassie asked as she pulled her keys from her purse.

"How about Italian?" Lily suggested.

"Sounds good to me."

Within ten minutes, they were settled at a corner booth in *Linguini's Italian Eatery* two blocks from the police station. With their order for ravioli placed and a basket of bread and an olive oil dipping sauce, Cassie and Lily settled in for their meal.

"No desire to get back to your journal now, huh?" Cassie said.

"Oh, I have the desire, especially if she tells us where that treasure is! But I am a bit deflated over the fact that Clifton dies young."

Cassie raises her eyebrows. "Oh, Clifton, is it? Not Black Jack? I'm shocked you're so upset over this thug."

Lily shrugged and offered a coy smile. "I don't know him as a thug or as Black Jack. I know him through Henrietta's eyes. Or Ri or Riri as he calls her."

"I thought she hated him?"

"Thin line between love and hate," Lily answered, as she took another bite of her oil-dipped bread. "Actually, I don't think she hated him. She must have been angry with him over something, but he seems pretty protective of his big sister."

"Hmm," Cassie murmured. "Interesting."

"I told you, sibling relationships are different. You can go from being very angry to defending them at the drop of a hat."

"What was she angry about, I wonder?"

"She hasn't mentioned it yet. I'm not sure she will. Though I'd love to know, too."

"It's interesting because I've really only gotten the ruthless pirate vibe from Susan's stuff," Cassie said. "So I find him rather intimidating. Like an 'I wouldn't want to run into him in a dark alley type of guy.'"

"He seems like a big teddy bear. At least with his sister," Lily answered.

Cassie screwed up her face. "How in the world was he a feared pirate?"

"Maybe he reserves his gentler side for his family."

"Sounds like an interesting fellow. I might have to read that journal when you're done," Cassie said.

"You should have stuck with it, instead of trading for the broken carousel," Lily joked.

"Haha, I like the carousel. Even if the thing won't work."

"That's a shame. I wonder what happened to it?"

"It hasn't beaten me yet. I'm going to look at it when we get home. Right after I dive into this ravioli!" Cassie smiled down at the plate delivered by the waitress moments earlier.

With full bellies and a to-go dessert for later, they headed for home as the afternoon hours waned to evening. Willy greeted them at the door, threading himself through their legs as they shed their coats and shoes in the foyer.

"Yes, I'll get you fed, buddy," Cassie said, as he rubbed his head against hers. "What's your plan for the evening, Mom?"

Lily checked her watch. "Looks like I've got some time to read about my new favorite rogue!"

Cassie chuckled as she rose from her crouch. "Meet you in the library with the lemon cake after I feed Willy and change."

"Make it the living room and you've got a deal," Lily answered.

The two women were settled on the couch with lemon cake slices within twenty minutes. Cassie pulled Susan's journal onto her lap, after she balanced the cake plate on the sofa's arm. She bit into a slice of her cake as she flipped open the small book. Tiredness crept over her and she settled back into the couch's cushions. "Hope I can stay awake long enough to finish my cake," she mumbled.

"I'm tired, too," Lily admitted. "All this drama is really draining me."

Cassie glanced down at the bubbly handwriting on the page.

I'm really excited! I finally made it to something concrete in Henrietta's journal. She's got a map and a note hinting at the treasure's location. I can't make heads or tails out of it but I'm going to ask a few people about it. I won't show them the real map but I'll make a copy of it and see if anyone can figure it out. This could be the key to finding the treasure!

I'm going to hide the real map in my secret hiding spot. Not the one where I put the letters, but my new secret spot. I can't wait to see if this pans out!

CHAPTER 25

*C*assie bolted upright, nearly toppling her cake. "Mom!" she shouted. "Is there a treasure map in that journal?"

Lily, who had just found her place in the book, frowned and answered, "I'm not sure."

"Susan said she found a map and a note showing the treasure's location."

Lily flipped through the remaining pages. "I don't see any drawings or anything."

"Nothing tucked in the covers or anything?"

"Nope."

Cassie read the entry again. "Wait, she said she hid it. I didn't come across anything that looked like a map while we were cleaning out her room, did you?"

Lily shook her head. "No, not that I recall."

Cassie knit her brows and Lily added, "Does she say where she hid it?"

"It says her secret hiding spot–not the one where she put the letters, but her new secret spot."

"So," Lily said, narrowing her eyes, "she has two hiding spots?"

"Apparently." Cassie's eyes floated to the ceiling. "I'm going up there to check it out."

"I'll come with you."

The women rose from the couch and trudged up the steps, slipping into Susan's old room. Her furniture still sat awaiting pick up from the local charity, though the space was devoid of any other belongings.

"I'll check under the bed," Cassie said. She flicked on her phone's flashlight and shined it under the bed frame. Nothing but dust bunnies met her beam's sweep.

"Check between the mattress and the box spring, too," Lily said, as she pulled open desk drawers and searched the bottoms of each.

"Okay." Cassie slid her arm up to her shoulder in between the thick mattress and the box spring. She reached her arm forward and back, sliding it up and down under the mattress searching for anything hidden.

"Nothing," she said, as she pulled her arm from under it.

"I didn't see anything secret in the desk, but you can check again if you want."

Cassie pulled out a few drawers and searched. Lily pulled the grate off of the floor heater vent. She shined a flashlight down the vent's shaft. "Nothing down here," she reported.

"Maybe the cold air return?" Cassie suggested, pointing to the vent high on the wall. "I'll get a step stool."

She darted from the room as Willy wandered in. "Oh, good, I'm glad you came to help us," she overheard Lily say to the cat.

Cassie returned a few moments later, lugging a three-step step-stool. She set it up against the wall and climbed up. Cassie tugged at the vent. "Ugh," she groaned. "Screwed in tight, and I can't turn the screws with my fingernail."

She clambered down the three steps and to the floor. "I'll grab a screwdriver." Cassie disappeared from the room again as Willy reached his paw under the bi-fold closet door and tugged to pop it open. He disappeared into the closest.

"Your cat's in the closet," Lily reported when she returned. "Don't lock him in there when we leave."

Cassie glanced at the closet door. "Must have wanted a dark, warm spot for a nap." She thudded up the steps and set to work on the screws. After removing both, she yanked the register cover from the wall. Standing on her tiptoes, she shined her flashlight inside.

"Well?" Lily questioned.

Cassie's nose scrunched up. "Nothing," she reported with a sigh.

"Are you sure?"

"You are welcome to climb up and double-check me," Cassie said.

"Nah, I believe you."

Cassie shoved the vent back on and secured it to the wall. She backed down the step stool and glanced around the room.

"I checked the dresser drawers. Maybe under it or behind it?" Lily suggested.

Cassie made a sweep with her flashlight both under and behind the dresser. "I don't see anything. Let's inch this out a bit."

Together they shifted the corner forward. Cassie gave the back another sweep with her beam. "Nothing," she said as her shoulder sagged.

"Well," Lily said as she dusted her hands off. "That's that. No secret hiding places in her room. Maybe it's somewhere else in the house."

"Maybe. If it is, we won't be finding it tonight."

"I'm ready for bed anyway," Lily answered. "Let's go, kid."

Cassie nodded. "Don't forget your cat," Lily reminded her.

"Right," Cassie said, as she glanced into the closet. She flicked on the light inside and glanced around the space, expecting the cat to be curled in a corner. Instead, he stood on his hind legs pawing at a divot on the wall.

"What's this?" Cassie questioned. She stepped into the small space and ran her finger along the depression.

"What did he find? Another bug?" Lily asked, as she leaned her head into the closet.

"No, some kind of indentation in the wall."

"I hope it wasn't caused by an animal. Though that would explain some of the strange noises we've been hearing."

Cassie felt around the dent, pressing against it. The piece gave way and a panel slid open above it. Cassie stumbled back a step, her jaw unhinging. A gasp escaped her.

"Whoa!" Lily exclaimed.

Cassie's face lit up in a smile and her eyebrows raised. "Maybe this is her secret hiding space!" She toggled on her flashlight and shined it into the dark area.

"What's in there?" Lily questioned.

"Papers! This could be it!"

Cassie grabbed a handful of papers from inside the small rectangular chamber along with a few objects. Her pulse quickened as she pulled the items from the nook.

"Bring them out here," Lily prodded.

"Okay, okay," Cassie answered. She stepped from within the closet and hurried to the desk. She tossed her phone to the side and spread the documents on the surface. She counted five different missives. Along with them were a snapshot of four girls, a woven bracelet and a keychain.

Lily picked up one of the papers from the pile and unfolded it.

"Is it a map?" Cassie inquired, as she glanced over her shoulder.

"No," Lily said, as she scanned the page. "Looks like a love letter to Henrietta from The Captain."

Cassie wrinkled her nose. "Meh," she said as she turned her attention to the other notes. She unfolded all of them, discovering more of the same. "They're all love letters."

Cassie dropped onto the desk chair. "No map," she said, flinging her arms out. "Maybe I missed it." Lily studied the other papers as Cassie hurried back into the closet. She scanned the space, running her fingers over every surface. She shined her flashlight around the cubby, but found nothing more. She pressed the indentation again and the panel slid closed. She toyed with the button several more times in the event that it rotated through a series of compartments. The same alcove opened over and over.

Cassie frowned at it and wrinkled her nose. She slogged out of the closet to join Lily.

"No map?"

Cassie shook her head. "Nope."

"Well, she did say she had another secret hiding spot, so maybe it's there."

"She did. At least we found one."

Lily stretched and yawned. "I'll leave the other until tomorrow. I'm exhausted."

"I think I'll take another look around in here before I hit the hay."

"Good luck. Don't wake me unless you find the treasure. Some of us have to work in the morning."

Cassie offered her a wry glance. "Work or not, some of us can't sleep after all this excitement."

Lily kissed her daughter's cheek. "Don't stay up too late."

Lily wandered from the room with the love letters in her hand. If she couldn't sleep, she'd read those and hope they put her to sleep. She worried she'd suffer from a similar phenomena, but with a few body aches from the strain of the past few days, she preferred to stretch out in bed.

She tossed her robe across the foot of the bed and climbed under the covers. After flicking the light off, she lay back on the pillows. Her open eyes darted around the darkened space.

With a sigh, she closed her eyes and tried to relax. She blew a long breath out of her mouth as she concentrated on relaxing. An unimpressed expression crossed her face as her eyes popped open. Lily twisted onto her side. "Go to sleep, Lily," she willed herself.

After a few moments, she began to relax. Her mind began to drift, when something startled her. She snapped her head up and listened hard.

With narrowed eyes, she strained to hear what woke her. A muffled rustling noise reached her ears. She shook her head before letting it fall back on her pillow.

The sound continued. Lily rolled onto her back with a huff. "What is she doing in there?"

With a groan and an eye roll, she tossed back the covers, slipped into her slippers and draped her robe around her shoulders. She shuffled across the floor and yanked the door open.

"What are you doing over..." she began, before realizing Cassie stood at the top of the stairs, motionless.

Cassie's wide eyes focused on her. She gestured down the stairs and mouthed, "I think someone's on the porch."

CHAPTER 26

*L*ily gazed over the railing to the floor below. The rustling noise sounded as though it came from outside the front door. A light bobbled around on the porch.

Lily set her jaw. "I've had just about enough of this." She pulled her robe on fully and tugged the tie tightly around her waist.

"What are you going to do?" Cassie asked, as she stormed past her and barreled down the stairs.

"Strike a little fear into his or her heart," Lily called over her shoulder. She whipped the bat out of the umbrella stand and began to unlock the door.

"Mom, wait!" Cassie said.

"No, Cassie. This has to stop. I'm sick of these people thinking they can get away with this harassment." Leaving the chain on, she inched the door open.

"Listen, whoever you are, I've had enough of this."

Lily heard footsteps pound past the front door. She released the chain and sped out the door after the black-hooded figure. She raised the bat as the individual sprinted past Cassie's car and down the driveway. "And stay away!" she shouted, waving the bat at them.

She returned inside, slamming the door, locking it and dumping the bat in the umbrella stand.

Cassie's incredulous face stared her down.

"What?" she questioned.

"Are you crazy?"

"No, I am not crazy. Sometimes, though, Cassie, you have to take matters into your own hands. I've had enough of this nonsense! First, they sneak into the house, then they bust your window, then the shop's window, and now they're prowling around on the porch, presumably because they couldn't get inside with the new locks. I'm sick of it. What gives them the right?"

Cassie's eyes widened at Lily's lecture and her jaw popped open. "We could have called the police."

"By the time they got here, they'd have been long gone. And we'd be right back to where we started. I'm tired of feeling helpless. Maybe now they'll think twice before they try to scare us again."

"What were they doing out there?"

Lily shrugged. "I didn't see, but it sounded like they were going through the bags."

"Susan's stuff? I'm beginning to think Wyatt was right. I think this somehow ties to Susan."

"And maybe to the treasure. She was researching that. Speaking of, did you find anything else?"

"No. Though I barely started my search before that person appeared on the porch and started rummaging through the bags."

"Well, now that I'm wide awake, I guess I can help you."

The women spent another thirty minutes searching Susan's room for any other hidden locations. They found none. "Well, that's that. I'm still not tired," Cassie said.

"Nope, me either. How about a hot chocolate?"

"Yes, please!"

Cassie collapsed on the couch for a few moments. Her thumbs flew across her virtual keyboard on her phone as she waited for her warm drink. Her right thumb hesitated over the send button as she puckered her lips. She clicked off the display without sending the message as Lily entered carrying two full mugs of hot chocolate piled with miniature marshmallows and drizzled with chocolate.

"Wow, you went all out!"

"Yeah, and I even frothed the milk." Lily handed a mug off and collapsed on the couch next to Cassie. "Does Facebook have anything interesting on?"

"I wasn't checking Facebook. I was typing a message to Wyatt, but then I wasn't sure if I should send it."

"About our garbage picker?"

"Yeah."

"I suppose it could wait until morning if you don't want to send it in the middle of the night. He or she seems to be gone now."

"Okay, I'll send it tomorrow morning over breakfast." Cassie settled back into the cushions as she sipped at the warm chocolatey milk.

"Something else on your mind?"

"Yeah, Susan's other hiding spot."

"Cass, that could be anywhere in this house."

"I know! We may never find it!"

"Then we're no worse off than we were before."

"No, but perhaps finding and sorting this out will stop these nuisances." Cassie paused for a moment before adding, "Or your bat-wielding skills will."

Lily raised her mug in approval of the comment.

They finished their hot chocolate and, with the hopes of a few hours of sleep, both headed upstairs. Lily shuffled to her bed and crawled in after doffing her robe and slippers. With a sigh, she pulled the covers up around her and closed her eyes.

Moments later, she slammed balled fists against the mattress with frustration. With a grumble, she flicked the light on and pulled herself up to sit. Her eyes slid to the brown leather journal on her night table.

"Come on, Henrietta, let's see what questions you have." She pulled the journal onto her lap and paged to her spot.

"Well, out with them. What questions have you?"

"First, how do you propose to bring this so-called treasure here?"

"We must be careful. I propose docking in the dead of night."

I cocked my head at him. "And smuggling it ashore?"

He nodded.

"Where shall we place it? How large is it?" I paced with my finger pressed to my lips. "And who is guarding it now?"

"A trusted associate."

"Then why move it? Why insist I guard it?"

"Its location is growing less than secret. Because even trusted associates can be bribed."

"And I cannot?"

He narrowed his eyes at me. "We are blood. Family. I trust you. Our history proves it."

"Despite our estrangement?"

"A blip. A spat between siblings, nothing more."

"All right, so you sail under the cover of night. We smuggle the treasure ashore." I paused in my pacing, my palm up facing and finger extended to him. "How large is it? You never answered."

"I fear it may sink the ship."

My eyebrows shot up. "You jest."

"I do not. I told you I have been very successful in my endeavors."

"I suppose," I said, collapsing onto the bed, "I should be more reluctant in aiding you given the way you came into your fortune."

He shrugged and wiggled his eyebrows. "I have never wronged anyone who did not deserve it."

"What does that mean? You robbed trade ships, did you not? And let us not speak of what you did to the sailors aboard."

"Those trade ships were captained by crooked men already on the take. Men who mistreated their own sailors and those they traded with. I relieved them of their command and offered their men a new life. I'm rather a hero if you really consider it, Ri."

"Crooked men?" He nodded, an amused expression on his face. "So you have robbed the robbers?"

"Rather a Robin Hood, I'd say." He smirked at me. Clifton always had a way of talking himself out of most trouble. And his charming grin tended to disarm most everyone in its path. No wonder he could be a pirate and still accepted into society, I mused.

I shook my head at him. "You have a high opinion of yourself," I teased.

"Someone must, why not me?"

"All right, so it is large enough to sink your ship. And what of the contents?"

"Gold, silver, jewels and the like."

"I thought you robbed trade ships?" He nodded. "Trade ships carrying jewels and gold?"

He rolled his eyes. "No, Ri, you rob the ship, and then sell the contents for gold and jewels. And there was the occasional raid of a ship carrying some valuable contents of the European nobles."

"Stop," I said, holding my hand up, "I should hear no more of this."

"Why? The stories may prove interesting when you take up writing again."

"If I find myself in need of inspiration, I shall ask."

A bemused smile crossed his face. "Fine. What other questions have you then?"

"I am curious about something else you mentioned rather unrelated to our current discussion."

"Which is?"

"You mentioned a plan when I said I would be expected to remarry."

A naughty grin crossed his face. "If you continue your current course of action, no one will suggest it."

My brow furrowed. "My current course of action?" I inquired.

"Yes," he said nonchalantly, waving his hand in the air. "The grieving widow who refuses to believe her husband will not return. Pining away for him. You could even parade about on the widow's walk. Make a real show of it, Ri. You've always enjoyed acting."

I offered him a wry glance. "What?" he questioned. "I have vivid memories of sword fights, murders and more in my childhood bedroom every evening. I'm sure reluctant widow is something you can pull off."

"So, you propose I pretend to await my husband's return from sea in order to remain a widow?"

"It is the perfect plan!"

"Mother and Father will disagree."

"They usually do. You've never seemed to mind."

"I do not," I assured him. "Though that will not stop them from badgering at me."

"Nor you from pitching one of your famous fits. Father always gives in to you then. And Mother only wrings her hands because she does not know what to say or do."

"In an effort to win me to her way of thinking, she did rather spoil me. I am not certain she expected this result."

"In any case, it works to your advantage. Use it."

I offered a coy smile. "Then it sounds like we have a plan."

"Not quite," Clifton answered.

My brow furrowed and my grin vanished. I cocked my head at him.

"We still need a hiding spot."

Lily's eyelids drooped and the book slipped from her hands. A soft puff of air escaped her lips as she drifted off to sleep. The journal began a slow slip down the covers and clattered to the floor below. Lily jolted in bed as the sound echoed.

She shook her head and lifted the journal from the floor to her night table. After flicking off the light, she turned onto her side and nestled into the covers. "We'll find that hiding spot tomorrow," she murmured, as she drifted to sleep.

* * *

Cassie staggered up the stairs and into her room. A yawn stretched her jaw to its limits, and she plodded to her bed. Willy had claimed a spot near the middle of the bed. Crawling under the covers, she did her best to wrap herself around the cat so she could fit on the mattress.

Her mind continued to whirl as she shut her eyes. Where else could there be a hiding spot in the house? She tried to imagine the spots a teenager may seek out or frequent. The living room? Perhaps the library? Maybe the attic space held a secret.

She wiggled to find a more comfortable spot. With a deep sigh, she realized she couldn't sleep, even after the relaxing warm drink. She turned on her back to stare at the ceiling. Her eyes darted around the darkened space and landed on the carousel. She'd used it before to relax her into sleep–until it broke.

She frowned as the thought danced around her mind. She'd stripped down the unit to its gears and found nothing obstructing its movement. What was the problem?

With another sigh, she tossed back the covers and hurried across the room on her bare feet. She descended the steps and tiptoed to the pantry. A chill wafted past her bare arms.

She shivered, her flesh puckering with goosebumps. She hurried back to her room and tossed the toolkit onto the bed, before grabbing her robe and wrapping up in it.

She rubbed her arms as she flicked on the lights and stared at the carousel. "What's stopping you from working?" she asked.

The tiny horses stared back, unspeaking. Their painted eyes were wide, and their manes were frozen in a wind-whipped position. Cassie grabbed the object and her toolkit and took them over to her window seat.

She pulled her lips to the side as she narrowed her eyes. She'd already removed the bottom. There were no problems with the mechanisms there. She flipped the carousel over and stared at its ceiling. The poles disappeared into the carousel's top where she assumed the mechanism to make the horses bob up and down existed.

Setting the carousel down, Cassie studied the red and white striped top. She eased a flathead screwdriver into the top and attempted to loosen it. It didn't budge. Cassie glanced underneath again, squinting at the shiny top. Tiny golden screws held the top in place.

Cassie searched through her toolbox for her tiniest screwdriver and set to work removing the small fasteners. With the screws removed, she flipped the carousel upright and carefully wedged the flathead screwdriver under the red and white top. She gritted her teeth as she pried as carefully as she could, inching her way around the top until it finally gave way.

Cassie lifted the metal piece off and set it aside. She peered in at the inner workings of the mechanism that controlled the horse's movement. A dust cloud billowed as she blew on the parts. Nothing appeared to be wrong with it. She poked around at a few components, but found nothing to prevent the carousel from functioning.

With the cover off, Cassie wound the music box and studied the top as she allowed it to attempt to play. The gears tried to push the horses ahead, but slowed to a stop almost instantly. Cassie's shoulders slumped and she muttered to the device, "What is wrong with you?"

She checked each gear again to ensure nothing prevented it from moving. As she peered at one near the interior cylinder, she caught sight of something tan.

"Ah-ha!" she exclaimed. "Are you the culprit?" She squeezed the thin object between her fingernails and tugged. It slipped from her tenuous grasp. With a frown, she tried again with the same result.

"Okay, this isn't working," she said with a huff. She hurried into her en-suite bathroom and searched through her vanity's drawer. At the back, she found a pair of tweezers. She snatched the forceps and raced back to the carousel.

After a few failed attempts, she caught the edge of the thin material and freed it from the gear's path. Immediately the carousel began to spin. Music filled the room.

"Hooray!" Cassie said, as Willy raised his head and squinted in the direction of the noise.

The offending material still stuck up from the central cylinder. "I'm going to remove you before you cause any more problems," Cassie warned it.

She set the tweezers aside and grasped hold of the corner with her thumb and forefinger. As she tugged on it, she found it to be part of a large piece of paper. It spiraled upward before giving way and popping from the cylinder. Another smaller paper fluttered to the floor.

Cassie furrowed her brow, wondering if it was the instructions for the carousel. "Why hide them in here?" she muttered.

Cassie set the paper aside as she reconstructed the carousel. "And now, I am going to put these somewhere

where they won't break my carousel again!" she said to the papers. She planned to store them in her small filing cabinet containing other user manuals.

She gathered up the two pieces of paper and carried them downstairs. The edges of both continued to curl after having been stuffed in the carousel's inner cylinder for decades. If she wanted them to lay flat, she'd have to set something heavy on top of them.

She set the curled papers on the desk and sought a heavy book to place on top of them. Finding a large dictionary, she pulled it from the shelf. Balancing it in one hand, Cassie struggled to unroll the larger paper. It snapped back twice before she set the dictionary on one edge, and retraced her steps to retrieve another large volume from the shelves.

With another thick book in her hand, she unraveled the curled paper. Her eyes went wide at what she saw. The book slipped from her trembling hand and clattered to the floor with a loud thud.

Cassie's jaw dropped open. This wasn't an instruction manual for the carousel. This was a treasure map!

CHAPTER 27

A loud bang startled Lily from her slumber. "Now what?" she moaned, as she strained for any other sounds. She heard none. Maybe she hadn't heard anything. She rolled onto her back. With a shake of her head and a sigh, she tossed back the covers and climbed from her bed. She shrugged her robe around her shoulders. Given the events since they'd moved into Whispering Manor, she wouldn't sleep another wink unless she checked out the supposed noise.

She pulled her bedroom door open and glanced around. Across the way, Cassie's door stood open. Lights blazed inside the room. Was she still up, or had she heard the noise too?

Reluctant to call out to Cassie in case someone was lurking in the house, Lily took a few steps toward her open door. Something downstairs caught her eye. Light spilled into the foyer from the library. Shadows danced on the floor. Someone was moving around in the library!

Lily tiptoed past the stairs leading down and scurried to Cassie's bedroom.

"Cass! Cassie!" she breathed. She found only Willy curled on the bed. Cassie's carousel sat on the window seat next to her toolbox.

She must be attempting to fix it. Perhaps she went in search of another tool or a screw. The bang must have come from her. Lily retreated into the hall and leaned over the railing. She peered into the library. "Cassie? Is that you?"

"Yeah," a shaky voice answered her. A moment later, Cassie appeared at the door. Her eyes were wide and she looked stunned.

"What's wrong?" Lily inquired as her stomach did a back-flip. "What happened?"

Cassie swallowed hard. "Come down here and take a look at this."

Lily tied her robe around her as she dashed around the railing and down the stairs. "What? What is it?" she asked, as she flew through the door.

Cassie pointed a shaky hand to a beige paper laying on the desk. Two large books held down the edges. "I found that in Susan's carousel. It's what was preventing it from spinning."

Lily furrowed her brow, not understanding why this was of any consequence. She stepped to the desk and eyed the paper. Her head snapped to Cassie. "Is this what I think it is?"

"I think so!" An amused grin crossed Cassie's face.

"Looks like you found Susan's other special hiding spot."

"It came with this note."

Lily read through it, her forehead wrinkling. She stared at the yellowed paper again. A crude and vague map was drawn on it. Tan ink marked borders and boundaries. Of what, though, Lily pondered? A few squiggles seemed to represent water. Was it the ocean?

Other symbols dotted the barren landscape. Trees, rocks,

openings, houses. What did it mean? On the left, a large black "X."

"Oh, you've got to be kidding," Lily groaned.

"'X' marks the spot, right?" Cassie said with a shrug and a grin.

"I can't believe it's that cliched." Lily squinted down at the map. "Though I'm not sure it helps us much. Where is the 'X?'"

Cassie shrugged again and shook her head. "This doesn't provide much context, does it?"

"No. There isn't even a compass rose."

"Some pirate Black Jack was. Didn't even put a compass on the map," Cassie joked.

"You said there was a note with it?"

"Yeah," Cassie said. She shifted the dictionary and pulled a smaller piece of paper from under it. She handed it to Lily.

Lily shook her head and held a finger up. She pulled open the desk drawer and dug around for a moment, retrieving an item. She flicked open the arms on a pair of reading glasses and shoved them on her face. "That's better," she said.

"Now that you can see it, I hope you can make sense of it."

Lily pulled the glasses from her face and shook her head. She scrunched up her face. "This is just as vague. Though I can tell you this is Henrietta's handwriting."

Cassie nodded. "I couldn't make heads or tails out of it."

Lily stared at it for another moment, holding her glasses up in front of her face. After a moment, she tossed her hands out. "I don't know. Maybe with some sleep, we can figure it out. I'm not exactly thinking clearly. I was asleep until I heard a bang."

"Yeah, sorry. I dropped the book when I realized what this was. I thought it was instructions for the carousel."

"I don't think we should leave this lying around."

"No, I agree," Cassie said. "Susan died after she found this. I don't want the same to happen to us."

Lily swallowed hard and gave a slight nod. "And don't tell *anyone* you found this."

"Okay," Cassie agreed.

"Not Amber or Chloe or Tom. Not Pearl or Meghan or Genny. No one, Cass. Not even Wyatt."

"Wow, are we a little paranoid? Not even the sheriff?"

Lily shook her head. "I just don't want to tell the wrong person, or the wrong person to overhear. You're right, Susan died shortly after she found this. I don't want the same to happen to us."

"Where should we put this?"

"Back in the carousel?"

"No, I don't want it to wrap around the gear again and…"

"I was only kidding. We'll put it in the safe in the pantry."

"Okay," Cassie agreed. "Just a second." Cassie hurried from the room and returned moments later with her cell phone. She snapped a few pictures of the map and the note.

"You sure that's a good idea?"

"Well, I'd like to have a copy, and I don't want to go in and out of the safe every time I want to see it. I won't show it to anyone."

"Send those to me." Cassie raised her eyebrows. "I won't show it to anyone either. Cross my heart."

Cassie smiled as she tapped around on her phone. "Okay, done. Let's put these in the safe."

"And get some sleep!"

Despite the excitement, after the long day, both women managed to sleep after securing the map and note in the safe.

They met in the kitchen a few hours after crawling into bed, both bleary-eyed.

"Did you get any sleep?" Lily asked Cassie.

"I did, despite all the excitement. How about you?"

"I was out."

"I can't believe we found a treasure map," Cassie said, as she poured steaming water into two mugs and dunked tea bags in each.

"A rather useless one."

"Maybe not. Maybe we were just tired."

"Yeah. I'm sure in the light of day after a few hours of sleep, we'll be able to figure out which rock and tree are on the map."

"Haha, very funny, Mom," Cassie answered dryly.

"It's entirely possible the landscape over the centuries has changed, and the map is useless," Lily said.

Cassie puckered her lips but nodded in agreement. "And the note does little to help. No wonder no one has found the treasure."

"Read me the note again," Lily instructed, as she slathered her toast with strawberry jam.

Cassie dug her phone from her robe's pocket and tapped around. With a flick of her fingers, she enlarged the scriptwriting and read, "Over Land and Sea, Under the Hollow, Through Thick and Thin, Beyond the Border, The Cave. Then underneath, all in capitals, it says HENTON."

Lily screwed up her face. "It makes no sense to me."

"Could Henton have been a street name?"

"We could check."

"I'll check Google Maps," Cassie said as she tapped around on the phone again. She crinkled her nose. "Not showing up as a road here."

"Maybe it was a street name in Henrietta's era."

"We could check. Maybe Pearl would know."

"Try not to arouse too much suspicion if you ask her."

"Even if we find out it was, what's the rest of this mean?"

"Maybe there's a cave off of Henton Street," Lily said.

The crease in Cassie's forehead deepened. "Then what's

the rest of it about? Over land and sea and the hollow and all that?"

"Maybe it refers to the journey they took to bring the treasure here. Maybe the map was the route?"

"Hmmm. Maybe."

"I do know one thing, though."

"Oh? What's that?" Cassie inquired.

"If we don't get moving, we're going to be late for work."

Cassie offered an unimpressed glance at Lily as she stood to clear her breakfast dishes. The treasure map would have to wait.

Within an hour, the ladies were heading out the door and to the shop. A note taped to the counter near the register stated the glass company would be out to repair the door this morning, rather than this afternoon.

Cassie reviewed the previous day's sales as Lily checked the shelves. "The lighthouses are nearly gone, Cass! I hope you got an order in," she called from between the shelves.

"I did! Phil said he'd have another two dozen for us by tomorrow. He also said he was going to try a few Christmas-themed ones for us."

"Great! I can't believe we sold out of those in a week."

The conversation ended as the repairman arrived with the new glass pane for the door. He set to work under Lily's watchful eye. Cassie used the quieter morning hours to make a phone call to the library. As she waited for Pearl to come to the phone, she contemplated how best to ask her question.

"Hello, Cassie," Pearl's voice sounded on the other end of the line.

"Hi, Pearl! How are you?"

"Doing just fine. And yourself?"

"I'm okay." With the pleasantries out of the way, Cassie decided to dive into the heart of the matter. "I hate to bother you, but we've been looking through the resources you sent and some of the things in the house, and we came across an odd reference and wondered if you could help."

"I can try. What's the reference?"

"It's Henton. H-E-N-T-O-N. It seems to refer to a place or a location. Ever heard of it?"

"Henton? Hmm," Pearl murmured as she went silent. "Can't say it rings any bells."

"We were wondering if there was, perhaps, a Henton Street. Maybe in the town's early days."

"Well, I can certainly check a few old maps we have here in the library and let you know, but I am not familiar with it if there was. Are you sure it's a road?"

"No, but I can't imagine what else it could be."

"What's the reference? Maybe it's something else."

"Uh," Cassie stalled. Her eyes floated to the ceiling as she tried to think of a cover story. Her mother's words rang in her head. "My mom found it. Maybe in Henrietta's journal. I guess the way Henrietta referred to it, she figured it was a road. I'll ask her if it could be something other than a street."

"Okay," Pearl said. "And let me know so I can expand or change my search. In the meantime, I'll check the old maps and get back to you."

"Thanks, Pearl."

"You're welcome. And have a nice rest of your morning."

Cassie ended the call. Henton didn't ring a bell with Pearl. So, if it was a street, even one with a changed name, the librarian didn't know of it. What else could it be?

The arrival of Amber carrying a pizza and drinks for everyone stunted any conversation on the subject. With the glass repair almost concluded, the ladies dug into their lunch.

As Cassie downed the last of her root beer, her phone rang. She assumed it was Pearl returning her phone call and swiped at the screen without glancing at the display.

Wyatt's voice surprised her on the other end. "Hey,

Cassie," he said, his voice sounding grim. A shrill ringing sounded behind him.

"Oh, Wyatt! I didn't expect it to be you. What's up."

"We've got, ah, a situation at Whispering Manor. Are you able to come out?"

Cassie's pulse quickened. "What kind of situation?"

"Just get here as soon as you can."

The line went dead.

CHAPTER 28

*C*assie's heart thudded in her chest and a lump formed in her throat. She swallowed hard and hastened across the shop's floor to her mother, who was thanking the repairman.

She waited a moment as her mother shook his hand and said another thank you before grabbing her elbow. "A word," she murmured, as she pulled her away.

"What is it?"

"Wyatt called. He said there's some kind of situation at the house."

"What? What kind of situation."

"He wouldn't tell me over the phone. He said to get there as soon as possible."

"You've got to be kidding," Lily groaned, her posture slumping. "Well, let's get going."

"Hey, Amber," Cassie said, as she pulled their purses from behind the counter. "We've got to run out to the house. The sheriff called and said there was a problem. Will you be okay here alone?"

"Sure," Amber said. "Tom should be here in about two hours, I'll be fine."

"Great, thank you!" Cassie called, as they flew through the rear door and to the car.

She traversed the town's streets as quickly as possible as she headed for the ocean. Several police vehicles came into view as she pulled from Ocean Drive into their driveway.

"This doesn't look good," Lily said. The sounds of the ringing alarm still pierced the air.

"No," Cassie murmured, as she shoved the shifter into park and set the emergency brake. She flew from the car toward Wyatt, who sat on the porch steps. Lily disarmed the alarm with her app. The piercing noise quieted.

He stood as she approached. "Hey, Cassie. Really sorry to meet this way again."

"What is it? What happened?" she questioned as Lily hurried toward them.

"We got an alarm code from the house. When my deputy arrived on the scene, he found several of the items from these bags strewn across the porch and the front door pried open." He held his hands in front of him. "He entered the house and did find someone inside."

"So, you got him?" Lily asked, breathless.

Wyatt pursed his lips and gave his head a slight shake. "Unfortunately, the perp came barreling down the front stairs and knocked him over. He fled before the officer could get a good look at him or discharge his weapon."

Cassie's shoulders sagged and Lily bit her lower lip, offering a head shake. "I'm sorry, ladies."

"No," Lily answered, as she waved her hand at him. "It's not you. I'm just frustrated with this entire situation."

"Is your officer all right?" Cassie inquired.

"He seems to be," Wyatt said, with a glance over his shoulder. "Though he's not very pleased about having let the perp get away."

Cassie offered a half-smile. "I did a walk around the place when I got here," Wyatt continued. "It doesn't look like much is disturbed or missing, but I'd like to have you both take a look."

"Okay," Cassie said with a nod. With an unsteady breath, she climbed the stairs and entered the house alongside Lily. They wandered through the downstairs rooms, finding a few items out of place, but nothing missing. They climbed to the second level and split up, each going to their own bedroom spaces first.

Cassie rounded the corner of the banister and headed into her bedroom. For the most part, nothing seemed disturbed. Perhaps the thief hadn't made it to this room before his or her work was disturbed.

Her eyes performed a quick circuit of the bedroom. She focused her attention across the room, noting one item missing. "Hey, Wyatt," she called over the banister. "I can identify something that was stolen."

Lily emerged from her room. "Me too," she said.

Lily joined Cassie at her bedroom door as Wyatt climbed the stairs. He flipped open his pocket-sized notepad. "What's missing? Jewelry? Cash? Passports?" Wyatt clicked his pen, ready to write.

Cassie shook her head. "My carousel."

Wyatt froze, his pen pressed to the pad but not moving. His eyes darted side-to-side before they rested on Cassie. "The carousel? Susan's carousel?"

"Yep," Cassie confirmed. "Susan's carousel."

"Nothing else? From your room, I mean. Lily, I'll get to yours in a minute."

Cassie retreated into the bedroom and lifted her jewelry

box lid. She pulled open a drawer and pushed a few items around. "Nothing else. Just the carousel."

"Okay. And, you, Lily? You said you had something missing, too?"

Lily nodded. "Henrietta's journal."

Wyatt scratched his head before scrawling "journal" in his notebook. "Henrietta's journal? Like Henrietta Blanchard?"

"One and the same," Lily said. "Cassie found her journal shortly after we moved in. I'll confess I've been using it for some light reading. She was an interesting woman. Anyway, I had it on my night table and it's gone."

"Anything else?"

"Wait, Susan's journal is missing!" Cassie exclaimed. She darted into the room. "I had it right here on… oh, wait. Here it is." She bent over and snatched the journal that peeked out from under her ruffled bed skirt. "Willy must have knocked it down. Your guy must have interrupted our thief before he or she could find it."

"I must say, this is the most interesting set of pilfered items I've ever seen." He swung the cover of the notebook shut and stuffed it into his pocket.

"Any luck on finding out who smashed the shop's door?" Lily questioned.

"Nothing yet. No hits in our database. Though given his interest, I'd doubt he's your average criminal."

"Do you think it could be someone related to Susan? A family member who didn't agree with the sale of the house or something?" Cassie questioned.

"It's not a bad theory, though I'm not certain there's really much family left. At least not close to Susan." Wyatt shrugged.

"He does seem drawn to Susan's things. Someone was prowling around the bags on the porch last night. I chased them away with a baseball bat."

Wyatt's eyes shot wide. "You what?"

Lily shrugged. "Quite frankly, I'm getting fed up with this nonsense. And tired of being harassed."

"You should have called us!" Wyatt countered.

"That's all we do is call the police! Most of your resources are tied up with your latest arrivals in town. I'm tired of reporting crimes," Lily retorted.

"Don't be. You could have been harmed or worse! This is best left to the professionals."

Lily sighed. "All right," she said, holding her hands up in surrender, "next time someone's going through our trash, I'll call you."

Wyatt nodded. "That's more like it. Now, if there's any more trouble, I expect a call." He shot a glance at Lily, who shrugged and raised her eyebrows. "In fact, it might be best if the two of you head over to the Hideaway Hotel for a few nights."

"No," Lily said, waving her finger at him. "That's where I draw the line. I will *not* be chased out of my own home!"

Wyatt opened his mouth to argue, glancing to Cassie for backup. She shrugged, her palms facing up. "I don't think you're going to win this one," she said with a chuckle.

"Am I the only one? Would you prefer to go to a hotel?"

"No," Cassie admitted. "I don't want to leave Willy and honestly, I think whatever they're after they may have gotten."

"Until they realize it doesn't have what they need," Lily muttered.

Wyatt's eyes darted between the two women. "Well, keep the alarm on even while you're in the house, just in case, okay?"

"That I can promise," Lily answered.

Wyatt's team finished their work with the photographs and dusting for prints. As the last of the police vehicles pulled from the driveway, Cassie and Lily collapsed onto the couch.

"I suppose we should head back into the shop," Lily said with a sigh.

"I checked with Amber and Tom. They're fine. She told us to take the rest of the day off with everything going on."

"Oh, that's nice. At least we got a nice set of kids to run the shop."

"I guess it could be worse," Cassie answered. "Our thief could have trashed the place or stolen more than he did."

Lily nodded. "Yeah, but your carousel. And you just fixed it."

"Oh well," Cassie answered. "Though I suspect he'll be sorely disappointed if he was looking for the map inside."

"And how would he know about it?"

"I'm not sure," Cassie said. "I certainly didn't tell anyone. Though it seems that this might explain what the thief was after when he smashed our store window. I almost left the carousel there that night."

"Yeah, then you'd never have found the map."

"Nope," Cassie said. "Not that it does us much good anyway. Pearl has never heard of Henton Street. She asked if it could be something else."

"What did you tell her?"

"I said I wasn't sure. You came across it in your reading and assumed it was a street, but it could be another location."

Lily sat with her arms crossed staring into space. She chewed her lower lip. After a moment she said, "You don't think... nah." She waved off her comment with a chuckle.

"What?"

"You don't think Pearl's involved in this, do you?" Lily asked.

"What?!" Cassie exclaimed. "Really?"

"Well, think about it," Lily said, laying out her case. "One of the first people you talked to about Susan and the pirate treasure was Pearl. We started to have problems shortly after that. And today, just after you spoke with Pearl, the house was broken into and two pieces of information related to Susan and the treasure were stolen."

Cassie's eyes widened. "*And* Pearl was the last person to see Susan Davies alive. Oh my goodness, do you think Pearl is a murderer?"

"Or a treasure hunter."

Cassie's jaw gaped open as she processed it. She shook her head and flailed her arms in the air. "Whoa, wait a minute. Before we get too far into accusing gentle old librarians of murder, let's think this through. We know it wasn't Pearl on that CCTV footage."

"Pearl's son? Nephew? Cousin? Hired help? There's any number of ways to connect the gentle old librarian as you call her to the criminal."

Cassie considered the new information. "I will be so disappointed if sweet little Pearl is a killer," she murmured.

"I'm not saying she is. But if we look at the information, she's involved a good bit every time something goes wrong, dating all the way back to the disappearance of Susan Davies. She had a good amount of information about what Susan was researching, since she helped her with it. And she was the last person to see her alive." Cassie slouched a bit further as the case against Pearl built. "And, I'll remind you, we were ready to accuse Frida of the same."

"Well…" Cassie began.

"Just because she's not as sweet to your face as Pearl doesn't mean she's a criminal, Cass."

Cassie's shoulders slumped. "Yes, I know. I'm not a great judge of character either, so I can't say for sure."

Cassie's phone chirped and she glanced at the display. "Speak of the devil," Cassie said. "It's Pearl."

Lily raised her eyebrows. "Ask her if she stole your carousel," she whispered with a snicker as Cassie swiped to take the call. Cassie waved her comment away and shook her head.

"Hey, Pearl."

"Oh, hi, Cassie," the woman greeted her. "How are you?"

"I'm okay, what's up?"

"Oh, good. I heard there was a spot of trouble out at Whispering Manor. I'm glad it's nothing serious." Cassie frowned. Pearl had already heard about the trouble? Was that because news traveled that quickly in a small town, or because Pearl had a hand in it? She didn't know for sure but the comment bothered her now that her suspicions were raised.

"Thanks," Cassie said with a nervous chuckle. "Wow, news travels fast around here, huh?"

"Indeed it does, dear. Anyway, I looked into your Henton question."

"And?" Cassie prompted.

"There's never been a street named Henton from what I can see. I also dug through some records to see if there was a family surname of Henton or any famous Henton locations, but I didn't come across any references."

"Oh," Cassie said, the disappointment clear in her voice. "Well, thanks anyway."

"Maybe if you provide me with more context, I can dig a little deeper?" Pearl suggested.

"Ahhh," Cassie murmured, as her brain scrambled to come up with an explanation. She didn't want to reveal too much to Pearl, but she didn't want to look suspicious either. "You know, I'm not sure of the context and with all the commotion, I haven't been able to ask my mom. But as soon as I do, I'll get back to you and then maybe we can track it down."

The librarian chuckled. "All right, dear. Well, take care and I hope to hear from you soon. I hate not being able to put a matter to rest."

"Me too. Thanks again. Have a great afternoon, bye!" Cassie quickly ended the call, and breathed a sigh of relief.

"Well?" Lily asked.

"She didn't find anything, but she kept prodding me for information. And now I'm starting to wonder if she *is* guilty! Why the interest?"

"Well, you did ask her. Maybe she's just trying to be helpful."

Cassie screwed up her face. "You're the one who suggested she was guilty!"

"Suggested, not accused. Now I'm playing devil's advocate."

Cassie dropped her head onto the couch behind her in a dramatic display. "Ugh, I hope Wyatt catches the person soon, I'm tired of suspecting everyone in town."

"We've only suspected two people thus far," Lily reminded her.

"Yes, and I'm already over it."

"Well, what do you want to do with your newly gained time off?" Lily asked after a few minutes.

"How about a walk on the beach?"

"Okay," Lily said. "I just need to grab my sunglasses."

Cassie nodded and they parted ways at the top of the stairs. When Cassie returned, she held her sunglasses and Susan's journal in her hand.

"You're taking the journal?"

"Yeah. No way am I leaving our last piece of evidence unguarded!"

CHAPTER 29

They left the house through the sliding door leading to the beach. The afternoon sun shone brightly in the pale blue sky. A few fluffy clouds dotted the horizon, but did little to dampen the sun's rays.

Cassie squinted despite wearing sunglasses as the light reflected off the water in a brilliant display. The roar of the rolling ocean serenaded them as they wandered the sandy shore.

Cassie pulled her phone from the pocket of her leggings and swiped at it.

"Will you get off your phone?" Lily moaned.

"I'm bringing up the map. I thought something might strike us as familiar while we walked."

Lily hovered over her shoulder and glanced at the screen. Cassie shielded it with her hand against the bright sunlight. Both of them glanced at their surroundings, then back at the crudely drawn map.

"I don't see anything that fits," Lily said, as she scanned the horizon in both directions.

"Me either," Cassie said with a shrug. "Let's keep going."

They meandered another quarter mile down the beach before they gave up their cursory search. "Let's head back. I'm hungry," Lily said.

They arced toward the house and meandered back, coming across nothing along their way. After settling on sandwiches for dinner, they bustled about the kitchen fixing their meager meal.

Cassie sighed as she sank onto the kitchen chair. "That supposed treasure map and clue is driving me nuts."

"I didn't see anything that matched it while we walked."

"Me either," Cassie admitted.

"Maybe after we eat we can read some of Susan's journal. It's the last possible clue we have," Lily suggested. "She may have come up with something."

"Okay," Cassie said.

"Good going, Willy, for hiding that," Lily said, as she bit into her PB&J.

"Yeah," Cassie agreed as her phone rang again.

"Who is it? Pearl again? Heard we've been scouring the beach for clues?"

"No, it's Wyatt."

"Oh, heavens, now what?"

Cassie swiped to accept the call and put it on speaker. "Hey, Cassie," Wyatt's now familiar voice said. "I talked to Chloe earlier about the guy you think may be the vandal. She drew up a sketch of him. I wanted to run it by you and see if you think it looks like him. If it does, I'll send it through the database to see if we can match him to any other crimes."

"Okay. Did you need us to stop down?"

"No, I'll email it…" Cassie heard a voice in the background. "Oh, right, I'll text it to you."

"Okay, sounds good," Cassie said.

"Just give me a minute." Rustling noises sounded on the

other end. "Just a second." Wyatt said again before she heard him shout, "Hey, Ruby!"

Ruby's voice sounded on the other end of the line. "Just select Cassie's name and press Message, then press the plus sign and find the picture and attach it. Then press the arrow to send it."

"Okay, thanks."

Cassie held in a chuckle as Wyatt muttered, "Press the arrow. And, okay, I think I've got it sent. Did you get it?"

"Yes," Cassie confirmed. She navigated to the new text message and opened the image. "Oh, yeah, that looks just like him."

Lily nodded. "Yeah, she's done a great job. That's our guy."

"Okay, great. I'm going to run this through a larger database to see if we get any hits against it. I'll let you know as soon as we find anything."

"Thanks, Wyatt."

Cassie ended the call. "Hopefully something comes out of that," Lily said as she eased herself into her chair again.

"Or this!" Cassie said, waving Susan's journal around.

Following their meal, the two women settled on the couch. With Lily peering over Cassie's shoulder, they parsed through the remaining entries in Susan's journal.

I'm really frustrated! I have tried EVERYTHING with this map and nothing works. I have explored up and down the beach. I even brought friends along twice and told them I was looking for sea caves to find sea glass. Then I asked a few people who've lived around here for a long time. I showed my drawing of the map and said I was doing a scavenger hunt with friends.

I went to the library and looked at old maps. Nothing. And then this stupid note with it makes no sense. I tried to follow the clues and looked around the beach, I looked for hollows and caves. I even tried going into the woods around the town and searching there since it says over land, but nothing.

I'm ready to give up. I can't find this stupid treasure!

The entry ended. "Looks like she had as much luck as we did," Cassie said.

"Yeah," Lily agreed. "Though I hope our outcome is significantly different from hers."

"You and me both!" Cassie said as she turned the page to the next entry.

Okay, I'm back on the case. I'm not a quitter! AND I found some help! While I was studying at The Bean Machine, this guy came up to me and asked if he could sit with me. He said Pearl told him I was researching the pirate Black Jack. I was really surprised he was researching him, too. He's like six years older than me, so he's been at it for a much longer time than I have been.

He's spent years learning about the legends and he's even writing a book about it. He's a history major at Pembrook U just outside of town. I asked him if he could share his research to help with my project and he agreed!

He said we could meet at the library at Pembrook and go over notes together. I'm going to meet him tomorrow after school!

"Uh-oh," Lily groaned. "I don't trust this guy."

"Neither do I," Cassie said.

I met with Harold today! He had a TON of information on Black Jack. I took lots of notes. Some of the stuff he had wasn't written down, he just told it to me like a story. He's so interesting to listen to. He says the treasure is definitely hidden somewhere in Hideaway Bay. And it was never found because both Henrietta and Black Jack died young.

Apparently, there was another pirate looking for it. I didn't see anything about that in Henrietta's journal but I haven't read the whole thing yet.

Harold asked me a bunch of questions about what it was like to live in Henrietta's house and if it was really haunted. I told him it wasn't. He asked if I found any clues in the house about the treasure.

I told him about finding a few things but said it didn't help at all so far. He kept asking me to show him anything I found. It was weird. He was really being a pest about it. I got a funny feeling like maybe I shouldn't, so I told him I had to get home for dinner.

Then he got really nice again and said he hoped we could keep sharing research together. He said I was the cutest research partner he's ever had. I think I might have blushed a little. He's kind of cute, in like a pirate-y sort of way. He's got this really red hair and really dark, dreamy eyes. I bet we'd have a really fun time together since we both like history.

"It gets worse," Cassie groaned.

"Yep. This guy is using her."

Cassie snapped the book shut.

"What's wrong?" Lily inquired.

"It's just… these must be her last few entries. I'm not sure how I feel about reading these. Especially the last one."

"I'm not sure there's going to be anything gruesome in them, Cass," Lily said, tucking a lock of Cassie's hair behind her ear.

"No, I know that, but… Come on, one of these entries is the last time she wrote in this journal, and then she died or was kidnapped or something. I just… it's upsetting."

"Look at it this way: maybe this will help shed some light on her murder."

"Maybe. No one ever mentions this guy, Harold. Do you think anyone knew about him?"

"I'm not sure but…"

"What?" Cassie asked, as her mother's voice trailed off.

"His description. Red hair, dark eyes."

"Right. That describes millions of people."

"It also describes our suspected vandal."

Cassie's brow furrowed. "You think her Harold is our vandal?"

"Think about it. The ages fit. I'd say he's older than you. Which means he could have been a college student when she was in high school."

"Wonder if he's related to Pearl?"

"Yeah, I see her name came up again. Odd coincidence or not, I guess we'll see."

"Okay," Cassie said with a sigh. "Let's keep going."

I met Harold on the beach again today. I didn't show him the map or anything, I just said it was likely the treasure was hidden somewhere off the coast. He looked at me kinda funny but I didn't say anything else and he didn't either. We scoured the beach but we didn't find any clues or markers or anything.

When we were finished, we walked into town and went to The Bean Machine. Harold kept asking me if I found anything else in the house. When I told him no it seemed like he got mad at me. I said I had to go and he apologized and said he was sorry if he seemed mad, but he's at a dead-end with his research and he's worried he's going to fail his history class because of it.

I told him I didn't think they'd fail him if he couldn't find Black Jack's treasure. But he said I didn't know what it was like in college. That made me kind of mad, but I just shrugged and said I was sure all the research we did so far would give him a great paper to turn in.

"It would be even better if we found the treasure," he said. "I bet I wouldn't even have to finish my classes, they'd just give me a degree."

"Wow, this guy is a real jerk," Lily mumbled.

I bit my lower lip while I thought about sharing the map with him.

"Don't do it, Susan!" Cassie exclaimed.

In the end, I decided not to. While I was deciding, he leaned forward and grabbed my hands and was like, "Can I come over and look for clues?"

I didn't know what to say. I told him I had to check with my parents and he freaked out. He said I shouldn't do that. He wanted to come over when no one was home. I thought that was weird. He said my parents wouldn't understand and think he was too old for me to be friends with. He's probably right, which is why I've never mentioned him to them. But having him at the house while they're out made me a little nervous. At least when we are researching, we're in a public place. I don't know why, but he seems so pushy all of a sudden. I think I'm just going to go back to researching on my own.

"Best decision you can make, Susan," Lily said, as the entry came to an end.

Cassie turned the page and bit her lower lip. "Last entry," she said with a grimace.

"Let's see what she has to say."

CHAPTER 30

Lily peered over Cassie's shoulder as they read the final entry in the journal.

I've been avoiding Harold for a few days, but I talked to Pearl in the library after school last night. I can't make any sense out of anything on the map or the note so I'm going to go through all the information she has on Black Jack again. I'm meeting her later today. I'm going to go through everything again and see if I find any clues about this map or the note. Maybe I'll find a reference to HENTON or a cave that I missed before.

I'm determined to find something. I'm going to find that treasure, not Harold! I'm going to be famous!

Cassie bit back a sob as she read the final words in the diary. Susan had no idea how famous she'd become. Just not in the way she wanted.

"Chilling last words," Lily said, breaking the silence.

"Yeah," Cassie said after a hard swallow. "What a shame. Well, that's that. No insights into the map or the note."

"No, and she, too, went to Pearl for help."

"Pearl never mentioned Henton, so maybe she didn't mention it to her."

"Or she did and Pearl's not so innocent."

Cassie sighed. "We may never know. Well, what now?"

Lily glanced at the darkening sky outside. "How about a hot chocolate and some reading to unwind?"

"I'll take the hot chocolate, but I don't know what we're going to read."

"There's a library full of books in there," Lily said, gesturing toward the foyer. "I'm sure we'll find something. Maybe we'll find another journal."

"From who?" Cassie said with a laugh as she stood and stretched.

"Clifton," Lily answered.

"Clifton? Black Jack himself? He doesn't seem like the diary kind of guy."

After creating their warm, frothy concoction, the women browsed the shelves in the library.

"Hmm," Lily said after a moment, "someone was a gothic mystery fan." She waved a book in the air. "Look, Cass, a girl running away from a castle book."

Cassie chuckled. "I saw that before. There's a few of them over there."

"Might be a good read," Lily said, as she flipped the book over to read the blurb.

Cassie scanned the books on the shelf across from the window seat. Willy sat next to her, swishing his tail on the floor. After a moment, he darted toward the bookshelf, pawing at its corner.

"You love this bookshelf, don't you, buddy?" Cassie said. She scratched his head when he settled back to his haunches.

"Got a book you want to read there, Willy?" Lily inquired as she studied the inside jacket of a hardcover novel.

Cassie bent over and scanned the titles on the middle

shelf. Several books had no titles on the spine. "Wonder what these are?" Cassie murmured.

"Hmm? Find another journal?" Lily inquired.

"These don't look like the journal. They're bound books, but they look old." Cassie pulled one from the shelf and studied its plain front. "With all the shenanigans going on after we moved, I never got the chance to finish exploring these shelves."

Lily joined her and peered at the book over her shoulder. Cassie handed it to her and pulled another from the shelf. Setting down her almost empty hot chocolate mug, Lily flipped through the book. A plume of dust rose as she let the pages fall.

"Old and dusty," she commented with a cough.

Cassie pulled the cover of her book open and paged through to the title page. In scripted writing, it read *Under the Hollow*.

"*Under the Hollow*," she read. She set the book aside and reached for another.

Lily's page-flipping finished and she gazed at her title page. "Mine is *Over Land and Sea*."

"Wait, what?" Cassie froze mid-reach, her face a mask of shock.

Lily's eyes snapped to Cassie's. Her jaw opened wide and she glanced at the book in her hand. "*Over Land and Sea*," she repeated.

Cassie pointed to the book she'd discarded on the nearby table. "That's *Under the Hollow*." She pulled another book from the shelf. With trembling hands, she pulled the book open and paged to the title. "*Through Thick and Thin*!" she read, excitement building in her voice.

Lily snatched the next book and leafed to the title page, while Cassie opened the image of Henrietta's note on her phone. "*Beyond the Border*," Lily reported.

Cassie's eyes brightened as she grabbed the last book. "I'd bet *this* is *The Cave*." She opened the book and flashed the title page at Lily. With a grin, she said, "It is!"

Lily studied the title page on a few of the books again. "These were all written by Henrietta," she said.

"Really?"

"Yes. I gather she was an author. One of the first things she asked Clifton when he asked her to guard the treasure and told her she could be free was if she could write again."

Cassie's excited grin turned pensive. "You don't think this is the treasure, do you?"

"The books?"

"Yeah," Cassie said. "What if this is the treasure they were referring to? Like her stories were so good, they were a treasure."

Lily shook her head in disagreement. "No. In the conversation between Henrietta and Clifton, he said he worried the load would sink his ship."

Cassie screwed up her face. "Seriously?"

"That's what he said. Henrietta questioned it and he insisted it was large. Gold, jewels, the whole nine. It's not books."

"Okay, so how do these play in?"

Cassie glanced at the books. Willy stood on his hind legs, inspecting the gap left on the bookshelf. He sniffed at it and batted his paw, before descending to all fours and rubbing against the decorative trim of the bookcase.

Cassie toggled on her flashlight and shined it into the hole between the books. She squinted as she panned the light across the back.

"There's something back here!" she said, her voice catching a bit in her throat.

"What is it?" Lily peered over her shoulder, craning her neck to get a better view.

"I can't tell. There's something metal. Like a cover."

Cassie reached into the space. She shook her head. "I can't see a thing while my hand's in there."

"Let's clear the shelf," Lily suggested.

Cassie nodded and removed the books from one side, while Lily pulled them from the other. With stacks of books on the floor, Cassie shined the light in again. A brass rectangle with scrolled decorative trim met their gaze. No other markings existed on it.

Lily reached back and pressed on the metal rectangle. Her lips formed a grimace as she struggled to budge it.

"Stuck," she puffed out.

"Let me try."

Lily made a face at her but removed her hand. "If I can't get it, you won't budge it."

Cassie pushed against it at various angles. "Nope, nothing."

Willy stood on his hind legs again, peering between them at the metal box. Lily ran her hand across the shelf and up the side.

"Think there's a trigger to open that panel?"

"Maybe."

Cassie followed Lily's lead, searching the surrounding wood for a trigger button. "Maybe it's just a tag from the bookcase maker."

"Doesn't have his name on it, so it's a pretty poor tag."

"Good point."

After a thorough search of the surrounding area, they came up empty. Lily stared at the brass panel. After a moment, she reached forward and pressed the flower making up the top center of the decorative trim.

With a click, the panel slid open, retracting behind the bookcase's back piece. "Ha! You did it!" Cassie exclaimed.

She shined her flashlight at what lay behind the panel. Six

brass cylinders were lined from left to right. "What's this?" Cassie queried.

"Looks like an old-fashioned combination lock," Lily suggested.

"But with letters instead of numbers."

Cassie snapped her head to look at Lily. "HENTON," the two women said in unison.

With a wide smile, Cassie reached back as Lily held the light. She spun the dials to read H-E-N-T-O-N. As the final dial landed on "N," a clang resounded and the bookcase's right side popped away from the wall. Willy scurried to the corner, giving it a sniff.

Cassie and Lily scrambled to their feet. Cassie found a handhold on the bookcase's side. She dug her fingers in and pulled. With Lily's assistance, they nudged the large cabinet several inches into the room.

"Ugh, this thing is heavy," Cassie groaned.

Lily swiped the back of her hand across her forehead. "Whew, yeah. Probably rusted from years of disuse. I need a second." She collapsed into the chair.

"Take a rest, I've got to move the books and this table out of the way."

As Lily fanned herself in the armchair, Cassie shoved two piles of books against the wall and slid the table away from the bookcase's path. She stretched her back as Lily climbed to her feet.

"Okay, let's see if there's a treasure behind this!"

They labored with the large structure for several more minutes, before a cool gust of air burst from behind it as the back end slid away from the wall. A damp, musty smell filled their nostrils.

"Can you see anything?" Lily grunted as they continued to push.

"Not yet, but I can wedge my hands behind the bookcase now to pull."

"Okay, let's keep at it. On three!" Lily counted and they gave the cabinet another heave. It rolled another foot.

"I can get behind it now and push!" Cassie exclaimed. She positioned herself behind the bookcase and leveraged herself against the wall. With a groan, she shifted it back several more feet.

"What's in there?" Lily inquired, craning her neck to peer around Cassie.

Cassie stared into the black hole gaping behind the now open bookcase. "I can't see a thing, it's pitch black!"

Lily swiped Cassie's cell phone from the nearby table and toggled on the flashlight. She shined the light into the hole. It did little to illuminate the deep space.

"I don't see any treasure," Cassie lamented.

"Me either. But this tunnel seems to extend quite a ways. The light dies before it reaches the back."

"Shall we?" Cassie asked, her eyebrows raised high.

"Maybe we should get a better flashlight," Lily suggested.

"Good idea, I'll grab two from the pantry."

She disappeared from the room and returned within a few moments with two large flashlights in hand. They toggled them on, the bright LED light filtering through the darkness. The chamber still continued beyond the reach of their lights.

"Should we go for it?" Cassie asked.

"Why not? We'll never know what's in there if we don't look."

Cassie drew in a deep breath and nodded. Together, they stepped into the dark, cool tunnel. Both of them waved their flashlight beams around as they traversed forward. The passage wound around as it descended into the earth. The wooden walls turned to gray stone.

Cassie shivered. "It's cold in here."

"Yeah," Lily agreed, as she pulled her sweater tighter around her. "Seems like we're going down."

"Yeah. And this is pretty winding. I wonder where we are?" Cassie glanced up to the ceiling. "Are we under the house?"

The passage took a sharp left before it started to ascend gradually. The climb leveled off after a few moments of walking, and the tunnel widened.

"It's getting wider in here. Maybe we're coming to the end," Cassie said.

"I hope so. It was getting a little tight back there," Lily answered, hinting at her claustrophobia. Cassie clutched her arm and squeezed.

After another few steps, the walls dropped away from their sides. Cassie stepped into a large cavern. She swung her beam around. A few glints of light reflected back.

"Trunks," Lily murmured.

Cassie nodded and approached one. A thick iron hasp held the trunk closed. Cassie flipped it up and yanked on the lid.

"Heavy," she grunted, as she strained to swing the lid open. Lily hurried over and slipped her fingers under the lid's edge. She pushed while Cassie pulled until the top swung open. Clinking noises sounded as something dropped from the chest's interior to the stone floor below.

Cassie aimed her flashlight's beam inside the chest. Her jaw dropped open.

"Oh, wow," she whispered, her voice hushed with awe.

Glints of gold beamed back. A few gold coins had spilled over the edge of the trunk and lay scattered at their feet.

Cassie scooped up a handful of pieces, allowing them to fall through her fingers into the chest. Lily grabbed one from the trunk. She stuck it between her teeth and bit.

Cassie screwed up her face. "Did you just bite that?"

"Had to make sure it wasn't chocolate," she said with a grin.

"I can't believe this," Cassie exclaimed. "Is this Black Jack's treasure?"

"I imagine so." Lily swung her beam around the room.

"There have got to be one hundred trunks here."

"He said it'd sink his ship, it was so big."

Cassie wandered to another trunk and pulled it open. A golden chalice lay atop a stack of gold bars. She wrenched another open, finding gems and jewelry piled high.

The women darted around the large cave, opening crates and chests. After opening a few chests, Lily's flashlight beam rested against the wall. Large boulders and stones were piled high. A cool breeze blew between the slivers between them. Lily leaned closer. "I hear the ocean. We must be near the beach," she said.

"I wonder if this was a sea cave in Black Jack's time. They probably brought everything in through there."

"And then tunneled from the house," Lily suggested, finishing her thought.

"Yeah," Cassie said as she glanced around again. "I can't believe this. We found a pirate treasure!"

"We found a pirate treasure!" Lily exclaimed, pumping her fist in the air.

They clasped hands as they squealed with excitement.

"And not a moment too soon," a voice said from the entrance of the cave.

Both women froze. Cassie swallowed hard, as her pulse quickened and her heart thudded in her chest. She swiveled her head toward the entrance. A bright beam blinded her. She shielded her eyes with her hand.

With their eyes narrow slits, both women struggled to identify the man. Cassie shined her beam toward him.

"Put that down and raise your hands," he instructed.

"No!" Cassie shouted back, wiggling the beam to find his face.

A loud blast sounded, deafening them as it echoed in the cavernous space. Cassie's beam swung wildly toward the ceiling as she clamped her hands over her ears and squeezed her eyes shut. Instinctively, she ducked.

When she opened her eyes again and lowered her hands, the man said, "That was a warning shot. Now put your flashlights on the floor and raise your hands."

Cassie and Lily slowly lowered their flashlights to the ground. Cassie aimed her beam toward the ceiling to illuminate the space.

"Now back against the wall," he instructed, as he set his flashlight on the floor. He waved the gun toward the location he wanted them to go toward. He pulled something from his pocket. A small flame flickered as the lighter's wick burst into flame. He held it toward the wall and a torch burst into flames.

The dancing flame illuminated the space and the man's face. Cassie recognized him as their strange shop visitor.

"And now," he said, "I'll need to dispose of you."

"Who are you?" Lily demanded.

"That doesn't matter."

"It does to me. I'd like to know before I die who is responsible."

"Why? Do you plan on haunting me?" His white teeth gleamed in the meager light as he gave a wicked laugh. With his attention focused on Lily, Cassie risked reaching her hand into the kangaroo pocket of her hoodie. With trembling fingers, she tapped on her display. She offered a silent prayer that the light didn't shine through the pocket's fabric.

"If I'm given the chance, hell yes," Lily retorted.

"I already told you my name," he countered.

"Were you really named after a cartoon pirate?" Lily asked with a snicker.

The man narrowed his eyes. "Fine," he said, his face a mask of aggravation. "Why not?"

He paced the floor in front of them, waving his gun around as he spoke. "Harold O'Rourke is my name."

Cassie risked a glance in her pocket and tapped her message app. At the top of the screen was her latest incoming message from Wyatt. She swiped at it to initiate a call. She had no idea if she had service in the cave, but she prayed the call went through.

Cassie gasped at the name. "Harold?" she said. "Susan's Harold?"

He stared at her, confusion crossing his features. "Susan Davies. The girl who lived here thirty years ago," Cassie said, heat entering her voice. "She mentioned a Harold in her diary."

Cassie heard a muffled sound. Perhaps her call had gotten through to Wyatt.

"Oh," he said, with another derisive cackle. "Yes. Poor little Susan. She really shouldn't have trusted me."

"You killed her!" Cassie accused.

He shrugged. "Well, if the shoe fits," he stated.

"How could you? She was a child!" Lily shouted.

"I really didn't mean to," he said. "I realized she knew more than she was saying, though."

"And you killed her to find out?" Cassie questioned.

He shook his head. "I brought her to the beach to look for the treasure. We found a cave. It was a cold day and the rocks inside were slick. As we explored it, she fell and hit her head."

"So, the fall killed her?" Lily questioned.

"She was alive, but with a bad head wound. I couldn't let her go home–she knew far too much about me. And the little brat would tell.

"She was such a do-gooder. 'Oh, no, we can't meet alone without my parents knowing,'" he mimicked in his best girl voice. "She would have told. She needed medical attention. And I couldn't let that happen. So, I tied her up and left her in the cave."

Cassie's heart broke for the girl. "You left her to die."

"She must have washed out to sea when the tide came in," he answered.

"You monster," Cassie growled.

"Well, enough about me," the man said, turning his attention, and his gun, back to them. "At least now I've gotten to my goal. Her death and the deaths of her parents will mean something."

"The deaths of her parents?" Cassie asked, attempting to keep him talking.

"Oh, yes. That troublesome pair caught me lurking around in the house searching for that little brat's carousel. I'm afraid there wasn't much to be done about them. I made it look like a murder-suicide."

"Why are you doing this?" Cassie cried.

"It's owed to me!" he shouted in response.

"How do you figure that?" Lily questioned.

"I'm an O'Rourke."

"So?" Cassie said.

"So, I'm descended from Ronan O'Rourke."

The quizzical expressions on both Cassie and Lily's faces prompted him to continue. "Perhaps you know him better as Redbeard."

Cassie raised her eyebrows at the admission. "Black Jack's rival?"

"One and the same. And the one Black Jack stole from. And murdered. This bounty is Redbeard's. Mine. Now, it's time to claim it." He leveled the gun at them.

"How did you know about the carousel?" Lily questioned, attempting to keep him talking.

"Enough questions. You're only delaying the inevitable. Hmm, which of you first?"

Cassie reached over and grasped her mother's hand. Trembling fingers wrapped around hers and squeezed. She heard no more sounds from her pocket. Even if the call went out to Wyatt, he wouldn't make it in time.

Cassie mashed her lips together until they hurt. It was the only way to stop her bottom lip from quivering. His deliberation ended. He aimed the weapon at Lily. "You first, after your antics with the bat."

Cassie whimpered as her mother squeezed her hand and closed her eyes. Her brain registered movement, but she didn't process it immediately. Suddenly, Harold's neck crimped and his head lolled back. His eyes rolled upward and he stumbled a step before he fell face down on the floor. Standing behind him was Frida Friedman, bat in hand.

"Looked like you two ladies needed a hand," she said, her voice still gruff as ever.

A tear spilled onto Cassie's cheek as Frida kicked the gun away from the man. "Got any rope?"

"Thank you," Lily said. "How did you find us?"

"Came to drop off a basket of pastries and cat treats. Heard you two weren't getting quite a warm welcome to town. When I showed up, the front door was wide open. The cat was sitting there and then hurried into the library. He kept staring down the tunnel. Figured it wasn't like you to leave your front door wide open like that, so I followed the passage." She waved the bat. "Grabbed this first, just in case."

"Good thing you did," Lily said with a sigh of relief. Cassie scooped the gun from the floor.

"Cassie! Lily!" a voice shouted.

"Down here!" Cassie called back, as she aimed the weapon at the unconscious man on the floor.

Wyatt rushed in from the passage. With his weapon drawn, his eyes darted around the space.

"This fella here," Frida said, pointing to the man sprawled on the floor, "had these two ladies at gunpoint. He aimed to kill 'em, he said."

Wyatt holstered his weapon and pulled handcuffs from his belt. He secured Harold before radioing for EMTs. Additional officers raced into the chamber a few moments later. Wyatt relieved Cassie of the weapon, before ensuring both she and Lily were unharmed.

"We're both fine, just a little scared," Lily answered.

Wyatt glanced around the dimly lit space. "Is this…"

"Treasure," Cassie said. "Black Jack's treasure."

Wyatt blinked a few times as though his eyes deceived him.

"And yours, I suppose," Lily said to Frida. "At least partially. Aren't you the last remaining Nichols descendant?"

Frida waved her hands in the air. "I don't want any parts of any cursed treasure."

"Let's discuss this later, ladies," Wyatt said, as the prisoner on the floor moaned and writhed.

EMTs entered the cave, led by one of Wyatt's deputies. They placed blankets around Lily and Cassie's shoulders before they led them from the cave.

Willy greeted them as they emerged from the tunnel into the library. Cassie scooped him into her arms as another tear fell. "Oh, buddy, I'm so glad to see you."

"I see he found the treats," Frida said with a huff. A package of treats lay on the library floor, dragged from the basket sitting just inside the door. A hole had been chewed into it and several treats were sprawled on the area rug.

"I suppose you deserve it," Cassie said as she nuzzled against him.

"And I suppose Mayor Tinsdale will be giving you two a medal," Wyatt said. One of his deputies led a grumbling, handcuffed Harold through the library and out to the waiting police cruiser.

"You can't prove anything," he shouted.

"You found the long-lost treasure!" Wyatt said.

"And solved a few more mysteries," Lily added. She pointed out the window as the deputy shoved Harold into the backseat. "That man killed Susan and her parents."

Wyatt's face reddened a shade. "I knew it had to do with Susan Davies. We found her carousel and Henrietta's journal in his hotel room. I was on my way to tell you when I got your call, Cassie. Smart thinking to dial me. I heard most of his confession, and recorded it too. Well, Ruby helped me with that."

Cassie chuckled. "You really are terrible with technology."

EPILOGUE

*assie waved to Frida as she ambled down Main Street, heading to *Buy the Sea.* It had only been a week since they'd found the large bounty hidden in a cavern attached to a winding tunnel hidden behind one of their library's bookcases. In that time, though, everyone in town had heard about the discovery.

Thrust into the limelight of the national news, Mayor Tinsdale appeared on several morning and evening news shows to discuss the find. Cassie and Lily allowed her to suck up as much of the air time as she wanted, desiring no part of the spotlight.

The local university's history and archeology departments had descended on the cavern to study the items. With a finder's fee offered, that Lily and Cassie insisted be split with Frida, the teams would remove, catalog and disseminate the items for museum displays across the nation and globe.

An excavation of the collapsed rock wall leading to the beach cave was already underway, as was the sealing off of the passage to Whispering Manor. Soon, the hubbub would die down, and Cassie and Lily could slip back into the quiet life they imagined when they purchased their seaside home.

Cassie entered their shop through the front door, carrying their takeout order. "Thank heavens," Lily said, "I'm starving."

"It took a little longer, as usual. There are about two people left in the town who haven't heard our story, and they both asked."

Lily chuckled. "Wyatt stopped by while you were out."

"Oh?"

"Yeah. He said their case is shaping up nicely against Harold. With his confession to us, they have him on multiple counts of murder, trespassing, and about half a dozen other things. Apparently, he's been the one 'haunting' Whispering Manor for the past few decades. He'd found an easy way to slip in by scaling the house up to the widow's walk. Everyone was so primed to believe the ghost stories, they assumed anything they saw was the ghost of Henrietta."

"Or Susan," she said.

"Yep. He also said there's no connection between Harold and our friendly neighborhood librarian."

"Whew," Cassie said, wiping her brow in mock relief.

"She is just a kindly, old librarian."

"Well, that should settle things down then," Cassie said. "No more hauntings, no more treasure hunts. Now we can enjoy our quiet little town."

"Yep. I mean, what else can happen in a small town like this?"

The End

Stay up to date with all my news! Be the first to find out about new releases first, sales and get free offers! Join the Nellie H. Steele's Mystery Readers' Group on Facebook! Or sign up for my newsletter at www.anovelideapublishing.com!

* * *

If you loved Lily & Cassie, look for their next book due out in 2023!

* * *

Want to know more about Clif & Ri's story? They have their own book series! Book 1, *Rise of a Pirate*, is available for purchase now!

* * *

Like cozy mysteries? Check out the Cate Kensie Mystery series. Misty Scottish moors and a quirky castle. Read Cate's first adventure, *The Secret of Dunhaven Castle*! You can also read Jack's version of the story!

* * *

Like supernatural suspense? Try the *Shadow Slayers* series, a fast-paced page-turner! Book one, *Shadows of the Past*, is available now!

* * *

Love immersing yourself in the past? Lenora Fletcher can communicate with the dead! Can she use her unique skill to solve a mystery? Find out in *Death of a Duchess*, Book 1 in the Duchess of Blackmoore Mysteries.

* * *

Ready for adventure? Travel the globe with Maggie Edwards in search of her kidnapped uncle and Cleopatra's Tomb. Book one, *Cleopatra's Tomb*, in the Maggie Edwards Adventure series is available now!

* * *

A NOTE FROM THE AUTHOR

Dear Reader,

Thank you for reading this book! *Ghosts, Lore & a House by the Shore* is the first book in a lovely mother/daughter series based off of the special bond shared by mothers and daughters (and heavily influenced by my own relationship with my mom!).

I hope you enjoyed reading this book as much as I did writing it! If you loved it, please consider leaving a review and help get the book into the hands of other interested readers.

Book 2 in this series isn't available yet, but look for it coming in 2023! In the meantime, you can read more about Clif and Henrietta in their series! Book 1, Rise of a Pirate, is available now!

All the best, Nellie

RISE OF A PIRATE SYNOPSIS

When two sibling's worlds are shattered by a single bullet, will they choose a path that leads to danger?

Henrietta longs for independence, seeking it by marrying into Savannah's elite society. But when her love interest is a philandering scoundrel, her protective brother Clifton's vows to stop her. And when emotions run high, an accidental murder threatens to rip their worlds apart.

A shattered and heartbroken Henrietta mourns for the life she's lost. Meanwhile Clifton, alone and devastated, escapes the reality of his tragedy through a series of dangerous choices. Physically and emotionally separated, the siblings find themselves on paths of reckless abandon.

Will their lives on water create a powerful pirate duo, or will the rough seas of their past make the waves that lead to death?

Rise of the Pirate is the thrilling first book in the pirate adventure series *Cliff and Ri on the Sea.* If you like redemption arcs, take-charge females, and treacherous waters, then you'll love Nellie H. Steele's ride across the ocean.

Grab Rise of a Pirate today!

RISE OF A PIRATE EXCERPT

PROLOGUE

1802

*W*ind whipped across the violent sea. Dark clouds raced up the coast, bringing with them an impending storm. Lightning tore through the night sky as thunder boomed overhead.

Hidden in the house's secret chamber, one meager flame fought to keep the darkness at bay. The hurricane lamp's light danced off the gold bars scattered on the floor. More gold glinted in the scant light as Henrietta pulled open a wooden chest. She snatched one of the bejeweled necklaces from the pile and shoved it into her dress pocket. She'd need it for the task that lay ahead of her. She'd need more, of course, but one was enough for now.

The chest slammed shut as she released the lid from her grasp. She climbed to her feet and dusted off her dress.

Reaching down, she grasped the hurricane lamp and spun to leave the chamber. A chill passed through her and she shivered. She squared her shoulders and strode from the room.

Henrietta navigated through the tight corridors to the end of the passage. She located the trigger to open the hidden corridor. The bookcase swung open and away and she stepped into the library of her home.

Whispering Manor sat seaside in the small northern town of Hideaway Bay. Henrietta had moved here after marrying Captain William Blanchard. The man flitted through her mind as she shoved the bookcase closed, masking the hidden corridor behind it.

She glanced at the clock on the mantel, ticking the time away. She had hours before her task.

Henrietta stepped into the manor's ample foyer. She grasped hold of the intricately carved wooden banister gracing the stairs leading to the second floor.

"Jane!" Henrietta called. "Jane!" She huffed when the woman failed to appear. "Jane!" she shouted again.

A mouse of a girl appeared at the rear of the foyer. Her blonde hair was tucked into a bun at the nape of her neck. She folded her hands in front of her apron which covered her black uniform. "Yes, Mrs. Blanchard?"

"Where have you been? I've called three times."

"My apologies, Mrs. Blanchard, I was scrubbing in the kitchen. With Elsie sick, I…"

"I do not wish to hear your excuses. Tea, please."

"Yes, ma'am. Will you take it in the sitting room?"

"No, in my bedroom. I must write. I feel a case of depression coming on and it will be all I can do to stave it off. I must pour out my emotions onto the page."

Jane nodded at her and spun to retrieve the tea. Henrietta climbed the large staircase. She veered left at the top and entered her bedroom. Seating herself at her writing desk which overlooked a window facing the ocean, she gazed outside. The ocean's waves churned and roiled, crashing against the beach with all the fury of the building storm.

Her mind, too, roiled, but not with the depression she'd confessed to Jane. No, she mused, that was merely a distraction. An act. She had fooled them all. And she would continue to do so.

With a half-smile, she focused her attention on her brown leather journal. It sat open to a blank page. She dipped her quill in ink and began to pen a journal entry.

She finished the entry, penning the last words

Tonight, I shall take the first steps in cementing my destiny.

As she set the quill down, a knock sounded at her door. Jane entered after she called to her.

"I am leaving for my walk before the storm hits, Mrs. Blanchard. Unless you need something," Jane said.

Henrietta arched an eyebrow and a smirk formed on her lips. Before she faced the girl, she let her features fall and slumped her shoulders. "Nothing else."

Jane nodded and departed from the room, pulling the door closed behind her. Henrietta stood and gazed at the stormy sea again. It was time. Time for death.

Want to read more? Buy Rise of a Pirate today!